DREAMS

Shadows of the Night

by

Olivia Claire High

Fireside

PUBLICATIONS
www.FiresidePubs.com

Fireside Publications
1004 San Felipe Lane
www.firesidepubs.com

Printed in the United States of America

ISBN: 978-1-935517-19-1

For additional copies of this book, please visit:
http://kadinbooks.com or
www.firesidepubs.com

OR
Contact the author at:
Joeclaire2424@comcast.net

Acknowledgements

Many thanks to Lois Bennett
for her assistance and expertise.

Dedication

To the love of my life, my husband,
My Joe.

Prologue

She watched in helpless terror as the water closed over their heads before they sank down deep where no sunlight could reach.

"Mommy! Daddy!"

Would they be cold? Afraid? A sob escaped her. Fear – so much fear for a seven year old child. She called again, but only heard the pounding of her heart. Her eyes squinted trying to see through the murky surroundings of her nightmare.

"Don't go. Please don't leave me," ragged sobs pierced the silence of the night.

Why weren't they listening to her? She knew she was only a child, but she saw things – awful things that terrorized her mind and made her heart pound.

Long, agonizing seconds passed while she burrowed beneath the sheet, but no matter how hard she tried to fight the nightmare, the frozen images of her parents' faces flashed before her eyes. They finally appeared – Mommy and Daddy floating toward her. She stared into their lifeless eyes – and screamed.

>>>>*dreams*<<<<

Catherine Ashley bolted upright in bed, awakened by the sound of her own screams. She pulled her knees to her chest, wrapping her arms around them, in an effort to ward off the chill that shuddered through her body. Her throat felt raw. Tears dampened her pale cheeks. It'd been twenty years since she'd first envisioned her parents' lifeless bodies floating in water. But the dream still managed to slip through her defenses from time to time, stripping away the layers of protection she'd carefully built up to block out the horror.

Other prophetic dreams still came occasionally, but none as frightening as her parents' deaths. They hadn't listened to her warning and two days later they'd drowned in a boating accident – forever fracturing her carefree childhood. She flopped back, fighting to regain control of her emotions until sheer will allowed her to drift into a more pleasant dream – a dream in which a mysterious auburn haired man appeared sporting a smile that lit up the darkness and made her insides quiver in the nicest way. But by the time dawn crept in washing away the darkness, she felt wary.

The fact that he showed up in a dream so soon after recalling a horrendous nightmare might not be a good thing – for either of them.

Chapter One

Josh Dallas surfaced in slow motion struggling through the fog that swirled inside his head, as a sliver of light crept beneath his fluttering eyelids. A woman leaned over him and he worked to bring her into sharper focus. Skin the color of fine porcelain, hair like pale sunlight, and unbelievable sapphire eyes. She had to be an angel. He was pleased to see she wasn't the alternative with pointy horns poking out of her head.

"Am I dead?" Despite the words being slurred with grogginess, his deep voice maintained its usual rugged quality that mixed well with his natural aura of raw sexuality.

"No, you're not dead. You had an accident, Mr. Dallas. You're in the hospital."

He thought her voice sounded a little shaky, but decided it could have something to do with the throbbing inside his head.

"Accident?" It took his brain a few seconds to process the information. He winced, remembering. "I rammed my truck into a lamppost."

"From what I'm told, you swerved to miss a child who ran into the street."

"It all happened pretty fast, but I guess I did. How's the kid doing?"

"He's fine. His parents called. They'd liked to come by and thank you in person."

"Tell them I'll have to take a rain check." He stared at her, enjoying the lazy pull of attraction that tugged at his stomach muscles and decided to go with impulse. "Have dinner with me Catherine Ashley," he said reading her nameplate.

"What did you say?"

"I want to take you to dinner when I get out of here."

"Is that so? Well, I'll have to give you a rain check on that."

Her humor made him grin. "I can be pretty persistent when I want something."

"So can I when I'm not sure something is a good idea."

"How do you know unless you try? I like to give the lady flowers on our first date. What's your favorite?" He held up a hand. "Wait, don't tell me. Roses? Daisies?

No, I've got it. Violets." Her expression told him he'd finally hit on the right one.

"Aren't you the clever boy?" She walked to the door.

"Top of my class in school. So how about that date?"

"Go back to sleep, Mr. Dallas. You've had enough excitement for one day."

"You have no idea how much excitement I can handle, angel nurse."

>>>>dreams<<<<

Josh scanned the hospital entrance waiting for Catherine to appear. He smiled recalling their lighthearted bantering, but his inner radar told him she possessed a sensuality simmering beneath her playful façade and he had every intention of exploring those intriguing depths.

He approached her as soon as she came through the glass doors.

"I was hoping I'd be in the right place at the right time," he said sliding easily into the courtship mode ready to take his wooing to the next level. "Looks like I got lucky."

Their eyes locked before she took a couple of steps back. "I beg your pardon."

He saw her flash of recognition and something else that looked like caution. If she wanted to pretend she didn't know him he was willing to play along. He treated her to his most winning smile.

"Don't tell me you don't remember me. I was in here a few days ago and you were my nurse. I'm Josh Dallas, the guy who rammed his truck into a lamppost."

"Oh yes. You're the man who saves little boys. How's the head, Mr. Dallas?"

"It's feeling better by the second, especially now that I'm here seeing you again."

A brow lifted.

"Don't tell me you actually get results with such a line, Casanova?"

He winced.

"A pretty woman like you shouldn't be so sarcastic. I like Josh if it's all the same to you, and I'm here to remind you we're going out to dinner."

"Strange, I don't remember agreeing to that and FYI: I don't date patients."

"Technically, I'm no longer a patient." He brought out the nosegay of violets he'd hidden behind his back. "I promised you flowers. Don't I deserve some kind of reward?"

A smile tugged at her mouth, as she took the flowers.

"You are outrageous."

"But loveable." His eyes took in her petite shape clad in pants and a cotton smock dotted with tiny red hearts. "You'll want to change. I'll pick you up at seven. All I need is your address." He waited while she gnawed her lip seeming to wage a battle with herself.

"Make it seven-thirty and all I need is to have my head examined," she muttered.

"Hey, I could be the man of your dreams."

She rewarded him with a shivery laugh. "Funny you should say that."

"Yeah, how so?"

"Let's just say there's a possibility we could both end up regretting this."

>>>>*dreams*<<<<

A cotton-candy pink dawn streamed in through the bare windows tinting the bedroom with its rosy illumination. Josh lay in his bed propped on one elbow watching Catherine's sleeping form. They'd been together four months now and just as he'd suspected there was a lot of fire hidden beneath her cool, creamy skin. She was so hot when they made love it was a wonder they didn't scorch the sheets. Not that he was complaining. He liked fiery women and was quite happy to let her ignite his pilot light.

But their lovemaking would have to be put on hold for a while. He'd signed on for a three month project in the Amazon and was leaving later today. He started to lie back when Catherine's arms and legs thrashed about and she began to cry out, her voice choking, her words incomprehensible. She began to flail about, clearly agitated by whatever she was dreaming.

He shook her gently.

"Hey, wake up, honey. You must be having a nightmare."

Her eyes flew open, glazed with fear before focusing on his face.

"Don't go," she begged, the piercing whine of her voice mounting as she grabbed for his arms.

"What? Don't go where?" he asked concerned by her desperate sounding plea.

"The Amazon. You mustn't go there,"

"Catherine, what are you talking about? I've already signed the contract."

"I saw you in my dream. You were lying unconscious surrounded by dense foliage. It was raining. You were covered in mud. This is a warning sign. I feel it."

He gathered her in his arms.

"It was just a crazy dream. I'm going to be fine."

"You don't understand. I never told you, but I sometimes see things in my dreams – things that come true. I saw you in a dream the night before you came to the hospital."

"No kidding?" he said, more intrigued than shocked by her confession. "This talent could be kind of handy. Can you predict whether or not I'll win the lottery?"

She tried to pull away from him, but he held on.

"I'm serious, Josh."

"So am I." He started to laugh, but stopped when her eyes filled with tears. "Hey, I've been all over the globe and the worst that's happened to me is getting blisters."

"You have to listen to me. The night before I met you, I had a repeat of an old nightmare and that was just before I saw you in my dream. It concerned people I loved very much. That dream ended badly for them and I believe I had it again because something terrible is going to happen to you, too."

"You had a bad dream because you're going to miss me," he teased.

"It's more than that." She hesitated. "I've seen death in my dreams before."

He jerked back.

"What the hell! Are you saying I'm going to die on the job?"

"I don't know, but I'm not willing to tempt fate. Please, please, don't go."

>>>>*dreams*<<<<

They sat in one of the airport bars. Josh hunched his long, lean body over a beer while Catherine sat in rigid silence next to him, ignoring the glass of wine he had ordered for her. He looked at her out of the corner of his eye, wishing he could think of something to say that would ease the tension between them. He began to consider apologizing when he inadvertently caught a whiff of exotic perfume nearby.

"Do you mind if I join you?"

They both turned at the sound of the sultry voice. Josh recognized the red haired woman standing there smiling – she'd been introduced at a recent meeting as the botanist going with the team on the Amazon trip. After dealing with Catherine's sullen mood, Josh was eager for any kind of diversion. He quickly rose to his feet and flashed a welcoming smile.

"Not at all. This is Catherine Ashley, Dr. Rabb," he said making the introductions.

"Marie," she amended and nodded toward Catherine before easing her supple body onto a bar stool. "Vodka, rocks," she told the hovering bartender before plucking a pretzel out of a nearby bowl. She waited until the bartender brought her drink and melted back into the shadows at the other end of the bar before she spoke again. "I don't mean to pry, but you seemed a bit tense at our last meeting. Anything you'd like to talk about?"

"I wasn't aware that I gave that impression. I'm fine, really."

"That's good. I thought you may be worried about the hired guns. My mistake."

Josh winced at Catherine's sharp intake of breath. He wanted to stuff more pretzels in Marie's mouth to shut her up.

"Why do you have to have hired guns?"

"It's only a precaution in case the locals get testy, but they never have before."

"How many times have you done this?" Josh asked, hoping to get off the subject of guns and ease Catherine's anxious expression.

"The Amazon? A few." She sipped her drink giving her lips an inviting sheen.

"A trip like this can't be comfortable for a woman. Why do you keep doing it?"

Josh didn't miss the quick gleam of excitement that leaped into her eyes.

"There's plant life in the Amazon still waiting to be discovered. I'm willing to put up with living in a tent for a few months each year because I want to see as much new vegetation as I can."

"There's certainly nothing uncivilized about the pay."

She rejected his comment with a quick wave of her hand. "Money doesn't last. I like the idea that I have the opportunity to contribute something valuable to mankind – something that will endure long after the pay envelope is empty."

"That's commendable of you," Catherine said.

"I guess I must sound pretty mercenary in comparison," Josh mumbled.

Marie smiled. "You're just being honest and this is your first trip. Wait 'till you get there. There's a certain mystique about the place that might appeal to you."

"I'll have to get back to you on that, but I'll do my job no matter what."

"I'm sure you will. You have a reputation for being a first-rate geologist and from what I've read you've been around." She drained her glass. "Thanks for the drink."

He didn't miss her innuendo about his travels, and the look on Catherine's face told him he wasn't the only one. "Would you like another?" he offered trying to be polite.

"Thanks, but I'd better not. I have some notes to go over and I need a clear head." She swiveled her body off the stool in one graceful motion and looked at Catherine. "Don't worry about Josh. I'll be happy to keep an eye on him."

"Oh, I've little doubt of that, but I'm putting my money on the hired guns."

Marie raised her brows and shrugged before turning to Josh.

"I'm looking forward to working with you, Josh. I have a feeling we're going to make a very good team."

"Wouldn't that depend on the game?"

"Oh yes." Her velvety laugh drifted over her shoulder, as she strolled away.

Josh knew being around an attractive female like Marie would be a test for any man's willpower. She literally sizzled with sensual energy and a guy would have to be dead below the waist not to admit to being tempted to dip into all that heat.

He allowed himself a brief image of them rolling around naked and sweaty before turning back to Catherine. But there certainly wasn't any heat coming from his little fireball now. She glared at him with enough ice to send chills prickling along his spine.

"I can see why you didn't want to cancel the trip now that I've met your teammate, or should I say playmate? I'm sure she's quite good at mixing work and play."

"Well, it's not going to be with me. I have no intention of messing around with her. She's just a big flirt. I'm going on this trip because I want the field work and it pays a lot better than my desk job." He hadn't told her, but he also planned to put his generous salary toward building a nest egg if marriage ended up being in their future.

She grabbed her purse off the bar. "I hope the money will be worth it. Take care of yourself, Josh. I've tried to warn you by telling you about my dream, but the irony here is I can't protect you from yourself. Promise me you'll be careful."

He couldn't let her leave with this coldness hovering between them. He grabbed her before she could walk away and took her mouth in a deep kiss.

"You can count on it."

11

She looked as though she wanted to say something else, but shook her head and walked away. He watched until she was out of sight. It bugged him that she was so hung up on her dream. Having her talk about death was creepy, and he didn't like the way she'd made jagged nerves saw at his gut. Just because he'd be leaving civilization behind and entering the unknown didn't mean something bad was going to happen to him.

Chapter Two

Marie's breasts brushed against Josh's arm leaving searing points of hot pressure against his bare skin, as she reached in front of him for a notebook. His quick shot of adrenaline came from anger, rather than lust. He knew she enjoyed this little game of flirting and it usually amused him, but he wasn't in a mood for her playfulness today.

He snatched up the journal and shoved it at her. "Here, take the damn thing."

"Oh! Oh! Somebody got up on the wrong side of his tent this morning."

"That somebody is ready to get started working." Exasperation nipped at him like tiny pinches. "Do you have a problem with that?"

"Well, excuse me!" She turned her back and jammed the book in her backpack.

"Wait, hold on a minute." He touched her arm. "I'm sorry for snapping at you, Marie. I guess I'm feeling a little out of sorts today."

"That's okay. I think I know what's bothering you." Her angry expression melted.

He lifted a brow at her. "And that would be?"

"You miss your lady friend, Catherine."

"I miss a lot of things, including a comfortable bed."

"Don't we all? But seriously Josh, I really do think it's nice for anyone to know that he or she has a special person to go home to when we're finished here."

"Does that mean you're expecting a private welcome home party yourself?"

She hesitated a moment. "That will depend on me." She slipped her backpack over her shoulders. "Let's go see what surprises the jungle has in store for us today."

Josh winced at her words. This would be the first time they planned to venture so far from the base camp and he didn't want to tell Marie the prospect was part of the reason he felt on edge. One of the guides had found several footprints the day before by a spot in the river where no one from camp had been. Despite Marie's lack of concern and the team leader having assigned an extra security guard to accompany them, Josh couldn't shake the feeling that those testy locals Marie had mentioned might decide to make an appearance today. He just hoped they'd be in a friendly mood if they did.

Although this work was providing the change he'd craved from his desk job, Josh found himself marking off the days until he returned to Catherine. He took it as a good omen. He admitted he needed the time away to test his feelings for her. When a man had marriage on his mind he'd better be sure he was hooking up with the right woman.

>>>>*dreams*<<<<

Later as Josh stopped to examine a rock formation beside the trail, a startled sound slipped through his consciousness.

"Ooh Dios!"

He jerked up and recognized their guide's voice.

"Come, Senior! You must come now!"

Josh ran toward the moored boat. His body froze at the sight of the two security guards lying unmoving on the ground, each with a long slender primitive looking dart protruding from his chest.

The guide continued to yell, his arms flailing frantically while Josh looked desperately around. "Marie! Where the hell are you?"

She burst from behind a cluster of tall plants. He grabbed her arm, turning her away from the grisly scene on the river bank, and ran with her to the boat. They'd barely scrambled aboard the small craft when a group of men rushed through the wall of thick foliage, with rifles clutched in their hands aimed and ready.

One, apparently the leader, stepped away and shouted to the others in rapid Spanish. Three of them rushed forward; one man dragged a struggling Marie back onto the bank while the other two seized Josh. The leader spoke harshly to the guide who'd fallen on his knees holding his hands out in tearful supplication.

The terrified guide stopped babbling and carried out the order to untie the boat. Josh watched, as the small craft maneuvered out from the bank taking away their only means of escape. He cursed and struggled until he felt the tip of a rifle thrust in his face. Realizing rebellion could get him killed, he forced himself to clamp his jaw shut and submit to being bound.

Marie's hands had already been tied. She stood trembling while darting frightened glances at the men who surrounded her. Josh recognized the sheer terror on her face and felt his own raw fear kick in. The man issuing orders led them away from the river and in a matter of seconds the entire group was swallowed up by dense vegetation.

The leader set a grueling pace with ruthless disregard for the welfare of his captives, leading them ever deeper into the all-enveloping jungle. Time and miles crept by. Muscles burned with fatigue while sweat drenched their clothing in the sauna-like atmosphere. After watching her stumble and fall for the third time, Josh tried to communicate to the leader that Marie needed to rest but his efforts earned him a hard jab to the shoulder with the butt of a rifle.

When they finally broke through a thick wall of plants and entered a large clearing, he and Marie both sank to their knees panting with exhaustion. In front of them, an assortment of rustic dwellings constructed from crude wooden poles and slender saplings clustered together. Overlapping leaves formed roofs, but as a concession to the torrid climate, the huts had no walls. Mesh sleeping hammocks hung from rafters.

Wide-eyed natives stood silently watching, as one of their captors kicked Josh in his ribs motioning him to get up and another hauled Marie roughly to her feet ignoring her gasp of pain.

Rough hands shoved them into one of the huts where they collapsed onto the dirt floor. Tears slid down Marie's face leaving grimy tracks through the sweat that clung to her cheeks. The gloss and teasing Josh had come to associate with her had disappeared.

"Oh, God, what are we going to do?" she moaned. Anxiety robbed her voice of its usual cool self-confidence.

"All right now. Hang on – just hang on." Josh inched himself as close to her as he could, hoping his nearness might help to calm her. But as fear slid through him like a slithering snake, he realized he wasn't feeling too steady himself.

He looked at his surroundings with a helpless feeling and a vulnerability that he'd never experienced before, as he watched the armed men bullying their way around the encampment. Josh knew he'd been seduced by the lure of the unseen challenges he and Marie had talked about, but none of his other jobs over the years had prepared him for this terrifying turn of events.

Any lingering exhilaration he'd felt for the work vanished with the ominous threat they now faced. He'd discovered jungle living did not come without danger when one considered the insects, wild animals, and possible exotic illnesses. He had known there would be risks before he took the job, but as long as they had their armed guards to protect them, no one on their team had anticipated that the worst threat would come from humans.

"I just can't believe this is happening," Marie whispered.

Josh nudged her gently with his shoulder, knowing it wouldn't do any good to mention he'd had a bad feeling about leaving camp this morning.

"I'm sure our guide is back at camp raising the alarm," he said, in a futile effort to reassure her. "Our people aren't going to waste any time coming after us."

"I hope to God they hurry," she said and began to cry in soft little sobs.

"They will." Josh hoped he was right because he'd never felt more unnerved. He let her have her cry hoping it might help to relieve some of the strain. "I know you're scared Marie, but I need you to focus," he said when the tears finally stopped. "You speak Spanish. Do you know what these thugs want with us?"

She sniffed and wiped her face on her shoulder.

"I'm not usually such a crybaby."

"Nobody's keeping score."

"They want a ransom. Apparently Orlando has a beef with Americans and feels the money will help to soothe his wounded sensibilities."

"Who the hell is Orlando?"

"He's the leader of the men who brought us here. I heard him tell our guide that people like us owe him for invading his country. He wants a million dollars from our company or he'll return us to camp in little pieces."

Josh watched the color drain from her face and felt as though a hand had reached inside his chest to squeeze his heart.

"Jesus! It's not like we're doing anything wrong."

"It's just his excuse to get money. I'd be willing to bet that we care more about this land than Orlando and his scum. The other people are indigenous natives and they're not happy to have the outsiders here, but they appear terrified by the guns."

"But weren't those native darts that brought our two men down?"

"Yes, but whoever used them was probably forced to. My guess is that Orlando didn't want to fire a rifle and take the chance he'd alert anyone from our team."

Josh struggled to take it all in. Everything had happened too fast, like an unexpected punch. "Better not let this Orlando know you speak Spanish, so he'll continue to talk freely in front of us."

They stopped talking when a native woman ducked into the hut. She bent down and using a knife, cut through the ropes that bound their wrists. Marie groaned and Josh hissed out a breath, as the blood began to flow painfully back into their swollen hands. The woman took turns briskly rubbing their wrists to help ease the discomfort.

She left and returned a short time later accompanied by a young girl. They each carried a cup with water and a plate of what looked like some kind of stew. Josh had no idea what the ingredients were and he didn't care. The aroma wasn't bad and he was hungry enough to gnaw on his shoe. But thirst was his most immediate concern. He drained his cup and instantly wished for more. He wiped the back of his hand across his mouth and saw Marie wrinkle her nose after taking a tentative sip.

"What's the matter?"

"This water hasn't been treated. Despite having shots it could still make us sick."

"I'm sure it's okay. I saw some of the natives drinking it."

"We can't go by what they eat or drink. Over the years their bodies have built up immunity to any microorganisms. Bacteria that could make us ill most likely wouldn't have any effect on them at all."

Josh stared into his empty cup and swore. "Great. An amoeba cocktail. That's all we need on top of everything else. I don't know about you, but I have to say so far this day really sucks," he said, trying to infuse a bit of humor into the situation for her benefit.

She rewarded his efforts with a weak smile. "I've had better."

They ate in silence and a tenuous calm gradually settled around the area. People had finished eating and began climbing into their hammocks for the night. The darkness beneath the jungle canopy reminded Josh of thick molasses. He looked at Marie where she lay sleeping curled on the ground with her head pillowed on her arm. Weary from the day's march, he settled himself on the dirt floor and folded his hands behind his head.

The jungle reminded him of a surly mistress sulking through each day punishing everything with her suffocating heat. As if that wasn't enough to make a body miserable, the rain and humidity could rot a man's feet inside his boots if he weren't careful.

He'd always enjoyed going to new places, but what happened today was undeniably the downside of being adventuresome. He hoped for Marie's sake things weren't going to get any worse. She'd turned out to be a lot more vulnerable than he would have expected considering she'd always acted so confident. But then that was before someone had pointed a loaded gun at her.

A tired sigh escaped as he wished he had clean water to drink, a shower, and a change of clothes. Most of all he wished to God he had taken Catherine's advice more seriously. Maybe if he hadn't been so damned determined to prove it'd take more than a nightmare to scare him off, he may have reconsidered taking the job.

Whether or not she had some kind of psychic connection with the future or it had been that mysterious woman's intuition thing that guys never understood, he'd obviously been wrong to ignore her. He shifted his body trying to find a more comfortable position on the hard packed dirt and closed his eyes.

He supposed he should at least be thankful she hadn't been right about his being unconscious, soaked to the skin, and coated in mud.

Chapter Three

Dressed in faded sweats, Catherine propped her bare feet on the coffee table and leaned her head back against the sofa cushions. She'd turned the TV on more for the sound of voices than any interest in the program. Images from the screen sent lights dancing over the carpet in flickering patterns.

It had been a long day. Two nurses calling in sick had made it necessary for her to work a double shift. The extra hours had left her feeling more tired than usual. But there was an added dimension to her weariness now – a disturbing sense that something wasn't quite right. The feeling had started as an unsettling mood when she'd drifted off to sleep last night and had slowly developed into a disturbing dream.

The details were too vague for her to understand much, but she did know it concerned Josh and he appeared to be surrounded by a group of armed men. Catherine assumed these were the security people hired to keep him safe, so it didn't make sense when fear continued to scrape at her nerves.

Setting the TV on mute, she closed her eyes hoping to block out the unwanted intrusion when three sharp raps at the door broke into her thoughts. Her eyes snapped open and her heart jerked in uneven thumps. She sat up and glanced at her watch. It was late for unannounced visitors. She slid off the sofa and walked warily toward the door.

When she saw Josh's close friend Tom Wolden through the peephole the strange feeling that had plagued her all day instantly developed into full blown distress. A cold shiver that shouldn't have been there in the warm room trembled through her, as she fumbled with the latch before flinging the door open to stare at him with anxious eyes.

"Something's happened to Josh. That's why you're here isn't it?"

He blinked in surprise. "Huh? No. As far as I know he's fine. I just came from a movie and was in the neighborhood, so I thought I'd stop by." He peered at her more closely. "But maybe this isn't a good time. Are you all right? Did I wake you up?"

"I'm fine and I wasn't asleep." She smiled at him feeling relief sink in, soothing her uneasiness. "I'm sorry for being a drama queen. It's been a weird day. Would you like a glass of iced tea? I'd offer you a beer, but I don't keep it unless Josh is here."

"Tea would be good," he said, as he entered and she motioned him to a chair.

She went into the kitchen for a moment, returning shortly with two tall glasses and handed him one before settling on the sofa with her legs tucked under her.

"What have you been up to besides going to the movies?"

He shrugged.

"Not much – working mostly. How about you?"

"The same, but it's not enough. I can't help missing Josh."

"Yeah, I know what you mean. His absence does tend to leave a big blank spot."

"He told me you've been friends since you were kids. Do you ever get a sense you might lose him when he takes off like this – that he'll want to stay away for good?"

"Nope. I believe he's like Dorothy in the Wizard of Oz. One of these days he'll realize everything he needs is right in his own backyard."

She wondered if Josh realized how wise his friend was. "Maybe you ought to remind him of that fact."

"I have plenty of times, but I've seen Josh take off on too many escapades to know I couldn't stop him from going to play Tarzan. Believe me I did try."

"So did I. It's so frustrating that we can't have any contact with him."

"I don't like it either. It's like having him drop off the face of the earth. But I bet he's counting the days until he can get back to you. Just think about the great reunion you'll have. You're his soul mate."

"Am I? Men and women often have different interpretations on what that means."

"I don't know much about women, but I'm right about Josh's feelings for you. He's kind of hard to understand sometimes, but if you're patient it'll be worth the wait."

"I'm trying." She took a sip of tea. "Josh told me you're shy around girls."

His face reddened and he shifted uneasily on his chair. "Josh has a big mouth."

She chuckled softly. "Have you ever had a steady girlfriend, Tom?"

"Not really. I kind of came close a couple of times, but they didn't work out."

"I'm sorry to hear that."

23

"Don't be – they weren't any big deal. One treated her cat better than me, and the other one baked me fruitcakes. What kind of a girl gives a guy fruitcake for Pete's sake?"

"Maybe one who likes to bake?" she said, smothering another laugh.

She studied him from beneath her lashes. Hair the color of dirty straw hung over his forehead in scattered waves and his brows hovered above his eyes like a pair of dark slashes. His slenderness made him appear frail and his modesty added to the illusion.

He and Josh were so dissimilar that Catherine found it hard to believe they'd become close friends. It wasn't only Josh's superior physique that set them apart; there was also his powerful persona. She couldn't imagine Josh being unable to get just about anything he wanted. She was a perfect example; one minute she was telling him she never dated patients and the next thing she knew she'd agreed to have dinner with him.

"Your families must have been quite friendly with you two growing up together."

"Not really. My parents weren't what you'd call sociable." His hand tightened on the glass he held. "I've always thought the concept of a family unit is a good one, but it has to have proper nurturing to develop into something meaningful. Sometimes there are too many gaps and missing pieces for things to work the way they should."

She sensed too much unspoken pain to ask more.

"Is Josh close to his family?"

"Very close, but I expect you'll find that out for yourself when he gets back."

"I know Josh had his share of women before we began dating. One of them sent me a nasty warning note that I was encroaching on her territory. No signature, of course."

"Really? Well, obviously he's not lived like a monk, but that's in the past. With you, it's not just physical. There's real emotion involved. What's your family like?"

"You're evading my questions. It seems males have their own code of ethics when it comes to discussing their buddy's old girlfriends with the current one."

"I don't know enough about any of them. I'd really like to hear about your folks."

She hesitated, swallowing down the familiar sick feeling that always came when she had to repeat how they'd died. "There's not much to relate. My parents drowned in a boating accident with my uncle when I was seven." She heard his sharp intake of breath. "I was an only child. My aunt raised me. She and my mother were sisters."

"God, I had no idea. I'm so sorry, Catherine. That must have been awful for you being so young. Do you remember very much about them?"

"Bits and pieces. It's been twenty years since the accident, but I do recall they laughed a lot and liked to hold hands." She had always hoped they'd been able to reach for each other in the end. Her cruel dream hadn't given her even that small comfort.

"I'm glad you have your aunt."

"I'm also close to her daughter. My aunt used to say if it hadn't been for the responsibility of raising two little girls she might not have gotten through the tragedy."

"Friends are nice, too. They can help make things easier when you're lonely."

It disturbed her to see his quick flicker of vulnerability. But even more disturbing was the look that suggested a need for intimacy. She couldn't allow that.

"Most of the time a friend is a friend, family is family, and a lover is a lover. Sometimes you can combine the three, but only to a point. It's usually not a good idea to confuse them."

Bright color flamed in his cheeks.

"Hey, I didn't mean to give you the wrong impression. I'm not hitting on you or . . . or anything like that," he said, stumbling over the words. "Josh is my best friend. He asked me to look in on you and maybe keep you company now and then. I'd never step into his personal arena."

"I'm sure you wouldn't, but it's important you realize where I'm coming from, too." She smiled to ease his discomfort. "What do you think he's doing right now?"

"Knowing Josh, he's probably swinging from some jungle vine having the time of his life." He looked at his watch and stood up. "It's late. I'd better let you get some sleep. Thanks for the tea. Is it okay if I call you sometime? You know, like Josh wanted me to. Maybe we can take in a movie or go for pizza. But I'll back off if you'd rather I didn't and there won't be any hard feelings on my part."

She raised herself from the sofa cushions and got to her feet.

"I would like us to keep each other company. I did not mean to scare you off with my little lecture, Tom."

"That's okay. It's always good to lay out the boundaries, especially for guys, so they know where they stand."

She had to smile.

"Are you always so agreeable?"

"I try. It makes life less complicated." He stepped outside. "Anyway, I'll be in touch. Think about what you'd like to do in the meantime."

"I will. Tom?"

"Yeah?"

"Thank you for coming by."

"You're welcome." He started to walk away, but stopped and turned to face her again. "Don't worry; Josh will be back before you know it."

Wanna bet? The silent words popped into her head so unexpectedly she didn't have a chance to hold back the quick shock that followed or the sudden queasiness that lurched into her stomach.

"Catherine?" Tom said, pulling her attention back to him. "Are you okay? Your face just went chalk white."

She made herself smile.

"It did?"

She rubbed a hand over her eyes.

"I guess I'm more tired than I thought. I'll be fine after a few hours sleep. Goodnight, Tom."

"Night," he said after a moment's hesitation.

She closed the door and stood leaning against it. His visit had chased away her earlier moodiness, but now that she was alone again she could feel the depressing feelings beginning to creep back. She looked around the empty room and found little comfort in the familiar surroundings, knowing how much she dreaded the dark secrets that might be revealed to her during another long, lonely night.

Chapter Four

Josh awoke to a strange gray-green light filtering beneath his eyelids. The sun's early morning rays crept down through thick vegetation to pluck at the ground with long golden fingers. Strong pungency from exotic blooms and half-rotting plants spiced the air with a cloying sweetness that bombarded his senses and made his nostrils twitch.

The heat was uncomfortable even at this early hour making his skin clammy and his clothes stick to him. Sore and stiff, he pushed himself into a sitting position and rubbed the spot in his shoulder where he'd been hit by the rifle butt. He saw that Marie was still asleep, but the murmur of other voices made him look around.

People were stirring and one by one leaving their hammocks. Josh turned his attention to the walls of dense greenery that circled the clearing. Even if he and Marie were able to slip away he knew they could easily lose their way in the formidable jungle.

He realized now that was why their bonds had been cut and no one had bothered to tether them for the night. They may as well be surrounded by iron bars. The grim reality was the environment would keep them here as surely as any prison cell could.

The same girl from yesterday brought two cups of coffee, which Josh assumed was an introduction to the camp by the kidnappers. She handed them to him. He thanked her and received a shy smile in return before she walked away. He gently nudged Marie awake and waited while she sat up before handing her a cup of the tepid liquid.

"A girl brought coffee."

They sat close together observing Orlando's every move. He strutted around snapping orders like some omnipotent dictator. They watched when he motioned to one of his men and engaged him in conversation. Josh leaned his head closer to Marie.

"Can you make out what they're saying?"

"No, but I'm sure it can't be anything good as long as Orlando's involved."

"Probably not, but remember we represent a lot of money to him."

"Haven't you ever heard the saying about wanting your cake and eating it, too?"

Josh had a feeling she was right and hoped whoever was in charge of their rescue wouldn't waste any time devising a plan to free them. He feared their situation could easily become a living hell if they were forced to stay in Orlando's clutches much longer.

>>>>*dreams*<<<<

Hamilton Spear sat at his desk staring at the data displayed on his computer screen when his secretary buzzed him with an urgent call from the team leader they'd sent to the Amazon. He snatched up his phone and listened in shocked disbelief to the voice on the other end. Grabbing a pen, he began to take rapid notes.

"I'll give the information to Mr. Marsh right away. Stay where you are until I can get back to you." He shoved himself out of his chair and hurried from the office ignoring his secretary's startled look when he rushed by her desk with his coattails flapping.

The company's CEO, Douglas Marsh, listened to Hamilton's disturbing news that two of their people had been abducted and that the captors were demanding a million dollar ransom. He pushed away from his desk and paced in swift, angry strides across the thick silver carpet, cursing under his breath until he abruptly stopped.

"What the hell kind of security did our people hire for God's sake? George Lang's the team leader, right?"

"Yes, and as you know he's a good, steady man and not one inclined to panic, but there's no mistaking his concern. According to what the guide told him, we're not dealing with some naive natives. The kidnappers are an armed, merciless lot. They've already murdered two of the security guards."

"Damn it! I want our men found as quickly as possible and in one piece. I'm willing to negotiate, but I'm not about to shell out a million dollars just like that." He snapped his fingers in mid air. "Call Lang back and make sure he hangs tough." He sat down again and scowled when Hamilton hesitated. "Well, what are you waiting for?"

"Mr. Marsh, you should know that one of the captives is Marie Rabb."

"What!" Douglas propelled himself out of his chair. "Are you certain it's Marie?"

"I'm afraid so. Also a man named Josh Dallas. This is his first trip to the Amazon."

"Good lord, man, why didn't you mention Marie in the first place? I assumed we were talking about two men being taken. Start setting up rescue plans at once. Get back to me as soon as everything's ready. Give me Lang's number. I want to talk to him myself."

"Yes sir." Clutching his notes, Hamilton wasted no time hurrying out the door.

Douglas sucked in a steadying breath before he walked across the room on leaden feet to a cabinet set against a back wall. He yanked open a door and reached inside for a bottle and glass. He poured a generous amount of whiskey out before going back to his desk, where he slumped onto the chair and rubbed a shaky hand over his square jaw.

"Oh my sweet, precious Marie," he murmured, as the idea of her being at the mercy of ruthless killers filled him with a gut churning sickness.

He took a long swallow from his glass and let the liquor burn its way down his throat. Other than the occasional drink at business lunches, he rarely drank during the day, but he needed the alcohol to blunt the tension that gripped him now.

He'd met Marie at a corporate Christmas party nearly five years ago. He'd been dazzled by her youth and beauty and hadn't been able to take his eyes off her. Douglas knew he was old enough to be her father, but the emotions she'd stirred in him had been anything but parental. He wanted her and intended to have her. He'd mapped out an ambitious wooing campaign, but gained only limited access to her life.

Her work kept her away from him too often, so he'd proposed marriage believing she'd be more apt to concentrate on him once she became his wife. But she had refused, claiming she wasn't ready. He'd been angry; his pride had taken a serious hit. They'd quarreled. He threatened to have her kicked off the team until she'd promised to at least move in with him when she returned from the Amazon.

The possibility of her being kidnapped had never entered his mind. He knew there was some danger involved going into the jungle, but nothing like this. Dear heavenly Jesus, never anything like this. Would the man kidnapped with Marie be able to offer her any protection? He answered himself immediately and felt his distress increase. What could an unarmed person do against a band of gun toting cutthroats?

>>>>*dreams*<<<<

Josh experienced a distinct tightening in the pit of his stomach when a furious Orlando barged into the hut with one of his men. Josh got to his feet and started toward Marie, but Orlando shoved him back. The other man pressed a rifle against Josh's back forcing him to walk away. He'd gone no more than a couple of yards when he heard a loud slap and Marie's cry of pain. He whirled around just in time to see Orlando slap her across the face again. Josh didn't miss the unmistakable gleam of pleasure that mingled with the anger in the man's expression.

Fury boiled up and rejecting his own safety, Josh lunged forward.

"No!"

He exploded in a fit of rage, flinging his body against the man with the rifle. Two other men immediately joined the fray. Josh lashed out throwing punches wherever he could reach, as the sound of Marie's screams pierced the air ripping into him like a serrated knife. Ignoring the blows from his combatants, he fought until a rifle butt landed behind his ear. Pain erupted inside his head seconds before he slumped to the ground.

Josh dragged himself out of unconsciousness by slow degrees. The metallic taste of blood filled his mouth. He shook his head trying to clear the fuzziness from his brain, but instantly regretted the action when pain clamped like a vise on either side of his head. One of his eyes had swollen to a mere slit. He concentrated on trying to focus the other one. He'd been hauled back and dumped in a corner of the hut. It took a few seconds to realize the moaning he heard wasn't coming from him.

His eyes found Marie and the sight filled him with pity. He staggered to his feet and limped over to her, grimacing at his body's painful protest. Her hands were tied and her shirt had a large tear in front. He lowered himself to his knees and began to work the knots loose with fingers that weren't quite steady. The coarse rope had rubbed the flesh raw, staining the fiber with blood and encircling her wrists like two bright red bracelets.

Josh blinked away the sweat that ran into his eyes and dribbled down his battered face. Gritting his teeth against the stinging perspiration, he continued to work the rope loose doing his best not to bring her any more pain than she was already suffering.

When she was freed she reached up and touched him gently on one battered cheek. "Oh Josh, look what they've done to you."

"Don't worry about me. They got in a few good shots, but I managed to land a few of my own," he told her, trying to alleviate her concern and although it caused him a great deal of discomfort, he gathered her close. His attempts to protect her had been useless. Regret burned inside him like a red hot poker branding him with the knowledge.

Tension swirled in audible waves around the camp gripping all those under Orlando's iron fist in a numbing fear. Josh propped himself against one of the hut's poles with Marie laying within the circle of his arms. He felt hot and sweaty and sore, but if holding her brought a measure of relief it was the least he could do.

Late afternoon shadows crept toward the hut when one of the native women stepped inside. She carried a gourd in each hand and had a cloth tucked beneath an arm.

Josh recognized her as the same one who'd helped them before. He wished he knew her name, so he could thank her in a more personal way. She motioned for him to lay Marie down, but when he began to ease himself away Marie whimpered and clutched his shirt.

He stroked a hand over her hair.

"It's okay. She just wants to help you."

Marie gripped his hands, as the woman soaked the cloth with water and began to gently clean the torn flesh. When she turned to Josh to wipe the dried blood from his cuts he looked into her dark eyes and saw deep sorrow. He decided to name her Sad Eyes.

She dipped her fingertips into the other gourd and gently smeared a pale sticky substance over their wounds. Josh had no idea what it was, but was grateful for its soothing coolness. Perhaps it was a medicinal plant known only to the natives. He felt certain if things had been different Marie would be interested in trying to find out.

As soon as the woman left, Marie scooted into a corner. Her tears had stopped and she appeared dazed. Josh hated these men for making him bow to their cruelty, but most of all he despised them for what they'd done to

Marie. He was suddenly filled with a terrible sense of guilt for being a male. He'd had a few women try his patience to the point of making him angry, but he couldn't imagine using physical abuse to get even.

Marie sat with her knees drawn up under her chin rocking herself back and forth in mute misery. She'd come here to find help for her fellow man, only to be brutalized by him. It saddened Josh to see this once vibrant woman be reduced to such a wretched state.

"Marie, did Orlando . . ." He cleared his throat trying to get the dreaded words out. He needed to know what happened after he'd been knocked unconscious. "Did he rape you?" he finally managed to ask, praying she hadn't had to suffer that humiliation.

She shook her head vigorously. "No! I told you he hates Americans and while he was hitting me he yelled that he loathes all women because his mother dumped him on the streets when he was barely old enough to fend for himself."

"Damned unlucky for you being both American and a female," he muttered.

"He was also angry because I hadn't let him know I speak Spanish. One of his men helped haul supplies for the last team I was on and recognized me. Orlando thinks I'm holding back information about his chances of getting the ransom money."

Seeing Marie's swollen face and split lip and feeling his own sore body, Josh had a sick feeling it wasn't just about money. The man obviously enjoyed inflicting pain, and it looked as though the ransom wasn't going to make him curb his sadistic tendencies.

His gaze wandered to Marie again. They'd become more than Orlando's hostages. They were his playthings, his amusement. This new insight added yet another ugly layer of fear.

Chapter Five

Josh lay on the floor of the hut watching discreetly from beneath half closed eyes while Orlando and his men filed out of camp shortly after daylight. He saw that one of the native men had been forced to go with them, assumedly as a hostage to insure that the rest of his people wouldn't abandon camp while they were gone. Josh felt instant relief at the thought of having this small bit of independence from Orlando's dominance.

He sat up slowly, ran his tongue over his teeth, and wrinkled his nose. His mouth had a sour taste, but as unappetizing as it was the thought of food made his stomach rumble with hunger. God, what he wouldn't give for a plate of ham and eggs right now.

He looked down at himself. Sweat and dried blood stained his clothes. He raked fingers through his matted hair and grimaced at the patches of dirt caked on his exposed skin. Since they had water to drink, he assumed the natives must have a place to bathe.

He looked at Marie. She slept on her back with her wounded wrists resting on her chest. He hoped in sleep she'd get a break from the disaster they'd stumbled into. Rolling to his feet, he stepped away from the hut. He spotted Sad Eyes and walked over to where she poured water into a pot. Others watched his approach, but no one stopped him. He pointed to the water and gestured as though he was washing himself.

She looked at him for a moment before filling a cup and lifting it toward his mouth. Josh shook his head and moved his arms through the air mimicking swimming strokes. Several children gathered around, obviously intrigued by his strange behavior. Sad Eyes frowned at him and shook her head, clearly unable to decipher his actions. Josh dropped his arms giving up his hope of a bath when one of the older boys suddenly began to jabber. He pointed to Josh and then over his shoulder until Sad Eyes nodded.

The child came up to Josh and took him by the hand. He began to pull him forward, slowly at first, and then with more insistence while other children joined in. Josh hesitated, not sure what he was letting himself in for, but Sad Eyes gestured for him to go with them. He looked at their eager faces before allowing himself to give in to their persistent pulling until they'd tugged him through an opening in the surrounding bushes.

When he looked down he realized they were on a well-worn path. The children rushed forward the last few yards and one by one jumped into a pool of water. Josh followed more slowly and watched until they motioned for him to join them. He needed no further enticement. Taking off his boots, he set them on the bank before easing himself fully clothed into the water.

Sunlight shot streaks of light through the sheltering foliage laying tints of amber over his dark auburn hair. He savored the coolness lapping against his heated body, thankful to find this small bit of relief in the harsh environment. He waited until the water had completely saturated his clothes before he removed each garment.

Gritting his teeth against the more painful areas, he began to gingerly scrub the grime from his aching body using his briefs as a washcloth. He scowled at the sight of the bruises and lacerations scattered over his skin.

"Nice going Orlando, you sadistic S.O.B. Thanks to you and your brute squad my skin looks like a rotten piece of fruit."

As soon as he finished bathing he took on the task of washing his clothing. He was in the process of draping everything on a nearby vine to dry when he realized some of the adults had come to the pool and stood on the bank watching him. His height, broad shoulders, and long muscular legs made a striking contrast to the smaller, more delicately built native men.

He experienced a twinge of self-consciousness when a couple of young women pointed at his genitals and giggled behind their hands. Flushing with unexpected modesty, Josh turned and waded back into the water to conceal his nakedness.

The children swam around him beneath the water, their heads popping up like corks bobbing to the surface. The others joined them in the water and Josh soon forgot he was naked and surrounded by people all bare as the day they were born. The adults splashed him and each other with a childlike innocence that made him laugh.

He lingered for several minutes enjoying their playfulness until he realized Marie might be awake and looking for him. Josh wanted to get her into the water. For a few precious moments he'd been able to forget about their nightmare and he wanted that for her, too. He pulled on his khakis and boots, but left the rest of his clothes scattered on his makeshift clothesline before retracing his steps back along the path.

She was awake, but resisted his efforts to make her leave the hut.

"Please, Marie. The water will make you feel better," he coaxed, as he gently tugged her to her feet.

"I'm not going to feel better until I'm away from Orlando," she insisted, but gradually allowed herself to be led away. "I took pleasure in my job when I was here before. That's why I wanted to come back, but not like this. He's ruined it for me."

"You mustn't let him take away something that was so important to you."

Her eyes darted around the enclosed area as soon as they arrived at the pool. "What if the ransom doesn't get paid? What if no one comes? We could end up dying."

He pulled her to him.

"They'll come," he insisted. His nose twitched at the combination of unpleasant odors that clung to her. "Let's get you into the water."

She stepped back and would have fallen had he not grabbed her.

"You okay?"

"I don't know. I feel dizzy and I ache all over, especially my head." She pressed fingertips to her temples. "God, I hope I'm not coming down with some jungle crud."

Josh forced down the shiver of dread her words brought and helped her out of her soiled clothes. He did his best to shield her from staring eyes and waited for her to wash herself, but she simply stood there until he took her passiveness as a signal to take charge.

He kept his hands as impersonal as possible. Marie allowed him to bathe her, accepting his help like a docile child and for the first time in his adult life Josh touched an attractive naked woman without any thought of making love to her. The others watched in silence seeming to understand that Marie was too fragile for their earlier frivolity.

Josh brushed a tangle of wet hair away from her face.

"Feeling any better?"

She leaned against his chest and whispered, "I just want to go home."

He didn't want to think about it, but the fear that she may be ill and they might not get away or that he wouldn't see Catherine again felt almost unbearable.

"I know."

>>>>*dreams*<<<<

Douglas stormed into the conference room and practically hurled himself into a chair. He leaned forward and scowled at the group of men that lined either side of the long conference table.

"Well?" he queried in a voice that snapped like a whip.

Hamilton took the lead. "A rescue team is being put together as we speak and . . ."

Douglas sliced through his words.

"You mean they haven't started looking yet?"

The other men exchanged uneasy looks and shifted in their chairs. "It takes time to find the appropriate people for this kind of thing, Mr. Marsh," one of them ventured.

"Don't give me that crap. We've got enough influence to get things moving a hell of a lot faster." He jerked to his feet nearly knocking the chair over in the process. "Get your asses in gear!" he demanded with a blistering glare and slammed out of the room.

Hamilton quickly pushed back his chair and hurried after him. "Excuse me sir, I know you want to keep things as quiet as possible, but families should be notified."

Douglas pinched the bridge of his nose between his thumb and forefinger.

"Get me their numbers; I'll make the calls."

>>>>*dreams*<<<<

Catherine and Tom were spending the day at the beach. A balmy breeze blew off the water and skimmed over the dry sand scattering a few granules. The sky, dotted with small popcorn shaped clouds, molded itself to the land like a pale blue cloth draped gracefully along the horizon. Gentle waves rolled into shore delivering jagged lines of frothy bubbles before rippling back leaving the sand slick and shiny in its wake.

Catherine looked at Tom, as he stared out to sea.

"You're awfully quiet."

"I was thinking how far away Josh is."

"More than miles separate us. I know he felt he had to go, but it still baffles me."

"Josh has always been an adventuresome guy. Even as a kid his inquisitive nature drew him into situations that the rest of us avoided either out of fear or common sense. He thrives on new challenges – new places."

"Even when there could be danger involved?" she asked while drawing little circles in the sand with her fingertip.

"I don't think it occurs to him. I've never seen him be fazed by anything. When we were kids I used to think if I hung around him long enough I might be able to absorb some of his nerve by osmosis. I can't help envying him his courage, even if I don't always agree with everything he does."

"If you ask me, I think his actions come more from egotism than bravery. I don't know how you and his family have continued to tolerate his narcissistic behavior."

"He doesn't give us a choice. Josh is what he is. I guess it sounds kind of weird to you, but that's always been part of what makes him so fascinating."

"I don't understand that kind of logic. If you walk on a tightrope long enough the odds are you're going to fall off sooner or later." She bit her lip. "I've been having bad dreams about Josh. I'm afraid something has happened to him; something terrible."

"They're just dreams, Catherine. Don't try to make anything more out of them."

>>>>dreams<<<<

Tom tried to dismiss Catherine's strange premonition as he drove home, but being stuck in traffic gave him too much time to think. He stared impatiently at the endless lines of vehicles, as they crawled along like sluggish speckled snakes. He had a feeling there must have been an accident up ahead that he couldn't see yet.

Coming from a small town in northern California where four cars in a row was considered heavy traffic, he'd learned to put up with the delays here in the more populous southern part of the state. He'd taken a helicopter ride right after arriving and thought how the freeways reminded him of giant spider webs with vehicles stuck like insects.

By the time he finally let himself into his apartment and took Douglas's call, he listened to the message with a kind of fatalism. Tom couldn't imagine what bizarre twist of fate had made Catherine sense that things had gone wrong for Josh before the rest of them had received word, but now he was going to have to let her know she'd been right.

Without hesitation he drove back to her apartment where he vigilantly stood in her living room waiting for the impact of his words to sink in. He watched her struggling to grasp his words, as shock became disbelief and disbelief slowly turned into desperate optimism.

"Kidnapped?" She frowned, creating tiny lines in her smooth forehead. "I don't understand how this could happen when he was with a team. He's going to be all right isn't he? I mean, the people he's working for are going to get him back, aren't they?"

"They're doing everything they can."

I knew something was going to happen to him, but he wouldn't listen to me." Her hand pressed against her stomach. "No one ever listens," she muttered.

He pulled her gently against him.

"Hey, Josh is tough. He'll get through this."

She leaned into his body and began to cry.

"Please don't cry, Catherine," her name slipping from his lips in a broken whisper, as the warmth of her tears slowly soaked into his shirt.

They clung to each other sharing their distress until her sobs had dwindled to soft hiccups. He eased her onto a nearby chair.

"I'll go make some coffee. Okay?"

She sniffed and wiped the back of her hand across her eyes.

"Yes, all right."

He poured out two cups and added extra sugar to Catherine's thinking it might somehow help. He carried them to the living room.

"Here you go. Careful, it's very hot."

She took a cautious sip.

"Does Josh's family know what's happened?"

"No. He always gives my number for emergencies when he takes off. I'm flying up there tomorrow afternoon. I didn't want them to hear the news over the phone."

"Would you mind if I went with you? I realize it's not the best timing considering the circumstances, but I'd like to meet them."

"I'd be glad of your company." He realized too late that his quick answer hadn't given him a chance to think about what repercussions her visit might create.

She drank from her cup again and set it aside. "I don't want to be a nuisance, but would you mind if I went home with you now? I'd rather not be alone tonight."

"Not at all. I'll take care of our cups while you get ready."

Tom had trouble understanding how Josh could leave her. If she was his woman he wouldn't be able to tear himself away. He'd told Josh as much before he'd taken off, and that's when Josh had asked him to look after Catherine. He'd said it in a joking way, but Tom hadn't wanted to pass up the opportunity to be around such a beautiful woman.

He took their cups to the kitchen, poured what was left of the coffee down the sink, and rinsed them out. He stood there staring into space, trying to absorb the fact that his best friend could at this very moment be trussed up like a hog ready to go to slaughter. The disturbing image made his hands grip the edge of the counter, but he forced himself to clamp down on his inner turmoil when he heard Catherine coming.

"You travel light," he said pointing to the small duffle bag in her hand.

"Are you sure it's okay if I go with you? I invited myself before I asked if you have a place for me to sleep."

His pulse raced at the idea of what it would be like to have her share his bed, quickly followed by a deep sense of guilt that made him ashamed.

"I'll take the sofa. I don't relish the idea of being alone tonight, either. Go get a jacket and I'll help you lock up," he said and took the bag from her, as they walked out of the kitchen together.

Chapter Six

Tom ran a damp palm down the side of his jeans before accepting Josh's brother-in-law's vigorous handshake. He resembled an enormous teddy bear with his wide body, oversized limbs, and small black eyes peering out of a large head.

"Thanks for meeting us, Jerry."

"Glad to. I guess you're feeling a little homesick for the family, huh?"

"You know me," he said ignoring Jerry's speculative look and edged closer to Catherine. "This is Catherine Ashley. She's... a good friend," he mumbled.

Bushy brows shot up.

"A friend?" he slapped Tom on the back. "Well, well, well." Huge fingers engulfed her hand. "Welcome to the boonies, Ms. Ashley."

She could see that he obviously thought she was Tom's girlfriend. She waited for Tom to correct the assumption, but to her surprise he remained silent.

"Please call me Catherine," she said filling in what had become an awkward void for her.

"That's a lovely name for a lovely lady. You two got everything you need, Tom?"

He held up their duffle bags. "Yes, we're all set."

"You can wait inside while I bring my truck around if you'd like, Catherine."

"Actually, I'd rather get some fresh air after being on the plane."

"Can't say I blame you. I hate to fly. All those people packed inside a tin can breathing each other's germs. Darned unhealthy if you ask me."

They walked out of the glass and steel terminal into a pale gray day. A slight wind stirred the air with the hint of cooler temperatures yet to come. They walked to the shuttle stop and waited. Catherine couldn't help noticing how nervous Tom seemed.

But she couldn't very well blame him. Facing Josh's family with such awful news was probably one of the hardest things he'd ever had to do. He'd become so subdued that he let her and Jerry do most of the talking during the hour and a half drive.

He had explained during the flight that Josh's austere mother, Ivy, had a tendency to measure and dissect people looking for weaknesses, and that he always felt intimidated by her and knew she only tolerated him because Josh wanted his friendship. Although she had two older daughters, Eleanor and Margaret, everyone knew Ivy favored Josh. She was a strong woman and could probably recover from anything, but not if she lost her beloved son.

Josh's father, John, greeted them at the door with a welcoming handshake. He was the antithesis of Ivy, generating genuine warmth with his friendly smile.

"Good to see you, Tom. It's been too long between visits."

Considering the reason for his visit, Tom couldn't very well say he was happy to be there. He camouflaged his discomfort by introducing Catherine. They followed John into the kitchen where the rest of the family sat at the table waiting. More introductions were made and time elapsed while Ivy served dinner.

They went into the living room where Tom stalled until they'd exhausted their store of small talk. Unable to wait any longer, he gathered his courage and delivered his disturbing news. His fingers dug into the sofa cushions, bracing himself for their reaction.

A collective gasp of shocked dismay rippled around the room quickly followed by Eleanor and Margaret bursting into tears, John clenching his jaw, Jerry reaching for Eleanor's hand, and Ivy staring hard enough at Tom to make him squirm. Catherine sat quietly, as the family began to fire questions at him with Ivy dominating the onslaught.

Looking like a soldier ill-equipped for battle, Tom swallowed his unease and answered them using the limited information he'd received. Once he'd given his meager store of facts, Ivy turned her attention to Catherine with a forbidding expression.

"Did you come to prop up Tom or do you have a specific connection to Josh?"

Catherine felt her heart sink at Ivy's brashness. She may be Josh's mother, but right now she sounded more antagonistic than maternal.

"Josh and I met a few months ago when he was a patient in the hospital where I work. We've been dating ever since. He means a great deal to me and I expect to continue our relationship when he returns."

"If that's true, why didn't you stop him from going to such a dangerous place?"

Shocked by the demanding question, Catherine stammered out a reply. "I . . . I tried, but he wouldn't listen."

"I see. Well, it would seem you obviously don't have quite as much influence over him as your little announcement would indicate. Are you sure he didn't go to the Amazon to get away from you?"

Resentment and temper burned in her throat.

"Excuse me?"

John came to her defense.

"For God's sake Ivy, leave the girl alone. You know very well no one can hold Josh back when he decides to take off on one of his jaunts."

Tom tugged Catherine to her feet in an effort to diffuse the tension filled atmosphere.

"I think it's time we leave you to discuss things in private."

"Yes you should, since it concerns our family. The two bedrooms upstairs on the right are ready unless of course you'll only require one. I leave that up to you," Ivy said ignoring Catherine's quick intake of breath and the strangled sound from Tom.

They said a hasty goodnight and hurried away. Catherine let out a long pent up breath.

"Well, so much for wanting to meet Josh's family. His sisters looked at me as though they'd like to strangle me, and his mother has definitely altered my perception of what I thought she'd be like. Is she always so hostile to strangers, or is it just me?"

"I told you she's difficult." He raked a hand through his hair. "I should have stood up for you, but I never know what to say to Ivy. I certainly didn't expect her to grill you like that, especially the crack about us sleeping together. But don't think she's singling you out. She believes in being direct with everyone."

"In general, or only when it concerns Josh? Is she jealous of me for crying out loud?" She shook her head. "Don't answer that. I probably don't want to know."

"I'm not excusing her, but it doesn't help with what's happened to Josh."

"You're right. I'm not being fair to her and I'm intruding. I shouldn't have come."

"Yes you should," he protested. "Josh would have wanted you to be here."

"I don't know how you can say that when I obviously wasn't important enough to have him so much as mention my name to his family. I wanted, needed Josh in my life, but it's becoming more and more apparent that while I was putting down roots in our relationship, he was barely skimming the surface. I assumed too much from him and coming here has made me feel like a fool."

"Josh is the fool for leaving. He wouldn't be in this mess if he'd listened to us."

"I know, for all the good it does, but we shouldn't be criticizing him considering what's happened."

"We're not criticizing, we're venting. That's what friends are for." He stopped by a door. "Take this room. I'll be next door if you need me in case you have a nightmare."

She squeezed the doorknob. "God, I hope not. I can't change the fact that Josh has been kidnapped, but the last thing I need is to be adding more bad dreams to the mix."

"You dreamed something was going to happen to him before he left, didn't you?"

"Yes and I tried to tell him, but he didn't believe me."

He swore under his breath.

"The stubborn idiot."

"Don't be too hard on him. You didn't believe me, either. It's hard to convince anyone what goes on in my dreams when I don't understand why it happens myself."

"That would make it difficult. So can you predict the future? Is it always bad?"

"Not the way you'd think. My dreams are subjective. They only concern the people I'm very close to and no they're not always bad. Hopefully tonight will be okay."

But she wasn't to be spared so easily. Despite her determination not to dream, her thoughts hurled her into another nightmare leading her down a torturous path filled with gore and blood and the sound of someone crying out in agony. She jerked awake and covered her ears. She struggled to clear the mists from her brain and when she did she knew that someone was Josh – and he was covered with blood.

>>>>*dreams*<<<<

Josh was engrossed in his own, more pleasant dreams. He lay on a bed of pristine sheets caressing Catherine, sensitizing her skin to his touch. He kissed her, savoring the sweetness before pressing his hard body against her silky skin. A groan of desire escaped him seconds before the dream was abruptly shattered by a hard kick to his buttocks.

He instinctively rolled away from the pain and his eyes popped open. Orlando had returned. Heart hammering, Josh felt queasy as anxiety washed over him – crawling across his skin like a meandering stream of icy water. Insides knotting with dread, he instantly looked for Marie and saw her crouched on the floor cowering like a cornered animal.

He scrambled to his feet intending to go to her, but two men jerked him back.

He watched with mounting fury, as Orlando seized Marie by the hair dragging her to her feet. She shrieked in terror and her eyes locked with Josh's begging him to help her.

He went ballistic. The need to tear into Orlando burned like acid.

"Damn your cold, black heart. Can't you see she's had enough? Leave her alone!" He twisted his body straining against his captors, tugging at the hands that held him back. His defiance awarded him a couple of vicious punches to his midsection robbing him of breath and sending him to his knees, gasping for air. Vibrating with rage and a glare of pure evil, Orlando snarled orders to his men before turning back to a sobbing Marie.

The men dragged Josh past solemn natives and slammed him against a tree trunk.

He struggled to catch his breath as they yanked his arms behind the tree and tied them with a heavy cord. Two men pummeled him with their fists then one of them tore the front of his shirt open seconds before the other began to whip him with a slender switch.

Each razor sharp lash flayed Josh's skin sending shock wave after shock wave of fiery agony throughout his body. White hot pain exploded, burning all the way to his nerve endings like streaks of lightening, searing and intense. The burly man's sweaty face gleamed with wicked pleasure, as the makeshift whip whistled through the air cutting into bare flesh while Josh writhed trying in vain to avoid the terrible punishment.

The tendons in his arms swelled and his muscles quivered when he strained against his bonds. His body jerked in reflex each time the switch landed against his bloodied chest, forcing out hoarse moans to mingle with Marie's pleading screams that ricocheted around the camp in a piteous duet of shared suffering.

Orlando called a halt to the flogging after several more excruciating lashes. Josh's legs buckled beneath him and his body hung helplessly, adding more strain to his burdened muscles. His head fell forward onto his mutilated chest while his breath heaved in and out in hoarse gasps. Orlando gripped Josh by the hair, forced his head back, and spit in his face. Despite his pain, Josh instinctively jerked away and hissed out a protest. Orlando laughed and sauntered away leaving him tied to the tree.

Some of the natives immediately rushed forward in an effort to help him, but were ordered back by the threat of rifles aimed at them. But even with the reprieve from his human torturers, Josh's suffering hadn't ended. He was left to endure the agony of voracious insects attacking his bloodied wounds, tormenting him anew as they fed off his torn flesh.

He lay in a crumpled heap while the merciless sun beat down on his unprotected body making sweat seep from every pore creating salty drops that burned into his wounds. He turned his head as if he could move away from the misery, but the pain wove a scorching path throughout his body consuming with relentless greed. Time crept by and as his agony increased, his body weakened, until he slid into blessed unconsciousness.

>>>>dreams<<<<

Josh awoke under the protection of the hut's roof with Sad Eyes leaning over him.

At least, he thought it was Sad Eyes. Pain and prolonged exposure to the sun had made him delusional. An image of Tom swam before him wagging a finger, insisting he not leave. Catherine appeared next, pleading and warning of danger. He felt her tears dribble onto his face, or possibly they were his own. He could not be sure.

A sudden spasm of pain made his body jolt forcing out a guttural groan. His face, bruised and cut from the men's pounding fists throbbed, and his throat felt raw. Sad Eyes lifted his head to trickle water between his torn lips. Somewhere in the dim recesses of his mind, Josh realized Orlando must have allowed her to take care of him because of the ransom money. Engulfed by excruciating pain, another groan escaped him before his swollen eyelids drifted closed, dragging him back into darkness.

Several hours elapsed before Josh managed to rouse himself again. The midday sun sent searing warmth through the air spearing the ground with spikes of heat. He assumed Sad Eyes must have retreated to her hammock for the midday siesta. Woozy with pain, he turned his head and saw a cup of water sitting on the ground next to him.

Gripped by nausea, he balanced carefully on one elbow and lifted the cup to his mouth with a trembling hand. He drank in small measured sips forcing back the bile that rose in his throat, as his muscles quivered from the raw wounds crisscrossing his chest.

He eased himself down taking shallow breaths in an effort to minimize the sting. The realization that his grand adventure had turned into an excursion into hell made his body throb as though all the physical and emotional misery in the universe centered on him. But it was too late for regrets. He closed his eyes. Although the air shimmered with heat, Josh felt cold inside. Surrounded by a jungle teeming with life, he thought of death.

He drifted in and out of sleep until thoughts of Marie brought his focus back to his surroundings. He spotted her in a far corner lying on her side curled into a tight ball with her back to him. Violent tremors shook her body and her breath came in ragged gasps. Josh thought he heard what sounded like teeth chattering. Either that or someone was playing castanets inside his head.

"Marie, are you okay?" he asked in a voice that reminded him of a croaking frog.

She didn't answer, but he wasn't sure if she'd heard his raspy request. He lay quietly, trying to focus beyond his body's throbbing sting while he calculated his limited stamina. When finally realizing his legs wouldn't support his sagging weight, he gritted his teeth and began to drag himself toward her in an arduous journey through a world dominated by pain.

He touched her cheek. She was burning up. His own flesh felt overly hot. He spoke her name with more urgency. She stared at him, but there was no sign of recognition in her feverishly bright eyes.

>>>>*dreams*<<<<

Douglas stood at the row of windows in his office outlined by a nimbus of gray light when a knock sounded at the door.

"Come!" He didn't bother turning when Hamilton stepped inside. "Let's have it."

"The rescue team has been assembled and they've started their trek into the jungle from the point where the kidnapping took place."

"It's about damn time," he growled before turning to face Hamilton.

"Mr. Marsh, we've hired the best men we could find, but I'm sure you're aware of the difficulty they face given the density of the territory. There's always the possibility they won't be able to pick up the trail. At least not right away," he rushed to clarify.

Douglas's eyes pierced like points of steel.

"I don't want excuses; I want results."

He faced the windows again, fists clenched with burning rage barely contained.

Chapter Seven

Tom's eyes felt gritty from lack of sleep. Flipping back the covers, he rolled out of bed and pulled on his jeans before opening the bedroom door. The scent of pine cleaner and floor polish filled the hallway. Oak floorboards protested beneath his bare feet, as he hurried to the bathroom. Anxious to check on Catherine, he took a quick shower, but decided not to shave, unknowingly making the stubble give his features a more masculine appearance.

He knocked on Catherine's door as soon as he'd finished dressing. The lavender tint that stained the delicate skin beneath her eyes told him sleep had eluded her, too.

"Looks like I'm not the only one that didn't get much sleep. More bad dreams about Josh for you?"

She nodded and stepped from the room, closing the door quietly behind her.

"Would it help if you talked about them? I'm a pretty good listener."

"I'd rather not, but he'd better be found soon," she said through trembling lips.

He didn't miss the look of concern in her eyes and felt his heart jerk.

"Oh, jeez."

>>>>*dreams*<<<<

John walked in as they entered the kitchen saving them having to be alone with Ivy. He sank onto one of the wooden chairs and looked around the room.

"I just got off the phone with the CEO, Douglas Marsh. There's no mistaking his concern."

Ivy's eyes glinted with fierce anger.

"If anything happens to my son, I won't rest until I make those responsible pay. We should go there to be in on the negotiations."

"There aren't any negotiations. The man demanded a million dollar ransom and disappeared. A rescue team has been sent to try and find Josh." He fixed his eyes on Tom. "Did you know that a woman had been kidnapped with Josh?"

Tom turned away from Catherine's startled look.

"Yes, she's part of the team."

Ivy didn't spare any sympathy for Marie.

"A woman has no business being in a jungle. It's probably her fault Josh was taken. Does this Marsh expect us to do nothing?"

"I told you Ivy, there isn't anything we can do at this point but wait. Mr. Marsh promised to keep us informed as soon as he hears anything new."

She started to protest, but Jerry arrived at that moment. John shared the phone call while Ivy slammed around the kitchen preparing breakfast. Catherine left Tom finalizing their departure plans and felt relief flood through her to finally escape Ivy's angry scowls. But when she came out of her room she saw them together at the end of the hallway. She waited for Ivy to leave before approaching him.

"I saw Ivy talking to you. It looked like she was bawling you out. I hope I'm not responsible for driving a wedge between you two."

"She feels I didn't try hard enough to keep Josh from taking the damn job."

"Blaming us isn't going to bring him back."

"Try telling that to Ivy. Let's get our stuff and get the hell away from here."

>>>>*dreams*<<<<

The hours crawled by for Josh. He watched Marie move in and out of periods of coherency and delirium, as he fought against his own body's growing weakness. Orlando and his group had left camp again. As near as Josh could understand he had been in a violent mood because no one had shown up with news about the ransom. He lay on the ground with his hand on Marie's arm hoping the contact might help to assure her of his presence. He closed his eyes and drifted into a kinder world.

He awoke, aware that something was different. His hand had slipped away from Marie while he slept. She was quiet – too quiet after hours of labored breathing. Her skin was chalky white. Heart pounding, Josh touched one pallid cheek. Flesh that had been burning with fever now felt icy cold.

"Marie! Marie!" He gathered her lifeless body in his arms and began to rock back and forth, constantly moaning her name.

Sad Eyes touched him on the shoulder. She pointed at Marie and then to the ground. Josh ignored her, refusing to let go of his precious burden. But she became more insistent until common sense finally penetrated his grief and he knew what had to be done.

Although the native men came forth to indicate they would help him, Josh refused their offer. This was something he wanted to do by himself. It would be his last act of compassion for the woman who had asked for so little, but suffered so much.

He buried Marie and slumped to the ground panting from the exertion. Sad Eyes appeared by his side again. She pointed to him and to Orlando's hut before gesturing toward the jungle. Josh understood she wanted to get him away before his tormentor returned, but he hesitated. Leaving now could jeopardize his chances of being rescued.

But then he realized if the people looking for him didn't come, and he remained, Orlando was going to be furious when he discovered Marie had died. Given the man's penchant for inflicting pain and his vile temper, he'd look for someone to vent all that anger on and, ransom money or not, Josh had a sick feeling he'd be the likely target.

He struggled to his feet and stared at the mound of dirt. He thought of why Marie had come. He hated Orlando anew for destroying her hopes – hated the senselessness of Marie's death, the waste. He touched the grave, and felt grief shutter through him.

Sad eyes tugged on his arm drawing his attention. Unable to deny her urgency any longer, Josh turned to follow her through an opening in the thick jungle growth and within seconds it was as if the small encampment had never existed.

He had little conception of time. The only thing he could be sure of was the dark nights. Sad Eyes stopped before blackness spread its inky cape over everything. They slept on carpets of fallen leaves at the base of thick trees amid the sounds of jungle nightlife. Each night he fell asleep, too tired to think about any danger that may be lurking nearby. He had no idea where Sad Eyes was leading him and the fact that neither of them could speak each other's language kept their communication to a series of gestures. All he could do was try to keep up, but Josh felt his fatigue increase with each passing hour.

He awoke early one morning in a pool of sweat. Too weary to bother swiping at the insects swarming around his exposed skin, he lay there listlessly staring up at the different strata towering above his head. Josh knew some plants and animals flourished there that never touched the forest floor. Each layer of life depended on the others in a unique and complex ecosystem.

He recalled Marie's enthusiasm when she'd talked about the undiscovered indigenous plants that might hold the key to unlock cures for diseases. She had wanted to give life to the dying, but in the end hadn't been able to save herself. Sad Eyes nudged him, pulling him away from his mind's wanderings. Josh grunted and crawled to his feet.

He braced a hand against a tree trunk when a sudden attack of dizziness hit him. His body wobbled, as he waited for the scenery to stop spinning. He pressed a hand to his head trying to still the deafening roar that filled his ears. Clenching his jaw, he pushed himself away from the tree. It was vital that he keep going. If Sad Eyes was leading him to someone who could help, he had to let them know about Marie.

>>>>*dreams*<<<<

Douglas stood waiting, his body rigid.

Hamilton stared at the floor for a moment before looking up.

"They found the encampment," he said quietly.

"And?" Douglas stood pressing both hands on his desk steadying himself.

"The leader escaped, but his henchmen are in custody. The natives said Josh Dallas disappeared into the jungle with one of their women."

"What about Marie?" Douglas had the look of a man who knew what he was about to hear would be almost too painful to bear.

"She didn't make it. I'm sorry, sir."

"Dead?" The word was torn from Douglas in a hoarse whisper.

"Yes. I'm sorry."

He slumped back onto his chair, swallowed by his grief. "I should have gone with the rescue team. I might have had a chance to see her before she . . ." He couldn't finish.

"She was already gone, and I don't mean to sound unkind, but you probably would have slowed the team down." Hamilton hesitated. "I know this has been a terrible shock."

"Tragedy most often is. Would it be possible to bring her body back here?"

The sadness in Hamilton's eyes deepened.

"She'd already been buried. They had no choice because of the climate. But I can make arrangements to have the team return and exhume her remains if that's what you want, Mr. Marsh."

Put into words, the idea sounded repugnant.

"Perhaps it had been fated that Marie would end her days among the unique plant life she'd been so eager to study. Let her be. But I do want you to see what our people can do about finding out more on Josh Dallas. I'd like to have something more conclusive to tell his family."

Hamilton nodded.

"I've already sent instructions."

>>>>*dreams*<<<<

Catherine smiled and handed Tom a glass of wine.

"Here, maybe this will help."

His fingers grabbed the slender stem like a lifeline and he immediately gulped down a couple of deep swallows.

"You should have told me your cousin was coming."

"Why, so you could start worrying that much sooner? Or end up not coming at all?" She patted his arm. "It's only dinner with a woman you haven't met before."

He swallowed more wine.

"I'd rather walk over hot coals in my bare feet."

"Oh come now, it won't be that bad and you needn't worry about her bringing you any fruitcake because my cousin doesn't bake," she said in a laughing voice.

"I'm lousy at socializing and I'm so nervous I can't even remember her name."

"It's Nancy Mills." Her smile faded. "We need to try and get our minds away from what's happened with Josh. I thought this evening might help us both, Tom."

"I know. I'm sorry for being such a wimp about this dinner thing."

"You're not. I need to check on dinner. I'll leave you to answer the door."

"Wait!" He started to grab her arm, but stopped when she lifted her eyebrows at him. "Okay, okay, I can do this." He drained his glass, as she walked away.

The doorbell rang a couple of minutes later. He took a deep breath and yanked it open before he could lose his nerve. He stood, rooted to the floor, facing the petite woman with hair the color of ginger and big brown eyes that suggested welcoming warmth.

"Hi, you must be Tom. I'm Nancy," she said cheerfully, holding out her hand.

The brief touch caused the air to leave his lungs in a quiet little whoosh.

She tilted her head to one side and grinned. "Aren't you going to invite me in? I do believe I'm expected."

"Huh? Oh! Sure." He stepped back and caught the scent of flowers as she moved inside. "Um, Catherine's in the kitchen," he mumbled thinking his voice sounded like he was talking through sponge rubber.

She gave him another smile.

"I'll go say a quick hello."

He watched her walk away. She moved with just enough sway of her slender hips to make a man want to follow her and right now he realized he was that man.

Later, as they sat at the dinner table, Tom could have been eating sawdust for all he knew. Nancy consumed his thoughts. He'd never reacted to a woman like this before.

It was a new and heady experience. He asked if he could walk her out to her car when the evening ended.

"I enjoyed tonight. Thanks for coming."

A soft light came into her eyes. "I was about to say the same thing. I don't usually do blind dates, but I made an exception because I trust Catherine's judgment. I'm glad I did. It's been fun."

"That's good." He blew out a little breath, gearing himself up to issue his request. "Um, may I call you sometime?"

"I'd be disappointed if you didn't." She pulled a business card out of her purse.

Tom watched her flip it over and write on the back before handing it to him. "That's my home phone, but you can call the shop, too. I own a boutique with my mom, Priscilla."

He fiddled with the card.

"I swear this isn't a line, but I feel like something special happened here tonight. For me, anyway," he added, as his cheeks grew hot.

"I certainly hope so. That's why I gave you my number." She scooted onto the front seat of her car, flashed him a final smile, waved, and pulled away from the curb.

>>>>*dreams*<<<<

An hour later in his apartment, Tom sat stunned listening to Hamilton's message. He phoned Catherine. "I just got an update about Josh. I'm coming back to your place."

"What did they say?" A sob caught in her throat. "Oh God. Is he dead?"

"No! He's not dead. Hold on until I can get there and I'll explain everything."

The drive back was sheer torture. He'd been ready to tap dance on the clouds. Now tension hung heavy, weighing him down. Catherine all but pounced on him when she opened the door. He led her to a chair and relayed his bad news.

"I met Marie Rabb the day they left. She was a very attractive woman, and I'm ashamed to say I was jealous thinking of how much time she'd be spending around Josh. But I admit, she sounded quite excited about the job and apparently very dedicated. Being kidnapped must have been horrible for her. I may not have liked her, but she certainly didn't deserve to die that way. Was Josh ill, too?"

"I don't know. He left with a native woman before the rescue team got to him and even the natives didn't have any idea where she was taking him."

"If only he had waited a bit longer he would have been there when the rescue team arrived. Are you going to go see his family again?"

"Not right now. The company CEO, Douglas Marsh, has already notified them personally."

"You'd think my nightmares would have prepared me better for this, but they never quite do."

"Knowing something ahead of time doesn't always ease the burden."

"No it doesn't." Her eyes clouded with sadness. "Josh and I had barely begun and now it looks like our time together is over." Silent tears slid down her pale cheeks, slender ribbons of grief.

He pulled her into his arms.

"It's not over. He's going to be in our lives again," he insisted in a voice that wasn't quite steady.

Chapter Eight

Josh blinked his eyes several times trying to bring his surroundings into sharper focus and caught brief glimpses of flashing colors through the masses of greenery. Birds? Flowers? He wasn't sure. The whole scene resembled a watercolor painting left out in the rain.

He held his hand up in front of him. It looked blurry around the edges and when he wiggled his fingers they appeared to melt together. He stared at them and found it strangely fascinating as though he were caught up in a psychedelic hallucination.

Light and shadows swirled around him twisting everything into odd shapes. He shook his head trying to clear it, but no matter how hard he tried he couldn't distinguish between what was real and what had become a product of his confused mind. Josh wasn't sure what was happening to him, but he sensed he was slowly coming unraveled.

A hodgepodge of sounds came at him from every direction, distorted and difficult to differentiate. Weariness bit into him like an animal clawing at his body. He stumbled often, falling to his knees or sometimes on his face when he wasn't quick enough to catch himself. Each rising to his feet pushed his waning strength ever closer to its fragile limit.

Sad Eyes seemed to understand his difficulty and often tried to help him, but her small stature was no match for his size. She sat by him patiently waiting while he struggled to right himself. His biggest fear was that he wouldn't be able to get up at all and he'd end up lying there until Orlando or some marauding animal found him. That and his need to get to wherever Sad Eyes was going gave him the will to go on. Sometimes she would reach into the mesh bag that held their meager supplies and pour out a small measure of water for him. But with the unquenchable thirst that raged throughout his body, it was never enough. She'd brought along a small cache of food as well, but Josh could barely manage to swallow a few bites.

He'd become so accustomed to being surrounded by the cocoon of thick foliage that when Sad Eyes suddenly led him through a break in the jungle barrier he stood swaying in confusion, as the impact of the sun in the open space hit him. Struggling to make sense of his new surroundings, Josh finally realized he was looking at what appeared to be a road of sorts. He turned to Sad Eyes wishing he could find a way to thank her; yet Orlando had left him with nothing more tangible to offer, just his gratitude.

Suddenly, huge drops of rain pounded against his sensitive flesh. He flinched as water quickly began slashing down in heavy sheets. Along with his blurred vision, Josh found it even more difficult to see but thought he could make out a few crude houses lining either side of the rutted lane. He began to understand that Sad Eyes had brought him to some kind of a settlement.

He touched her gently on one bony shoulder in a gesture of appreciation. She smiled shyly before gesturing toward the houses and pointing to the sky reminding him that darkness would soon envelop everything within its claustrophobic cloak. Josh waited for her to lead them on once more, but she shook her head and pointed to the houses again telling him in her own way that he no longer needed her.

He nodded and concentrated once more on putting one foot in front of the other; stopping briefly to wave a last farewell, as Sad Eyes slipped back into the jungle.

Josh set off again, staggering through the rain as his body reeled with illness and fatigue.

The downpour had turned the dirt road into a quagmire of soft mud that sucked at his boots. He kept losing his balance and slipping until he was spending more time on the ground than on his feet. Night's heavy shade slid down obscuring everything behind its murky darkness. Someone lit a lamp in the house nearest to him and Josh gratefully used the small beacon to guide him there.

When he arrived at the house he stood at the base of the small porch and reached out, trying to grab hold of the slender railing. But his hands were slick with mud and they kept sliding away from the wood. He sank to his hands and knees, laboring to get each breath. When he raised his head he saw someone walk by a window.

Realizing he didn't have the strength to go any farther, Josh gathered his rapidly waning energy and called out, but the sound of the rain on the tin roof muted his voice to nothing more than a hoarse whisper. He tried once more and waited, but still no one came.

Too weak to form the words again, Josh collapsed onto the ground. He lay silent and defenseless covered in mud and pelted by silver darts of rain. His heavy eyelids drooped closed. His body had given out and he felt his mind shutting down as well. He felt oddly at peace knowing he didn't have to fight anymore. His last coherent thought before everything faded into nothingness was that Catherine's nightmare had come true.

>>>>dreams<<<<

Raymond and Hannah Daniels had been serving as missionaries in South America for over twenty years, the last eight in the Amazon region. Unfortunately, no matter how hard they tried, most of the natives refused to be Christianized, but their faith and perseverance kept them there. The small settlement they'd carved out of the jungle was a humble monument to their dedication and determination to continue doing God's work.

Following his nightly ritual, Raymond sat reading aloud from a well-worn Bible opened on the table in front of him while Hannah relaxed in a rocking chair with her head leaning back. She listened to him as he strained to be heard above the din of the heavy rain, when a sudden, unfamiliar noise made her lift her head.

Certain she'd heard a sound beyond the rain and her husband's voice, she looked inquiringly at him, but he continued to drone on. He could very well have heard something, but he hated to have his reading interrupted. Requesting that he stop was like asking a dedicated athlete to break his stride, but curiosity compelled her to get up and walk to the window.

"What are you doing?" he demanded, looking up, and staring hard at her. The irritation in his voice was obvious.

"I thought I heard a moaning sound."

"It's probably some poor beast looking for shelter from the rain. Come sit down."

Determined to satisfy her curiosity, she peered through the glass. The heavy rains always reminded her of frenzied weeping. Straining to see through the thick veil of water, she saw a shape at the bottom of the steps. "Something's there! Please go look."

He abruptly pushed his chair back, scraping the legs on the wooden floor.

"Hannah, dear, I know you'd like to give aid to every poor animal that comes to our doorstep, but you must know we can't save them all."

"But what if it isn't an animal?"

"That's a strange thing to say. What else could it be?" He waved her reply away. "Never mind, I'll go because I know you'll continue to be distracted if I don't."

"Thank you, Raymond. It should only take you a few minutes," she added with a sheepish look. She thoughtfully handed him a rain slicker while he grabbed a flashlight off a shelf.

He snorted out an annoyed grunt and opened the door to the scent of rain. She watched from the doorway as he stomped down the steps to scan the dark form with his torch. He leaned down for a closer look, and the light almost slipped from his hand. He drew an audible breath. "In the name of God! Hannah, come quickly!"

Her heart jerked at the sound of his startled shout and she hurriedly pulled on a raincoat before rushing outside. Her hands flew to her mouth when her eyes followed the flashlight's beam. "Dear heaven! It's . . . it's a man. Is he alive?"

"Barely." Raymond knelt in the mud and ran his hands over Josh's body. "There don't seem to be any broken bones, but he's burning with fever. Let's get him inside."

Working together, they carried Josh into the front room where they lay him on the bare floor. Raymond flung off his slicker and kneeling down, began to unlace Josh's boots.

"We'll have to clean him up to see if he has any injuries. Get some water and towels while I start getting these filthy clothes off of him."

Hannah hurried away, shedding her raincoat. They set about easing Josh's ragged garments from his body. Neither spoke, as their bathing revealed the multitude of insect bites along with his cuts and bruises. But Hannah couldn't stop the hiss from her sharp intake of breath at the sight of his ravaged chest.

They cleaned his body as thoroughly as they were able to before carrying Josh to a small bedroom where they lay him gently on the single cot there. Hannah covered his nakedness with a sheet and tucked it around him.

"He's going to need careful tending."

Raymond nodded.

"Yes, I know. Try to get some sleep. I'll take the first watch."

Days blurred one into the other, as they nursed Josh. Hannah looked at Raymond while she prepared the daily broth they would trickle into Josh's mouth.

"How is he?"

"Still delirious."

"Oh, that poor man. I'm so worried about him, Raymond. I fear death is whispering at the door. How much more of this can his body take?"

"Man can endure many things and survive. Being young is in his favor."

"I wonder who he is and what he's doing here."

"Without identification we'll have to wait until he can tell us himself. But listening to his ranting, I'd say he's an American by his accent."

"I agree and I think he lost a woman close to him. When I was with him this morning he kept pleading for someone named Marie not to die and then he started sobbing."

Raymond closed his eyes for a moment. "May God rest her soul," he prayed.

She gnawed on her lip.

"How do you suppose he got those terrible slashes on his chest? They look to be fairly recent, since they're not fully healed. It upsets me every time I see them and my heart cries to think of the pain he must have had to endure."

"It's obvious the marks didn't come from something that happened in nature and considering his other wounds it looks to me as though he's been deliberately mistreated. He may well be fleeing from whoever abused him."

Her hand shook as she poured the broth.

"Who would do such a terrible thing?"

"Wicked people, my dear – very wicked people."

>>>>*dreams*<<<<

Plagued by the illness that raged through him, Josh thrashed about on the narrow bed. He often shouted out in anger and just as quickly cringed in fear. His fever finally broke on the morning of the sixth day, but by then he looked more dead than alive.

He lifted his leaden eyelids and strained to focus on the barren room. It had the distinctive odor of sickness mingling with the smell of dampness and mold. He stared at the plain wooden floor and rough unpainted walls before sleep took him once again.

The next time he awoke Josh noticed a woman kneeling at his bedside. She appeared to be praying. His brow pleated in a frown. He had no sense of familiarity for her or the simple room.

"Are you praying for me?" he asked in a raspy whisper.

Hannah's head jerked up and she struggled to her feet swooping toward him. She touched her palm to his forehead and sighed.

"Praise the Lord, your fever is gone."

Josh licked his dry lips. They felt like sandpaper.

"Water, please," he croaked.

Hannah raised his head and because he was too weak to help himself, she guided a glass to his mouth. He tried to drink in greedy gulps, but she doled out the precious liquid.

"I know how thirsty you must be, but it's best for your body to take in liquids slowly." She set the water aside and helped him lie back down on the pillow.

He didn't know what was wrong with him, but he felt incredibly weak.

"Who are you?"

She gave her name and told him about Raymond and how they'd found him lying outside in the rain.

His eyes slowly scanned the room. "How long have I been here?"

"This is your sixth day in our house. You've been quite ill; delicious with fever.

When did you arrive in the area?" she asked as she pulled the sheet up to his chest.

His frown deepened in concentration. "I'm not sure. Where exactly am I?"

"In a small Christian settlement along the Amazon," she answered, studying his face for a moment. "What is your name?"

The Amazon?

Josh thought surely the woman had to be mistaken or perhaps he'd misunderstood her. If he could just block out the sound of buzzing bees inside his head he might be able to think. She asked him his name again and where he was from, but it was taking too much effort to find the answers. Their brief encounter had exhausted his meager strength.

"My name?" He shifted restlessly and turned his head away from her persistent probing, wanting only to go back to sleep. "I don't know."

He felt too drained to be concerned at his lack of knowledge. Tomorrow was another day. No doubt the questions could be answered by then, but right now he just wanted her to go away and take her pesky questions with her. His eyes clouded over and closed despite her obvious disappointment.

Hannah rushed outside to tell Raymond as soon as she realized Josh wasn't going to answer her. She related their brief conversation, expressing concern that Josh didn't know who he was.

"My guess is that his memory loss is probably from the fever. I'm sure it's only temporary," he assured her and patted her hand. "Give him time; he's only just come to."

"I know, but I was so anxious for him to tell me. Surely he must have people looking for him. Oh

Raymond, what will we do if he doesn't remember who he is?"

"Only God can determine that. In the meantime we must pray that our young patient's mind clears, so he will be able to help us return him to wherever he belongs."

Chapter Nine

Too restless to sit, Douglas stood at the bank of windows staring at the assortment of towering buildings that loomed over the city. Rows of dark tinted glass stared back reminding him of huge sightless eyes. He stood with his hands folded behind his back. His appearance was that of a man enjoying the view, while in fact every muscle in his body was drawn tight with nervous tension. Marie's personal belongings left behind in camp the day she'd been abducted had been delivered to his office that morning.

His eyes strayed unwillingly to the two zippered bags – silent reminders of the last things she'd touched. He hadn't opened the bags. He'd leave that painful task to Marie's mother. He didn't envy her the dubious privilege. They'd never met, but had talked over the phone. Knowing he shouldn't delay any longer, he jabbed a button on the desk console and gave orders to his secretary to make travel arrangements to Oahu.

>>>>*dreams*<<<<

When Jenny Rabb opened the door to her condo, her resemblance to Marie left Douglas speechless.

"Thank you for coming." She stepped back. "Please, come in."

Dazed, he followed her into a miniscule living room, gave himself a mental shake, and found his voice.

"I realize it's rude to stare, but you . . ." He made himself stop.

"Look like Marie?" she finished. "So I've been told. I appreciate the compliment. May I get you iced tea or coffee, Mr. Marsh? I also have a bottle of Merlot if you'd prefer."

"Douglas, please. Tea will be fine, thank you. I've had enough shots of alcohol lately to float a battleship, and the only things I've gotten out of them are some nasty hangovers."

"I know what you mean. Make yourself comfortable, please. I'll just be a moment."

He settled his bulk onto a pale green loveseat. An old black steamer trunk with brass locks sat between the divan and two rattan chairs with brightly colored pads on their seats. The atmosphere reflected a coziness he found inviting. He was admiring an arrangement of framed flowers on a wall when Jenny returned carrying a tray.

She set it on the trunk. It held two tall glasses, a small wooden bowl filled with macadamia nuts, and yellow paper napkins with red hibiscus flowers on the front.

He took the glass she handed to him. "Thank you. Did Marie do those flowers?"

"Yes, pretty aren't they?"

"Very. Unique and lovely – like Marie."

"She was, wasn't she?" Jenny looked at her hands for a moment before focusing on Douglas again. "Marie did love you in her own way," she said in a soft voice.

His brows rose.

"I didn't know if you were aware of our relationship, such as it was given her reluctance to marry me. I suppose it makes me sound selfish, but I wanted her to myself." It was his turn to look away. "I shouldn't have pressured her like I did."

"She was afraid of commitment. You were special to her, but she saw too much of a bad marriage with her father and me to give you what you needed. People thought of her as a flirt, but it was her way of protecting herself. Inside she was a scared little girl."

"She hid it well." He felt emotion jam its way into his chest and settle there like an unwanted intruder. There would only be memories of her now, but memories were often lonely reminders of what might have been, and God knows, he did feel alone. He took a long sip of tea wondering what more he could say to this woman who looked at him with Marie's eyes. He shifted in his seat trying to think how best to remind her of the reason he'd come when Jenny saved him the trouble.

"Thank you for bringing her things personally. I know you're a busy man."

"I would never be too busy to do something like this. I have the bags in the car. Let me go and get them and then I'll be out of your hair, Mrs. Rabb."

She looked at him with a sad little smile.

"Douglas, you're the man who wanted to marry my daughter. Don't you think it's about time you call me Jenny?"

Douglas actually felt himself blush – something he hadn't done in a very long time. It was a bit embarrassing to remind himself that she was more suited to him age wise than Marie had been.

"Yes, I suppose you're right." She walked with him to the door, but he stopped before she could open it. "Would you happen to be free to join me for dinner this evening, Jenny?" he asked surprising himself with the impulse.

"As a matter of fact I am, but why don't you let me cook something here? It's the least I can do to repay you for coming all this way."

"Thank you, that's very generous of you," he said and felt the grip of loneliness lessen its hold. She wasn't Marie, but she was nice and he couldn't deny that he'd like to have her talk to him about Marie. It might even bring them both a measure of comfort.

She cut into his thoughts.

"I've wanted to ask you, did your people ever find the man that was taken with Marie? I'd like to meet him if possible."

"So would I, but unfortunately he was never found."

"Oh, I'm so sorry. I can't imagine the heartache his family must be suffering not knowing what happened to him."

"Yes. It makes one wonder how they're managing to cope."

>>>>dreams<<<<

Nancy stood next to Tom and watched the hospital entrance. "Mom and I are worried about Catherine. She's so down. Except for work, she stays home all the time."

He kissed her on the end of her nose. "That's why we're here, remember?"

"I know, but she'll probably refuse to let us take her out."

"We won't let her. Here she comes, put on your best smile."

Catherine hung back a moment before going to them.

"What brings you here?"

Nancy linked their arms. "Taking you out to pizza, you lucky girl."

"I can't," came her ready reply. "I'm too tired."

"We won't be late and you have to eat."

"I appreciate what you're trying to do, but I'm really not fit company."

Tom put a fingertip lightly over her mouth. "Humor our efforts to be useful."

She looked at their hopeful expressions. "Oh all right, but no anchovies."

>>>>*dreams*<<<<

Weeks turned into months and Catherine continued to dream about Josh. In one he appeared to be wandering through a maze of green. She reached out to him, but no matter how hard she tried, she couldn't make contact. Her depression dug in and clenched with an iron fist.

Nancy helped Tom cope. Mere weeks after their first meeting they'd eloped and were now expecting their first child. They were creating a new life for themselves while she clung to the old one. He'd encouraged her to stop pining for what might have been and give someone else a chance. Catherine hadn't been very enthusiastic, but had promised to try. She was leaving work one evening when a masculine voice called to her.

She stopped and smiled, recognizing the man coming toward her.

"Dr. Wade."

"I'd say it's acceptable for you to call me Ryan when we're not working."

Her face flushed a pretty shade of pink.

"Habit," she mumbled.

"Mind if I walk with you to your car?"

"Not at all."

Catherine liked Ryan. So did everybody else who worked with him. His easygoing manner also made him popular with patients. She remembered seeing his wife a few times before her death from ovarian cancer a little over a year ago. The staff had rallied around him while he struggled through the painful process of his devastating loss.

He tilted his head and looked at the sky.

"It's a beautiful night."

"It must be nights like this that make people sit out on their front porch swings counting the stars. That is if there's anybody around who still does that kind of thing."

"Oh I'm sure there are." They arrived at her car. "I realize we've only conversed on a professional level and my dating skills are a bit rusty, but I have a couple of tickets to a play for this Saturday evening. I wondered if you'd like to go with me and maybe have a late supper after the performance."

He looked so endearingly self-conscious that Catherine made her decision before she could change her mind.

"I'd love to."

He wiped imaginary sweat off his brow.

"I'm glad that's over." He glanced at his watch. "Would you be free now to pass another half hour or so over a cup of coffee?"

She dreaded going home to an empty apartment and guessed Ryan was probably suffering the same predicament. She knew he had a young daughter, but there was only so much you could talk about with a child.

She remembered her vow to Tom. Josh was only a hazy figure in her dreams now, but Ryan was here.

"A cup of coffee sounds great."

>>>>dreams<<<<

Hamilton stared at Douglas. "You're leaving us? Isn't this rather sudden, sir?"

"Actually, no. I've been thinking about it for a while. I just had to make a few more arrangements before I could trade in my three piece suits for beachwear."

"Beachwear?"

Douglas got up and walked around to stand in front of his desk.

"I'm going to try and put the past behind me and start fresh. There'll be no more regrets for the things I can't change."

Understanding dawned.

"You're moving to Hawaii."

"I am. When a man gets a second chance at love he'd be stupid to turn it down."

>>>>dreams<<<<

Douglas came into the living room and saw Jenny sitting on the sofa slowly turning the pages of a photo album. "What do you have there?"

She looked up, eyes bright with unshed tears.

"Family pictures."

He sat down and put his arm around her.

"Marie?" he asked, pointing to a photo.

"Yes, she was seven. It was taken after a dance recital."

"She was beautiful even then." He pointed to another photo of a man standing with Jenny and Marie. "Is this her father?"

"Yes. It's one of the rare times he bothered to come to one of her performances, or anything else she was involved in for that matter."

"She never talked about him."

"There wasn't much to say. They didn't have a good father/daughter relationship. He spent most of our marriage ignoring her – and tossing his affairs in my face."

"How sad he couldn't appreciate what he had. Didn't you realize what kind of a man he was before you married him?"

"I was young and quite naïve. I thought he loved me. It didn't take long to realize I'd made a mistake, but I did try to make the marriage work while it lasted."

"It must have been very hard, but at least he gave you Marie," he said gently.

"That's the one thing Alan did right."

"Does he live here on the island?"

"He did, but he was killed a couple of years ago in a car accident. I suppose it makes me sound bitter, but I didn't mourn his death – nor did Marie." She set the book aside. "She's been gone for months and I still feel so hollow inside. Maybe if there had been a burial things would be different. I need to have some kind of closure, Douglas."

"I know it's been hard. Do you have something in mind you'd like to do?"

"Yes, I've given it a lot of thought. I want to go to the place in the Amazon where your people had their base camp. I need to see the last place where my daughter was doing what she loved before everything ended for her. I'll understand if you'd rather not go with me, but I'd appreciate it if you would set up the trip."

He pulled her fully into his arms.

"On the contrary, I have a few ghosts of my own to bury, and I think it's only fitting that we make this pilgrimage together."

She leaned her head against his shoulder.

"Thank you. I know it isn't going to be an easy trip for either of us, but I'd appreciate having you go with me."

"I felt like I should have gone with the rescue team, but was politely told I would have been in the way. Since we're going, I'd like to make inquiries about Josh Dallas. Perhaps something new may turn up. It'd be nice to have some news for his family."

Chapter Ten

Josh's recovery was agonizingly slow. There didn't seem to be any part of his body that hadn't suffered from his ordeal. His shaggy hair and beard along with his drop in weight made him look worn and haggard like an old man whose vitality had long been used up. But regaining his physical health was only part of his battle to be well again. He also had to fight mental and emotional demons, and the worst part was not knowing who he was and why he'd come to be in the Amazon.

Vague fragments of wild ramblings flashed in and out of his weary brain with tidbits of information that teased, but never told him enough. Josh thought he'd seen a woman in his delirium; beautiful and delicate with pale hair that shimmered like a light in the dark corridors of his mind. He remembered finding comfort in the vision and reached out, wanting to hold onto the image. At other times another woman appeared. This one had red hair, and in his fog of confusion always seemed to be cowering and weeping.

Raymond felt Josh had subconsciously blocked out an ordeal so horrible his brain had buried it along with his identity to protect himself. Since he didn't know his name, they called him Paul. Raymond approached Josh and asked him the same question he asked every day.

"Has anything new come to your mind yet?"

"No. It's like swimming in a murky pool of water. I know something's there and I'm going as fast as I can, but whatever I'm supposed to find stays just out of reach."

"I confess I thought you would have regained your memory by now. You've been with us almost six months and I've made inquiries, but communication is sporadic at best here. I've been thinking you could have been sent to do some type of field work."

"Another one of your theories, Raymond?" he asked, not unkindly. "If that were the case then why has no one come looking for me in all these months?"

"They may very well have been, but this is such a vast area it would be rather like trying to find the proverbial needle in a haystack. I suspect by the state you were in when you came to us that you could have been running away from someone. Or, you might have wandered off and gotten lost from your group."

Josh snorted with self-disgust.

"If the latter is true, it makes me sound stupid."

"Not at all. Even experienced people have lost their way here. The vastness of the Amazon is a whole world of its own within the greater picture. Hannah and I haven't approached you about leaving our house because you've been so long in your recovery. But you won't find what you're looking for by staying here. Do you feel strong enough to travel now and go seek out some answers?"

"Yes, I'm more than ready. As long as I was so weak I was content to stay here in this protected environment you've provided, but I've been feeling restless lately."

"That's a good sign that you're ready to let the leopard out of the chapel."

"I beg your pardon."

Raymond chuckled.

"Oh, it's just a saying of mine."

"I gathered that, but what does it mean?"

"Your mind is the chapel and the leopard represents an unwanted intrusion. They aren't meant to go together. You must expel the beast, so peace may reign in its place."

"You're right. I do feel like there's a beast inside me trying to claw its way out, and as much as I need to know what that beast represents, I'm afraid of what I may or may not find. I suppose that makes me a coward."

"No man is a coward who could survive what you've been through, Paul."

>>>>*dreams*<<<<

Jenny had become so tense that Douglas gave her arm a comforting squeeze in an effort to help her relax.

"I told you this might not be a good idea. Do you want to stop?"

"We've come too far to turn back now. I'm uptight, but it's not just about Marie."

"What else is troubling you, then?"

"Have you noticed how that one guard keeps staring at me? He makes my skin crawl." She shuddered and rubbed her arms.

Douglas looked toward the man and scowled.

"I'll go talk to him."

He started to get up, but she put a hand on his arm to stop him.

"Better not. I don't want you to antagonize him."

He gave an indignant sniff.

"I don't give a damn if I do ruffle his feathers. I'm paying him to protect us, not use you as a sideshow."

"Is it much longer before we get to the town where we're meeting those people?"

He looked at his watch.

"About another hour."

"I'll just ignore him until then." She turned away, so her back was facing the gawking man. "Do you think the man we're going to see is Josh Dallas?"

"I know how much you want it to be him and so do I, but you must realize the chances are pretty slim. I hate to see you get your hopes up only to be disappointed."

"You have the fax from that missionary couple."

"Yes, but you know as well as I do it didn't elaborate. That's why I didn't want to say anything to Josh's family. All we know is that some guy who might have been in the area around the same time has been making inquiries. I thought as long as we were going near the town, we may as well talk to him, but you've got to prepare yourself for . . ."

She held up her hand.

"I know, but please let me have my fantasy while I can."

>>>>*dreams*<<<<

Douglas spotted the couple he assumed were the Daniels sitting in the reception area of the hotel where they'd arranged to meet.

"Reverend and Mrs. Daniels?"

They nodded and stood up.

"I'm Douglas Marsh and this is Jenny Rabb."

They shook hands.

Douglas looked around him.

"Where is the man we're supposed to meet?"

Raymond pointed to a couple of chairs.

"Please?" He waited until they'd settled. "We thought it best if Paul waited in his room until we had a chance to talk to you first."

Jenny stared at him.

"Did you say his name was Paul? Then he couldn't be the one who was with my daughter." Disappointment made her droop against the cushions.

"He could be. We call him Paul because we don't know his true identity."

A young boy arrived with a tray carrying a large pitcher of fruit juice and four glasses. Douglas waited impatiently while he poured and they were alone again.

"Look, I don't mean to sound rude, but we've come a long way to engage in a game of riddles."

"It is a riddle, but not a game, I assure you. If you'll bear with us, my wife and I have a rather unusual story to tell you. When we're finished we'll take you to see our friend and pray this will result in a happy ending for all concerned."

The Daniels took turns relating how they'd found Josh that rainy night at the foot of their stairs. They told of his long recovery from the illness that had very nearly taken his life. When they mentioned his memory loss Douglas and Jenny gasped in unison.

"You mean he's still suffering from amnesia?" Jenny asked in disbelief.

"Yes, and I feel compelled to tell you he's still very fragile – both physically and emotionally. So I beg you to please be careful with him," Hannah pleaded.

Raymond patted her hand.

"We feel very protective toward Paul. We've done what we can for him, but the effects of these jungle fevers sometimes linger for years."

Douglas nodded.

"The poor devil. I assure you neither Jenny nor I wish to hurt the young man in any way, especially considering what he's already gone through."

>>>>*dreams*<<<<

Josh paced the room. The fact that there were people coming here who might hold the key to his identity made it impossible for him to relax. He hitched up the khakis that slid low on his narrow hips and tugged at the shirt that hung loosely on his lean frame. Although he had gained back some weight, he was still much too thin for his height.

He stopped pacing and whirled to face the door when he heard a knock. He stared at it half in fear and half in anticipation, sweat beading his brow.

"Paul? It's Hannah."

His heart pounded and his hands shook, as he fumbled with the lock. She slipped inside and closed the door quickly behind her. She studied his taut features in silence.

"Did the people show up?" he asked, his chest heaving with agitation.

"Yes." She continued to watch him. "Perhaps they should come back later when you're more rested. The trip has obviously tired you out. Surely they'll understand."

He gave his head a vigorous shake. "No. I need to get this over with."

His voice throbbed with distress.

"Please Hannah, there's no point in waiting any longer."

"All right Paul, but remember Raymond and I are here if you need us." She gave him one last worried glance and opened the door to the others.

Jenny was the first to enter the room. Josh stared at her for several seconds before staggering backwards. All color drained from his face and his eyes opened very wide before he suddenly cried out.

"Marie!" He gasped. "My God, I thought you were dead!"

>>>>*dreams*<<<<

Seeing Jenny and her likeness to Marie had set off a chain of events inside Josh's brain. Facts burst inside his head making him savor each bit of information. He sat now meticulously assembling the pieces of the puzzle that had eluded him for so long.

His first thought was to rush home to Catherine and his family until Jenny asked if he would accompany them to the site of the base camp. He agreed for Marie's sake. He bid the Daniels an emotional farewell before boarding the boat Douglas had hired.

As soon as they docked the next morning Douglas started looking for the man who had bothered Jenny. Not finding him, he went to the guide who spoke English.

"Where's the other man?" he demanded.

"I sent him to check the surrounding area."

"Good. It's about time he does something I'm paying him for," he grumbled then walked over to where Josh and Jenny were standing staring at the ground.

She pointed, eyes glistening with tears. "This is the spot where her tent was."

He put his arm around her, offering his support, while simultaneously sharing her sorrow.

She gripped a metal box in her hands. "This is some of Marie's favorite potpourri and a cross from her first communion. I thought it would help me to bury something here that belonged to her."

Douglas pulled out his wallet and withdrew a snapshot. He showed it to Jenny.

"It's the only photo I ever had of Marie and me together. May I add it to your things?"

She gave him a watery smile.

"You're letting her go."

Feeling that he was intruding, Josh stepped back.

"I'll go help set up camp."

Jenny leaned up and kissed him on the cheek. "Thank you for coming here with us, and thank you for being Marie's friend. It helps knowing she wasn't alone at the end."

Josh had told her as much as he dared about Marie's last days, carefully leaving out the details of Orlando's abuse. But Douglas had taken him aside later, sensing there was more to his story. Josh wanted to spare him as well, but Douglas insisted on knowing everything. By the time he'd finished, Douglas cursed Orlando in a fit of helpless rage.

The group left Douglas and Jenny on their own, so they could have their private little burial service. Once camp was set up, the evening meal prepared and eaten, they retired to their tents, while the men Douglas hired opted to sleep on the boat.

Josh had trouble going to sleep and when he did finally drop off he ended up becoming enmeshed in a sweat drenching nightmare. He couldn't deny being grateful that Jenny had helped him remember who he was. But remembering had also opened up his mind to the trauma of his captivity making him relive the experience in vivid detail.

He knew he wasn't strong in many ways and needed to get home before he really cracked up. He lay fighting off the dregs of the nightmare while trying to ignore the sensation that the walls of the tent were moving in to wrap around him like a mummy.

A muffled noise startled him. He jackknifed into a sitting position and listened with an intensity honed from fear. The noise was there again. He fumbled around in the darkness for his flashlight while a hot ball of panic formed in his gut. Hoping it was one of the guards, he crept to the front of the tent and opened the flap with clumsy fingers. He stuck his head out and was immediately greeted with the cold steel of a rifle barrel pressed against his forehead.

Chapter Eleven

Faint rays of dawn slowly slipped through the jungle canopy, as Josh's assailant motioned for him to stand up. It was difficult to see his face in the shadowy light, but Josh felt a twinge of awareness. His eyes darted anxiously around the area when he saw the guard who'd been assigned to keep watch crumpled on the ground in a silent heap. The gun barrel dug cruelly into his back forcing him toward the surrounding jungle.

But despite the pressure of the rifle he began to falter, recoiling at the idea of having to step behind the wall of thick foliage. The man let out a savage growl and shoved Josh forward sending him sprawling to the ground. His vision misted for a moment with a horrible sense of déjà vu. Then the elusive recognition clicked into place and his attacker took on a name. Nothing could have stopped his enraged bellow.

"Orlando! You sadistic son of a . . ." he didn't give himself a chance to finish before lunging forward in mindless fury.

>>>>*dreams*<<<<

Douglas heard the shout and opened his eyes. He groaned at the instant pounding inside his head and reached up to touch the area where the pain seemed to be centered. Shocked to see the blood that stained his fingertips, he struggled to sit up. His stomach swelled with a surge of queasiness making him inhale deeply until the nausea passed.

Realizing he was alone, fear had him immediately crawling through the tent's opening when a gunshot echoed around the jungle like a clap of thunder roaring through a canyon. Unseen birds and beasts screeched in alarm at the unexpected sound. He staggered to his feet reeling with the throbbing pain in his head.

"Jenny! Where are you?" he called desperately.

"She is safe, Senor Marsh."

He whirled to face the English speaking guide standing over Orlando with a wisp of smoke curling around the barrel of his rifle. Blood, bright and red seeped its way across the dead man's chest staining his dirty shirt.

Jenny stepped from behind a tree and ran to Douglas.

Josh stood staring down at Orlando's body and pointed a shaking finger.

"He was the one who kidnapped us."

Douglas went ghostly white.

"My God, I hired him to protect us!"

The guide eyed Josh closely.

"Sit down while I get a flask of brandy out of my pack." He glanced at Douglas's and Jenny's strained expressions. "For you as well."

Josh sank gratefully to the ground and sat there watching the gaudy sight of his tormenter's blood draining into the soil. He'd made a grab for Orlando's throat wanting to kill the man, but had been saved the trouble when the guide's bullet found its mark.

Douglas touched a hand to his head making Jenny gasp when she saw the blood. "Oh Douglas, why didn't you tell me you were hurt?"

She rushed over to the tent and returned with a handful of gauze pads. Moving his hand, she pressed the material to the wound. She looked at Orlando before tearing her eyes away. "I saw him jab you with his rifle," she said to Josh. "What a horrible man."

"More than you know," he said, fighting to control the fresh feelings of loathing.

The guide returned with the brandy.

"Are the other men okay?" Douglas asked.

"Two were knocked out as they slept. They will be coming to any moment now."

"And him?" Douglas pointed to the guard on the ground.

"He was not as fortunate, I'm afraid. A knife was used on him."

Jenny shuddered and buried her face in her hands. "Oh, God!"

They sat huddled in a circle passing the brandy around. Josh drank and wiped a hand across his mouth.

"What was he going to do with me?"

"My guess is that he thought he'd keep you close by if his attempts to take her failed."

He pointed to Jenny.

"If nature hadn't called, I would have been in the tent. He must have hit you, Doug, but thank God that's all he did."

He put his arm around her trembling shoulders.

"How is it that you managed to keep clear of that monster?" he asked the guide.

"I have been suspicious of him from the beginning, and when he didn't return to the boat last night I decided to come ashore and watch for him."

"Thank the good Lord you did."

The other two men had buried their fallen colleague and were busy breaking camp. One of them signaled when everything was ready. The guide stood up.

Jenny pointed to Orlando's body. "What are you going to do about him?"

"He stays just as he is for the animals to peck at. The Devil's spawn does not deserve a Christian burial," he said in a cold voice.

Cruelty had its own payback and none of them felt compelled to argue with the harsh judgment. They walked away leaving Orlando's blood stained corpse behind.

Josh sat in the boat, as they pulled away from shore. He'd come close to dying here. The odds of him escaping had never been in his favor. The greed and cruelty of some had brought him to the brink of hell, while the kindness and compassion of others had plucked him from death itself.

Josh knew he wasn't the same man who'd left home in what seemed like a lifetime ago. Besides his lack of physical stamina, he felt the lingering fragility of his mental and emotional state. He shifted and felt the scars on his chest stretch. They were a harsh reminder of what his thirst for excitement had cost him. But all he wanted to do now was get back home.

Home! He never thought that word would ever mean so much to him.

>>>>*dreams*<<<<

Catherine stood in Ryan's living room studying several framed photos displayed on a table.

Ryan came out of the kitchen and handed her a glass of wine.

"Thank you." She smiled and pointed to one of the pictures. "Is that your daughter?"

"Yes. Her name is Kiren. She's ten."

"She's beautiful."

"She favors her mother." He nodded toward the photo of a dark haired woman.

"I see a lot of you in her, too. I like her name; it's unusual."

"It was my wife's maiden name."

They crossed to the sofa and sat down.

"She must miss her very much."

"She does, but her two grandmothers have been wonderful. As a matter of fact, she's at my in-laws right now. I don't know what I would have done without them."

"I'm sure it's been very hard for all of you."

"It's one thing to deal with death the way we have to sometimes when a patient dies, and it's never easy, but nothing prepares you for when it hits you personally."

"No it doesn't," she said quietly.

"You're very beautiful, Catherine, and I'm happy that you accepted my invitation, but I can't help wondering why you don't have someone special in your life."

She treated him to a ghost of a smile.

"There was someone once. His name was Josh Dallas. He was working along the Amazon when he and a female colleague were abducted. She died, but no one knows what happened to him."

Ryan's breath came out in a rush of sympathy.

"I'm so sorry. You read about that kind of thing in the news, but it never seems quite real. I can't imagine how difficult it must be for you. The not knowing must be unbearable."

"It is if I think about it too often. We'd only been together for a few months, but I felt an immediate, powerful attraction to him. I confess that I still miss him very much."

Ryan set their glasses on the table and took her by the hands.

"I know what you're saying. The first time I kissed my wife I knew I wanted to spend the rest of my life with her. We never really get over losing someone we love. We may move on, but they'll always be there in our hearts. It's the little day-to-day things that remind us of what we had and how nothing will ever be the same again. But I have to believe there is still a life out there waiting. We can't exist solely on memories hoarded from the past."

"A friend told me pretty much the same thing. That's why I accepted this date."

"I'm thankful they did. I understand about loss and I know this won't be easy for either of us," he said gently. "But I hope you'll give us a chance, Catherine."

She looked at their joined hands and pushed thoughts of Josh away.

"I'll try."

>>>>dreams<<<<

Catherine lay in bed that night and thought about how much she missed Josh and how Ryan still mourned his late wife. She fell asleep wondering if either of them would be able to get over their loss enough to help each other. She was still pondering the question when the telephone's shrill ringing broke through her slumber. Her hand fumbled for the receiver. She sat up and listened in disbelief to Tom's frantic voice.

>>>>*dreams*<<<<

Catherine stared at the tiny infant and smiled at the tuft of soft fuzz that topped his small head. He'd arrived a bit ahead of schedule, but thankfully in good health. A rush of tenderness flowed through her as she stroked a gentle finger along the length of his downy back. He made a soft mewing noise, bobbed his head, and went back to sleep.

She'd put together the details that had lead up to his unexpected birth with snippets of information she'd gotten from Tom and her aunt. Nancy had complained of tiredness and feeling achy at work. Tom awakened during the night to her moaning.

As Nancy's illness progressed so did the stress to the baby until the danger posed to her unborn child forced the decision for an emergency cesarean section. One of the hazards in working with the public was being exposed to unwanted germs. No one could say for sure, but some customer might have unknowingly passed this illness on to Nancy.

Catherine's stomach rumbled with hunger reminding her that she hadn't eaten in hours. Taking one last look at the baby, she told one of the nurses where she'd be and took the elevator down to the hospital cafeteria. But once there the smell of food made her stomach roll in queasy waves and she ended up settling for a cup of tea and a plate of dry toast. She sat sipping the tea and ignoring the toast when Ryan joined her.

"They told me I'd find you here," he said pulling out a chair across from her. "I wish I could say something to ease your distress, but any words that come to mind seem like tired clichés."

"That's how I feel every time I'm around Tom."

"He's taking this very hard."

"He can't help it. Nancy means everything to him. She's his life."

"In that case he'll take close watching if she doesn't pull out of this."

She looked at him with sudden alarm.

"Are you suggesting what I think you are?"

"I'm merely stating a possibility. When two people are that close they don't always handle it well when something happens to the other. You know that, Catherine."

"Yes, but Tom will have their baby. He could fill some of the void for him."

"That will depend on Tom. The baby may not be enough."

She looked at him, her eyes dull with worry and fatigue.

"He's got to be."

Ryan reached across the table and laid his hand over hers. "You look like you could use a good night's sleep. I know your aunt is planning on staying here. Why don't you come and stay at my house tonight?"

Instant color flooded her pale cheeks and she jerked her hand away.

"I hardly think that would be appropriate right now."

"Kiren is spending the night at a friend's. I was offering you her bedroom and the door has a lock."

"Oh. I didn't mean to imply that you were suggesting anything improper," she said, knowing that she'd done exactly that.

"Yes you were, and I'm not sure which one of us should feel the most upset by your assumption."

"That was very rude of me. I'm sorry, Ryan."

He pushed his chair back and stood up.

"So am I."

She watched him walk away and felt mortified by her careless words.

Chapter Twelve

While Nancy's health continued to decline, her baby grew strong enough to be released from the hospital. Priscilla went ahead to set up what she would need for her grandson, as Catherine convinced Tom to drive her and the baby home. Although the child wouldn't know, she wanted one of his parents to be involved in his homecoming.

Tom stood in deep thought, silently staring at his son lying in the bassinet Nancy had so lovingly chosen before her illness. He abruptly turned to face the two women.

"I have to go," he murmured. "Thank you for taking him."

Priscilla touched his arm.

"It's just until Nancy is well again," she said. "Then you'll both take your baby home with you." She spoke softly while blinking back fresh tears.

He seemed to shrink away from her offer of sympathy, as though he couldn't bear her personal grief coupled with his own.

Catherine, watching him and seeing his anguish, remembered how Nancy had cried telling her about Tom's troubled family life. He'd been an unwanted child treated with indifference by his father and scorned by his mother. He'd always thought he was unworthy to receive love until he met Nancy.

The telephone rang in the kitchen.

"That might be the pediatrician. I left a message that I have a few questions," Priscilla told them before hurrying away.

Catherine turned to Tom. "Have you told Josh's family what's happening?"

"No, they have enough of their own problems to deal with right now."

"That's true, they do. But I think they'd like to know that you have a son," she urged, silently vowing that she would call them if he didn't.

"Maybe later." His glance slid toward the sleeping baby then back to her. "I need you to promise me something, Catherine."

"Anything."

"I want you to take the baby when Nancy . . ." He stopped, unable to go on.

"You know I'll be here to help in any way that I can. So will Pris, but Nancy's a fighter. There's still a chance she could come out of this." They were empty words, and she knew it; yet she couldn't tell him she'd had a nightmare showing Nancy in a coffin.

He jerked her against him.

"Did you have a dream about her?" he questioned. "I don't understand how you know these things, but you do. Is she going to pull through this? Will she make it? Tell me!"

"I don't know."

His eyes narrowed.

"I think you do, and it's not good. You're lying to try and protect me. Or you're letting your personal feelings cloud your professional knowledge." He scrubbed a hand down his face. "I went into a curio shop in Mexico once and saw a death mask of a young woman's face. That's what Nancy's face reminds me of now."

"Oh Tom, don't."

"I need to know I can depend on you to take care of the baby."

"He'll still have you," she said hoping to penetrate the layers of his grief.

He let out a self-deprecating grunt. "Which isn't much.

"You mustn't say things like that."

"Why not? It's true. I'm an empty shell without Nancy. All my life I wanted to belong. She gave that to me, but now it's coming to an end. Watching her die is killing me bit by bit."

He gripped her shoulders until she winced.

"No matter what happens, I want you to be the baby's mother. Please Catherine, do this for me and for Nancy."

"Oh, Tom." She leaned forward offering him what comfort she could. "You know I will. He's part of me and Aunt Priscilla, as he is yours and Nancy's."

She brushed her mouth across his lips before he stepped back.

"It helps knowing that he'll have you both. I've got to go. Tell Pris goodbye and thank her for me."

"Will you come back here tonight?"

"It depends on what tonight brings."

She fought back her tears.

"We'll be here for you no matter what happens, Tom."

Catherine walked with him to the door and watched as he got into his car and drove away. She checked on the baby and started toward the kitchen when she heard the door open again. She stopped. The hairs on the back of her neck seemed to stand on end. She turned slowly and what she saw nearly sent her collapsing to the floor.

Josh stood framed in the doorway like a spectral vision that had returned from the dead.

"That was quite a touching little display."

In all her dreams of seeing him again, Catherine had always run into his open arms, but now she stood unable to move or utter so much as a sound. She didn't recognize the hot anger in his eyes or hear the low fury in his tone. His voice sounded distorted inside her head. It was as if the world had suddenly slipped off kilter.

"What's the matter sweetheart, cat got your tongue?" he taunted the cliché.

Jumbled thoughts raced along the edge of her brain. She stared at him noticing how his once sturdy body seemed so frail. He looked haggard, as though every bit of vitality had been sucked out of him. She felt a sob catch in her throat. Her prayers had been answered. He was here.

"Oh God Josh, you've come back."

"Slightly later than the three months I'd originally planned, but hey, who's counting?" His bitter attempt at humor only added to the tension in the room.

"Why didn't you let us know you were coming?"

"I wanted to surprise you."

Tears filled her eyes, as she reached out to him, but he stepped back. She frowned and dropped her hands to her sides.

"I can't believe it's really you. People were afraid you might be dead, but I . . ."

His voice sliced through her words.

"It would have been preferable at times, believe me."

She wiped a hand over her cheeks, brushing at the tears.

"We heard you were kidnapped and then you disappeared. What happened to you?"

"Maybe I'll write a book one day."

"I can see you're not well. Won't you come and sit down?"

"Save your TLC for someone who wants it," he snapped while his eyes burned with savage dislike. "All I could think about while I was rotting away in that hellhole jungle was holding you in my arms, but now I don't think I could bear to touch you."

His hostility made her take in a sharp breath. This wasn't how his homecoming was supposed to be. Where were the loving words, the warm embrace? The connection that had always been so strong between them was either gone or buried too deep to help.

"Why are you acting like this? I'm sorry I didn't give you the greeting you deserved, but you must know having you show up here unannounced after so long is a huge shock."

"More of an inconvenience from the look of things, I'd say. How remiss of me not to telephone first, so you could have gotten rid of your company sooner."

"Company? You mean Tom? If you saw him why didn't you come in? Surely you must know he'd want to see you."

"I didn't want to interrupt." His mouth tilted in a crooked half smile. "I'll say one thing for good old Tom. He's always taken his responsibilities seriously, and when

I asked him to look after you he's clearly been very conscientious with his extra personal touch."

The relief at his return was rapidly being defeated by his snide insinuation.

"Are you implying we've been doing something that we shouldn't have while you were gone?"

Josh lifted one shoulder in a casual shrug belying his obvious resentment.

"You tell me. After all, he's known you longer than I have. It looks like you and Tom were busy cozying up while I was trying to survive getting my ass kicked."

"What? No!" A gasp whistled through her teeth. "You're wrong, we never . . ."

He cut her off.

"Why didn't you wait for me, Catherine?" he demanded.

"I did wait. Months and months of living a half life, praying to see you again. Remember I did beg you not to go. I never really understood why you went."

"I'm sure Tom told you."

"He said you wanted the adventure."

"There was a little more to it than that, but he probably didn't want to jeopardize his chances with you. After all, a threesome would be kind of awkward."

"All this lost time. Why, Josh?" she asked again, ignoring his jibe.

"I wanted to build up a nest egg, so I could ask you to marry me." He scoffed at her surprised look. "Stupid of me wasn't it? I went through all that hell for nothing as it turns out. I'm not going to pretend that your disloyalty isn't eating me up inside, but I survived the damn jungle and by God I'll survive your betrayal, and Tom's, too."

She blinked in confusion.

"Wait. You have the wrong idea about Tom and me."

"Do I?" He shook his head. "I don't think so. I saw you kissing when I looked in the window. The sun and fever may have fried my brain, but I still have 20/20 vision."

"There's a rational explanation for what you saw. It's not what you think."

His upper lip curled back in a sneer.

"I'd say it was crystal clear."

"You're mistaken. Please don't do this, Josh. I was only. . ."

The baby began to stir at that moment, making Josh's head jerk toward the sound of the whimpering infant. Catherine lifted the baby out of the bassinet, not noticing how every last vestige of color had drained out of Josh's face as he watched her.

"A baby? Now tell me again how faithful you were, Catherine."

"No, Josh, no!" she cried, reaching out to him with one hand while holding the baby in her other arm. "You don't understand, he's not . . ."

"Get away from me!" he snarled, stumbling back out of her reach. Shocked at the flash of intense hatred in his eyes, Catherine put the baby down before rushing outside.

Priscilla joined her.

"I'm sorry I took so long. Did I hear Tom leave?" She shaded her eyes against the sun.

"Who was in that cab?"

"A ghost," Catherine whispered.

>>>>*dreams*<<<<

112

"Marsh," Douglas said, absently silencing the ringing phone a couple of days later.

"Mr. Marsh, this is Ivy Dallas, Josh's mother."

"Oh, yes. How nice to hear from you. How is your son getting along?"

"Not very well, I'm afraid," she said in her usual brusque tone.

"I'm so sorry, but I suppose it's to be expected given what he went through."

"We don't know what happened to him and Josh refuses to tell us anything."

"I see." He hesitated. "Perhaps it would be better if I talked to your husband?"

"I'm the one making this call. I want you to tell me everything you know." Waiting several seconds before he finally responded, she interjected, "No wonder his nerves are shot."

"What about Catherine Ashley? Surely seeing her again must have helped him."

"She's made things worse. It's her fault he took the job and look what happened."

"I'm afraid I can't accept your theory on that, Mrs. Dallas. Josh told me himself that he's always been one to take new jobs because he likes challenges."

"Not like this. My son gave up everything for that woman when he went to the Amazon and she repaid him by having an affair with his best friend while he was gone."

Douglas stubbornly continued to try and defend the younger man, disturbed as he was, by such allegations.

"Catherine? Are you certain? I got the impression she was very much in love with Josh."

"Love!" Ivy spat out the word as though it was something foul tasting.

"Josh doesn't want to have anything to do with her, and I personally, intend to see that he doesn't have to."

"Do you think it's wise to encourage that decision while Josh is ill? He may want to try and work things out when he's feeling well again."

"I can't afford to take that chance. A mother knows what's best for her child."

"Your son is a man Mrs. Dallas, not a child. Why don't you step back and give them time to discuss the situation on their own without your interference?"

Her voice exploded in his ear.

"How dare you give me advice about my son!"

"I beg your pardon. I merely thought Catherine might be able to help Josh."

"She tried to destroy him, but I'll see her in hell before she gets near him again."

Chapter Thirteen

Sensitive to the nearby presence of her family watching, Ivy fought to control the fury Douglas's words had caused, as she slammed down the receiver. She shook off the hand John gingerly placed on her shoulder.

His lips tightened.

"You're obviously upset. I told you I should do the call."

"And I told you I preferred to do it myself," she snapped.

"Hey, take it easy," Jerry quickly interrupted. "We're all on edge here, but attacking each other isn't going to help Josh. What did this Marsh guy say, Ivy?"

"After Josh escaped his kidnapers, he ended up staying with missionaries in the Amazon. He was there for so long because he suffered amnesia."

"Amnesia!" the others repeated in unison.

"Did Mr. Marsh mention anything about the scars on Josh's chest?" John asked.

Ivy's fingernails dug into the arms of her chair. Fresh tears threatened to flood her eyes.

"His kidnapers tortured him."

"Oh my dear God," Margaret wailed while the others groaned in sympathy.

Ivy stood up, her spine ramrod straight.

"We can't change what happened, but we must do everything we can to help Josh now, and the first thing I insist on is that no one mentions Catherine's name to him. Her defection has clearly torn him apart." She waited while they all mumbled in agreement before she left the room.

She climbed the stairs to Josh's bedroom and knocked on the door, waiting a few seconds before entering the room. He sat slumped in a chair staring into space. His eyes were dull with the terrible suffering of a heart broken by one dearly loved.

She pressed a hand into his shoulder.

"Josh?"

"I never want to see Tom or Catherine again."

>>>>*dreams*<<<<

As the days turned into weeks, Josh learned that physical wounds could heal in their own time and in their own way, but there was a part of him that remained dead inside. People came and went offering support and spoke of a brighter future for him. He thanked them for their well wishes, but took little comfort in words that rang hollow.

His mother constantly hovered around him nurturing and protecting. For a time he allowed her to slip back into her role as a parent taking care of her dependent child until he gradually grew tired of her smothering. He knew he had to begin to carve out a life for himself once again; a life he vowed would not include any serious attachment to any one person.

Once his health was fully restored, Josh took a job in a remote hamlet in Alaska. In the beginning he made little effort to socialize, but gradually allowed a woman in the company office to befriend him until they ended up in his bed one night.

He lay silent and unmoving, as she trailed her hands over his nude body followed by several open mouth kisses. Although he had invited her there, he took no pleasure in what she was doing. He continued to stare at the ceiling until she abruptly stopped.

"This would be a lot better if you were with me."

"Unfortunately, my mind is somewhere else. I'm sorry." He moved off the bed.

She sat back on her heels and watched him.

"Men deplore this question, but I've never been known for my subtlety. Have you seen a doctor about your impotency?"

Dark color rushed up to taint his cheeks.

"I don't need a doctor," he said through clenched teeth. "You may as well take off, Loni. We're both wasting our time here."

She scrambled off the bed and pressed her nude body against him, winding her arms around his waist.

"Let me stay. I won't bother you. We don't even have to talk."

"You won't bother me anymore than I bother myself," he said, unlacing her fingers.

She stepped back and walked to her clothes.

"Oh well, you can't blame a girl for trying. Besides being extremely well endowed in your male plumbing, you have a killer body. I admit I was looking forward to some action. I get a rush just looking at you."

"A hell of a lot of good it does," he snorted in embarrassment and pulled on a pair of jeans.

"I'd be willing to try again." When he didn't answer her, she pointed to the scars on his chest bathed in the moonlight. "Nasty looking body art you have there. They must have hurt like the devil."

His mind did a quick flashback.

"The pain is gone, but the memories remain."

"Now there's a cryptic reply that's bound to intrigue a girl. You're such a mystery, Josh. That's why people talk about you at work."

He cocked a brow.

"Is that so? What do they say?"

"They admire you professionally, but think you're a snob because you don't mix."

"Perhaps I should pat a few butts now and then to let them know how friendly I can be."

Loni chuckled.

"No, don't do that or they'll get you for sexual harassment. It's just that you're an enigma. You fascinate them because you never tell anyone anything about yourself. Personally, I like a good mystery, but it can drive most people nuts."

"They must be pretty hard up for entertainment if they have to use me for their amusement. Now you'll really have a choice tidbit to add some spark," he ground out.

"I don't get my jollies like that. I wish things could have been different between us, but I promise you tonight won't be added fodder for office gossip."

"I'd appreciate that."

"I wonder what secrets from your past have brought you here." She pointed to his chest. "It seems to me the scars inside have cut you deeper than those."

"Most people suffer from scars of one kind or another."

"Yes they do." She hesitated. "I hope for your sake you can get the woman you're running from out of your system, so you can stop running from yourself."

"What makes you think there's a woman?"

"Just a wild guess. I'll see you around," she said and closed the door.

His body ached with the need for release. He'd been so sure he was ready for Loni only to disappoint her and humiliate himself. Catherine's image haunted him no matter what he did. How was it possible to loathe a woman and yet hunger for her so? He simply could not get rid of the mind clogging, gut wrenching need for her.

The familiar sharp pain sliced through him, as he thought about Catherine and Tom being together. Seeing her with Tom's baby had tipped him over the edge mentally and emotionally. He'd often wondered if he would have handled things differently that day at her aunt's had his head been screwed on straight, but he'd never know now.

Feeling the need to make amends for last night's fiasco, Josh hoped to catch Loni before she left work the next day. Unsure of himself, he felt like a man getting ready to encounter a downpour with a leaky umbrella. He pulled into the parking lot after being in the field all day and saw her unlocking her car.

He hoped it was a good sign that she waited while he walked to her.

"Will you join me for a beer?" he asked, bracing himself for her refusal.

She shrugged.

"Sure, why not? I'll meet you at the usual place."

Loni had introduced him to her favorite haunt – a rustic bar with sawdust scattered across the floor and stuffed big game heads lining the wood paneled walls. She opted for a table in a corner while Josh walked over to the bar to get their drinks. She'd barely taken a seat when a woman in tight jeans and low cut sweater sauntered over to her.

"Hiding in the shadows, Lon? Not that I blame you for wanting to keep that gorgeous hunk to yourself," she purred glancing over her shoulder to where Josh stood at the bar. "How about you invite me to join you?"

Loni scowled at the woman's deep cleavage.

"How about you get lost?"

"Oh come on, don't be a spoilsport. All I'm asking for is a simple introduction."

"Yeah, right. We both know nothing is ever simple with you when it comes to men, Gloria. One minute the guy's standing and the next thing you know you've got him horizontal with his pants down around his ankles."

"You sound jealous, Lon. Not afraid of a little competition, are you?"

"Hardly, and even if I was you'd be wasting your time. He's not your type. The man has morals. Now go away. and peddle your raging hormones on someone else."

Gloria started to sputter a retort when a man came up and slung his arm across her shoulders, drawing her into the side of his body.

"Hey Glo, how's it going?"

She beamed at him.

"Much better now that you're here, honey. I was about to perish from boredom," she said with a pointed glare directed at Loni. "Why don't you buy me a drink and we'll see about perking things up."

He laughed and led her away.

Josh returned just as they left.

"I hope I didn't chase your friends off."

"You didn't and they're not friends – more like piranha." She held her glass in a toast as soon as he had settled onto his chair.

"Here's to all the lovers who got away."

They clicked glasses and drink.

"I wasn't sure if you'd take me up on my offer."

"I never turn down anyone who's buying."

"At least I can give you that pleasure."

"Don't worry about last night. Maybe I'm not the right kind of woman for you."

She tilted her head to one side and studied him.

"I keep asking myself why a good looking guy like you would take a job alone in such an out of the way place."

"Maybe I just like the snow."

"Or maybe I was right about a certain woman that's still out there." She raised her glass to her lips. "What's the matter did she run off with your best friend?" Her hand froze in midair when she saw his expression. "Oh crap! Me and my big mouth. I didn't mean to go digging around in private territory. I'm sorry, Josh."

He stared into the creamy white, floating in his glass.

"You're very astute."

"Yeah, I'm a real mind reader," she said sarcastically. "Want to talk about it?"

"There isn't anything to say that hasn't already been dissected to pieces."

"She marked up your heart real good. You must have loved her very much."

The softly spoken statement caused his insides to ache.

"I had an image of what I thought love might be, but images are often an invention of the mind."

"I don't know what happened and I'm not going to ask you again. My personal philosophy is simple; if you can't fix a problem, then you have to move on. All that unfinished business has a way of cluttering up life and making it difficult to let in any new stuff."

"Yes it does," he agreed in a quiet voice.

She leaned toward him.

"So why don't you try clearing the slate and start fresh?"

"I have a poor track record. I made some bad choices; trusted the wrong people."

"Welcome to the human race. We all make mistakes, Josh."

"Maybe, but in my case it's cost me dearly."

"Spilt milk. If you can't mop it up, it starts to stink after awhile, so you move on.

Hashing over things we shouldn't have done doesn't change the fact that we did them."

"I can't argue with that."

Josh looked around and suddenly realized he didn't want to be there with the canned music and voices raised in chatter and laughter. It reminded him that people were enjoying life while his remained stagnant. His nostrils flared at the mixed odors of spilt beer, cheap cologne, and stale sweat. He finished his beer and stood up.

"Thanks for the company and the advice."

"Anytime." She raised her glass. "Thanks for the beer."

"You're a good woman, Loni; too good to waste your time on a wreck like me."

"Wrecks can be restored, but I don't happen to think you fit in that category. For what it's worth, it would be a shame to allow any woman to get the best of you. You do, and she wins. You don't strike me as a man who's used to losing."

>>>>*dreams*<<<<

Minutes later Josh sat in his truck going over what Loni said. As long as he allowed Catherine to rule his emotions he gave her the power to defeat him; to keep him enslaved to his feelings for her. He slammed his hand against the steering wheel.

"Damn you, Catherine. When will I ever be free of you?"

Chapter Fourteen

Catherine made a concentrated effort to respond to Ryan's lovemaking, but knew she failed when she didn't feel so much as the tiniest spark of emotion. It wasn't that he repulsed her. He had a good build, a nice personality, and treated her with respect. That should have been enough, but she felt herself pulling away physically and mentally.

He stopped kissing her and stared at her for a few moments before moving away to lean his head back against the couch. She understood how tenuous his position was with Josh's shadow intruding between them. Using Ryan to fill in the lonely hours was unfair and made her ashamed. He was a decent man who shouldn't have to deal with the frustration he experienced every time he tried to get close to her.

"I'm sorry, Ryan. Maybe it'd help if we went into your bedroom?"

"Different room; same two people. Let's face it Catherine, the chemistry just isn't there between us. It looks like the best we can expect is that we'll be colleagues and maybe friends – just not lovers."

A wave of regret washed over her followed by her usual sense of guilt.

"I'm so worthless it's a wonder you even bother with me." She looked at him, her eyes swimming with unshed tears. "You deserve to be more than a consolation prize. I hate myself for hurting you like this and continuing to sabotage the good you offer me."

He sat up and took both her petite hands in his sturdy ones.

"Listen to me. You are not worthless because I don't turn you on. Please don't belittle yourself like that. You're a wonderful young woman who deserves more out of life than you seem to realize. It makes me sad to see the way you continue to use your vulnerability to Josh against yourself."

Her cheeks flushed with instant color.

"I don't do that. I'm fine," she insisted.

"Catherine, I'm not blind. I know what fine looks like, and I don't see that when I look at you." He paused a moment. "You're a hostage of your own feelings for him."

Josh's last visit flashed in her head. He'd been filled with anger, but beyond that it was his look of sorrow as though something inside him had died, that still haunted her.

"Look how Tom's deep love for Nancy consumed him. It's not healthy to make another person responsible for your individual happiness. I'm really more frustrated than sad, so I'm not sure what you mean about Josh."

"Yes you do. I've watched you for months dragging yourself through each day as though it were an ordeal. It's obvious that what you need, I can't provide. Why don't you take a few days off and try to resolve things once and for all?"

She tugged her hands free and shifted away from him. "What things?" she asked, hesitantly.

"I think we've just established that. I won't infringe on our friendship by insisting you share your private thoughts, since you would have by now if that was your intention. But it's important to be honest with yourself. It's for the best, Catherine. Trust me."

She heard the empathy in his voice and felt her insides collapse.

"It's easier to pretend that everything is okay," she whispered in a voice that wasn't quite steady.

"How well I know, but denial only prolongs the doubt. You're not going to be able to get Josh out of your head until you get him out of your heart. Go find him."

"I've thought of doing that a hundred times, but then I get scared. There's no guarantee I'll be able to do any good even if I can get his family to tell me where he is."

"True, but you owe it to yourself to try, and I'd be very surprised if you were the only one suffering." He stood up and held out his hand. "It's time I took you home."

>>>>dreams<<<<

Ivy knelt in front of a large flowerbed digging up any stray weeds that dared to invade the area. Her garden was important to her. People always said her yard was one of the prettiest around and she liked that distinction. It took a lot of hard work, but the rewards were well worth the effort. Her roses had earned her first prize at the county fair several years running and she liked winning at whatever she put her mind to.

She sat back to admire her work when she heard a car drive up and stop at the other side of the house. She frowned. She hadn't been expecting anyone, and she didn't appreciate people stopping by without an invitation. She stood up, removed her gardening gloves, and gave the front of her faded jeans a quick brushing down.

Catherine stepped out of the car and was stretching when Ivy appeared, walking briskly toward her. She saw the initial veneer of a friendly greeting drop away into a scowling expression and felt as though she should have brought a white flag to wave.

Ivy fixed her with a cold glare.

"You're the kind of intruder people put up no trespassing signs for. What are you doing here?"

Catherine was tempted to state that no signs would be necessary if Ivy used the searing dislike in her voice on anyone who dared to approach her. But she was here on a peace mission and couldn't afford to antagonize the woman.

"I hoped time might have softened your heart toward me, Mrs. Dallas, but I see I was wrong. Can't you try to understand how hard it was for me to come here? Won't you at least give me a chance?"

"A chance for what?" she demanded contemptuously. "To wreak more havoc?"

"I've never wanted to hurt anyone. I would like to know how Josh is doing."

"How solicitous of you," Ivy sneered. "You could have telephoned."

"I think we both know you would have hung up, just as you've done all the other times I've called. Josh and I were once very close. Is it asking too much to want to know that he's all right? Despite what you think, I really do care about him."

"He's fine, but no thanks to you I might add."

"Please tell me where he is," Catherine implored, further humbling herself.

"Begging now?" A look of triumph leaped into Ivy's eyes. "How pitiful you are."

Catherine's stomach churned.

"I came here in good faith. All I'm asking is that you look beyond your animosity toward me, so that I can set things straight with Josh."

"If you really want to make things right, you'll leave him alone. Josh has made a new life for himself and he obviously doesn't want to include you. Once you accept that we'll all be better off. What is this compulsion you have to keep complicating things?"

"I'm not trying to complicate the situation, but everything that happened has been based on fabrication. I don't want Josh to go on thinking . . ."

Ivy held up her hand.

"I don't care to hear any of your excuses. Your little fling with him hardly qualifies as a great romance. You need to get it through your head that you were merely one of his many women and your time ended long ago." She hurled the brutal words clearly intent on wounding. "I refuse to let you pester my son again."

"You couldn't understand what we meant to each other because you never saw us together. So with all due respect, I hardly think you're in a position to judge the quality of the relationship I had with him."

"You think not? I've seen enough females come and go in his life not to know exactly what goes through Josh's head. Apparently you're under the delusion that you were somehow different. If you were, don't you think he would have told his family? I'm sure you'll recall none of us had heard of you until the day you showed up with Tom."

"I don't know why he didn't mention me, but he loved me enough to want to marry me," she said feeling the need to establish how important she'd been to Josh, despite knowing she was clinging to an old promise that had grown cold with time.

"I don't believe you, but as it so happens he does have someone special. They're to be married and I won't have you spoiling it for them."

"Josh is getting married?" Color drained from her already pale cheeks. "When? To whom?" she couldn't help asking.

"That's none of your business. Now I'm through answering your foolish questions. I want you off my property, or must I call the police?"

"That won't be necessary, but will you at least please tell Josh that I wish him every happiness?" Her throat burned as she forced the words out.

"Why should I when the mere mention of your name infuriates him."

Unable to take any more of Ivy's surliness, Catherine turned away. Tears blurred her vision, as she backed down the driveway under Ivy's fierce stare. She'd just turned onto the main road when a pickup truck came behind her and honked.

She looked in her rearview mirror and saw to her surprise that it was Jerry motioning for her to stop. She pulled over to the side and quickly wiped the flat of her hand across her wet cheeks, as he jogged to her car.

"Coming from my mother-in-law's from the look of you," he said and snorted in disgust. "I think it's about damn time someone around here sets the record straight."

"If it's about Josh getting married, Ivy told me," she said, her voice quivering.

Both his brows shot up.

"Married!" He shook his head. "What will that woman come up with next to keep him in her clutches?

What you don't know is a lot and I for one am sick to death of this charade." He opened her door. "Move over, we need to talk."

>>>>dreams<<<<

The chunky heels of her boots echoed loudly against the cement, as Catherine made her way along the narrow walkway. The path wound its way between rows of small cabins that flanked her on either side. It sounded like someone was having a party nearby. Music and laughter drifted out into the night. Lights from the windows made a pattern of golden squares on the snow that reminded her of brightly wrapped packages.

She slowed her pace when the last cabin came into view. Despite the cold night air, perspiration trickled down her back beneath her sweater and coat. She walked a few more yards and stopped. She was so close now she could see someone's silhouette moving behind the curtains. Was it Josh? Jerry said he'd become a bit of a loner. At least she hoped she wouldn't be interrupting him if he was entertaining someone.

She stepped onto the tiny porch. Her hand shook when she reached to knock on the door. It opened so quickly she barely had a chance to take a breath. Josh stood there, filling her senses. Her pulse went wild, as she devoured him with her eyes. He looked tall and fit in dark brown cords and black sweater. Lost in a rush of sensual memories, she drank in the sight wanting to touch him so badly her fingers twitched.

Anger flashed, turning his eyes stormy and dark.

"What the hell are you doing here?" he demanded in a voice that matched the icicles hanging from the nearby eaves.

His brusqueness made her pulse hammer with fresh nerves.

"Jerry gave me your address. I came because I need to talk to you."

"I doubt if you have anything to say that I'd want to hear."

She hurried on before she lost her nerve.

"Your return from the Amazon was a miracle. I don't want us to continue to waste that miracle. You came to me first because you loved me. My heart belonged to you when you went away and it still does. It isn't fair that a misunderstanding should continue to keep us apart, especially when there's a way to make things right between us. You need to trust me."

"I made the mistake of trusting you once and I don't intend to do it again. What I need is for you to go away and leave me alone."

His anger felt like teeth tearing her apart. First Ivy and now Josh. It seemed she was destined to beg when dealing with the Dallas family.

"You've been alone too long already, Josh. Please let me talk to you. It's very important – and it isn't just about us."

"Put it in a letter," he snapped and started to close the door.

Desperate to get through to him, she lunged forward, tripped on the doormat, and grabbed the railing just in time to keep herself from falling at his feet.

"Tom's dead!" She blurted the words out hating the way she'd been forced to reveal the shocking news.

He yanked the door back.

"What did you say?" His voice sounded like someone had grabbed him by the throat.

"Tom, he . . . he died. That's why I had to see you."
Ignoring his dangerous looking scowl, she took a step
forward. "Now will you please let me come in?"

Chapter Fifteen

His nostrils flared. "What the hell are you talking about? Don't you think my family would have told me something as drastic as that? What kind of sick game is this?"

"Do you really think I'd make up something so terrible?" She rushed on before he could have a chance to answer her. "Your family didn't say anything because they didn't want to upset you. I don't relish being the one to relate the painful details, but you have a right to know. It happened a week after you left my aunt's."

"And you're just now getting around to telling me? It obviously wasn't a top priority for you. Why bother coming at this late date?"

"I couldn't come any sooner because I didn't know where you were until a couple of days ago. Jerry told me. He felt this conspiracy had gone on long enough."

"Conspiracy?" he rolled his eyes. "Jerry certainly didn't do me a favor by sending you. He should have called himself and spared me the aggravation of seeing you again."

His words hurt so much she thought her heart would shatter, but she swallowed the pain and forced herself to go on.

"This isn't the kind of thing a person should hear on the phone. Jerry thought you might want to have someone with you when you found out."

"He was wrong. I don't need anyone, least of all you. Are you finished now?"

"No, there's more." She peered over his shoulder. "Can we go inside?"

He shifted until his body blocked the doorway.

"I'm not in the habit of inviting unwanted people into my home."

She sighed, defeated.

"All right, if that's the way you want it. Tom drowned."

"Ha! Now I know you're lying. He's always been a very strong swimmer."

"Perhaps when he chose to be, but not this time. It wasn't an accident, Josh."

His eyes narrowed.

"Are you saying that he killed himself?"

"Sadly, yes. A man walking his dog on the beach witnessed everything. He saw Tom's clothes piled on the sand and spotted him swimming way out. He called for help on his cell phone and went in after Tom, but the currents and the waves were too strong. He had to turn back, but not before he saw Tom go under and not resurface again."

"Are you here to tell me it's my fault?"

She had not expected that reaction from him.

"No! Oh, God no, not at all."

"What did you say to him after I left your aunt's that day?" he demanded.

"I didn't say anything."

"I don't believe you. You must have at least told him I was there."

"I didn't have a chance. Tom never knew you had returned from South America."

Josh was quiet for so long Catherine began to wonder if he'd understood her. She saw how white his knuckles were where his hand squeezed the edge of the door.

"All right, you've delivered your message. I see no reason to continue this conversation."

He started to close the door, but she slapped her hand against it. "Don't send me away like this. I leave in the morning, and there's so much I need to tell you."

"It seems to me you've said enough already, most of which I'm sure are lies."

"No Josh. You have to listen to me. There are things you don't know. If you'll just let me come inside for a few minutes I'll explain everything that's happened."

"I told you I don't want you in my house." His chest heaved. "Need I remind you that you dumped me and trashed my relationship with my best friend? If you had any sense of decency at all you'd leave me alone instead of coming here turning the screws."

"I didn't come to hurt you. I'm here to straighten things out, so you won't continue to think badly of us, especially Tom. He thought of you as his friend to the end, Josh. I can't bear to think of you continuing to sully his memory with your bitterness."

"Then don't insult my intelligence with your wild tale. You're wasting your time if you expect me to apologize. Go back and tell Tom your little scheme didn't work."

"It's not a scheme. Please let me tell you the reason why he took his own life."

His anger flashed anew.

"Stop it!"

She thought he had the look of someone who would like to break something with his bare hands. Instinctively, she took a couple of steps back away from him.

"I know Tom, and he wouldn't have the guts to kill himself."

"He was your best friend," she reminded him. "Doesn't that count for anything?"

"Ex friend."

"I don't understand how you can be so unfeeling."

"I feel just as much as the next person, perhaps more than some. I've felt a depth of loneliness that has left empty places inside me that will probably never be filled. I wanted us to be together, but you made your choice. Go back to Tom and leave me be."

Crushed by his rejection, she allowed the door to slam in her face.

>>>>*dreams*<<<<

Josh spent most of the night tossing and turning. He still ached from seeing Catherine, and his anger had been the only thing that kept him from making a fool of himself by pulling her into his arms. But there were other things to worry about. What if she'd been telling the truth about Tom? They may not be friends anymore, but he didn't want the man dead. It didn't make sense that Tom would do such a thing when he had everything to live for. Josh rejected the idea to call his family. He didn't want them to know Catherine had managed to break through his defenses.

He was up and dressed at first light pacing until he could head for the airport and confront Catherine. He spotted her as soon as he entered the small terminal. His heartbeat immediately quickened. Her beauty had never ceased to rev up his system.

"Catherine."

She spun around at the sound of his husky voice and her eyes lit up.

"Josh! I didn't expect to see you here. I'm so glad you came."

"Either you're a consummate actress, or I'm a damn fool, but I took the hook.

We're going to finish this charade, or whatever it is, right now." He jerked his head toward an area dotted with small tables. "You have time for coffee before your flight." He chose a corner table away from foot traffic. "Do you still take it black with sugar?"

"You remembered," she smiled, not realizing how it made his pulse escalate.

"I can remember a lot of things, and maybe that's more of a curse than a blessing," he said in a hard voice making her smile fade. He returned and took a chair opposite her. "First off, you should know that I don't appreciate being here."

"Obviously, so why did you come?" she asked, matching his cold tone.

"Despite everything that's happened between us, Tom was like a brother to me. In many ways the bond we shared went deeper. That's why it tore me up when I saw you two together." His hand drew into a fist where it lay on the table. "Did you have an affair with him? I have to know. I've lived with that image inside my head eating at me."

"No Josh, it was nothing like that." She made her voice softer now. "We were lonely and we had you in common. We did not betray you. I can't bear to have you go on thinking otherwise. It's not fair to him. That's one of the reasons I had to come here."

"Then what did I see that day? Was I hallucinating? What about that baby I saw? He was the spitting image of

Tom. Are you going to tell me I was wrong about that, too?"

"No one who knew Tom would argue with you on that. He most definitely is Tom's son, but I didn't give birth to him."

His forehead wrinkled in a frown.

"If not you, then who is the mother?"

She reached in her purse, pulled a picture from her wallet, and slid the photo across the table to him.

"My cousin Nancy was. That was taken on their wedding day."

He picked up the picture.

"They look very happy. What do you mean by 'was'?"

"I introduced her to Tom and they fell in love. They were married within weeks of their first meeting and she became pregnant right away. But something terrible happened near the end of her pregnancy. She became ill and nothing the doctors did could stop it. They had to take the baby to save him. Tom was devastated. He spent every moment sitting by Nancy's bedside watching helplessly while she slipped away."

"How awful. I can't imagine what it must have been like for all of you."

"We'd just brought the baby home from the hospital the day you showed up. Tom was getting ready to go back to be with Nancy. What you mistakenly thought was an embrace between lovers was actually me trying to comfort Tom."

"I shouldn't have jumped to conclusions," he said in a voice filled with regret.

"Maybe if you hadn't been so ill yourself you would have noticed that Tom was in a pretty bad way, too. Nancy died the next day, and he couldn't get over losing her."

"Ah Jesus," he groaned. "Poor Tom. He finally finds a woman to love only to have her be taken away." He slid the picture back, as the first reluctant nudge toward acceptance began to take hold. "Then you were telling the truth; he's really gone?"

She nodded, and taking a moment, slowly tucked the photo back inside her purse.

"Yes Josh, he is. I'm so sorry," she said, her own sorrow making her voice wobble.

Josh pressed the heels of his hands against his eyes. "Just give me a minute here." His voice broke; a powerful shudder went through his body, engulfing his senses as raw grief replaced the months of anger he'd felt toward his friend. When he looked up his eyes were suspiciously bright.

"And who has been taking care of the baby all this time?"

"I have, with my aunt's help. I moved in with her right after he was born. Tom asked me to take little Tommy before he . . ." she stopped when Josh held up a hand.

"The baby's name is Tommy?"

"That's what Nancy wanted as soon as they found out they were having a boy."

"Although I wasn't in any shape to handle something so traumatic, I deeply regret not having the opportunity to see Tom before it was too late. I probably wouldn't have been much use to him, but someone should have at least told me what had happened to him once I'd recovered. I can't believe he's been dead all this time and I never knew."

"It's not your fault. I wanted to go to you, but your mother said you were too ill. You mustn't blame yourself for something you had no control over."

"You don't need to try and protect me by minimizing my behavior. Knowing Tom, I should have realized he never would have been disloyal to me. I've wasted a lot of time hating him. My only excuse is that I was so messed up I wasn't thinking straight."

"You'd obviously been through a lot. It's so good to see you looking well again," she said ignoring the remnants of suffering that still lingered in his eyes.

"Appearances can be deceiving. I may look okay, but I wouldn't say I'm completely healed. I'm finding it more difficult to close the wounds inside."

"You're not alone in that. I understand how you feel, believe me."

"I'm sorry for everything I said and did. I'm sorry that I ever went to that God forsaken jungle, but most of all I regret not being around when Tom needed me."

The hard knot that had twisted her insides for so long, unraveled. She reached across the table. He grabbed her hand.

"Would you like a chance to make it up to him?"

His brows arched.

"Of course I would, but he's gone, how can I?"

"You can be a father figure to little Tommy. I'm sure that's what Tom would have wanted." Her flight was announced at that moment. She reluctantly eased her hand away and stood up. "I have to go. I hope you'll give some serious thought to my suggestion."

Josh shoved his own chair back.

"Being a parent is a big responsibility."

"Yes it is, but it's also very rewarding. Tommy is a darling little boy and well worth spending time with." She picked up her suitcase. "Thank you for coming, Josh."

"No, I'm the one who should be thanking you. I've been in hell all these months believing you and Tom were together and that I'd lost you. I appreciate you taking the time to seek me out, Catherine, and I'm sorry for the way I treated you last night."

"You were entitled considering what you thought had happened. I didn't get to say this to you at my aunt's, but deep down I think I always knew you were alive. Love can make a person have hope even when everything tells you you're wasting your time."

Her words struck a chord within him, and he could feel the icy wall around his heart begin to give way.

"Yeah and hope is a hell of a lot easier to handle than hate."

Chapter Sixteen

Three days later Catherine left work and drove home to her aunt's. She stepped from the car, stopping for a few moments to inhale the scent of the climbing roses draped gracefully along the top rail of a white picket fence. She was at the front steps when she got her first glimpse of an unfamiliar pickup truck parked at the side of her aunt's house.

Priscilla met her as soon as she walked into the house. Her face was a study in harried lines.

"Josh is here. My God, it's like seeing a ghost after all this time." She pleated her apron with nervous fingers. "When I told him you weren't home from work yet, he asked if he could wait for you. He was very polite about it and I didn't know what else to do, so I let him stay." Her expression begged forgiveness. "I hope that's all right?"

Catherine felt her pulse quickened.

"Of course it's all right. Where is he?"

"He's been in Tommy's room ever since he arrived; acted like he couldn't wait to get there. But don't worry, I've been checking on them," she quickly added. "He's okay."

Heart racing, Catherine hurried down the hallway and found Josh sitting cross-legged on the floor stacking colorful wooden blocks with the baby. She paused in the doorway drinking in the sight.

"You're here. What a wonderful surprise."

His head snapped up at the sound of her voice. "How could I not after the things you told me?" His eyes shifted back to the baby.

"He's a smart little guy, isn't he?"

She heard the genuine warmth and what she was certain sounded very much like pride in his tone.

"Yes he is. Have you been here long?" she asked and entered the room.

"Half an hour, give or take. I hope your aunt didn't mind me hanging around."

"I think she's still a little shocked seeing you after so long, but she wouldn't have allowed you to stay if she didn't feel you had a right to be here."

"That's very generous of her considering my past history with all of you."

Bad memories wanted to crawl in and crowd out this special moment, but she steeled herself against them. The emotion of seeing him with the baby washed over her, swamping her senses. She scooped Tommy up, ostensibly to greet him and buried her face against his baby soft cheek needing time to control her feelings.

"Maa," he gurgled, trying the word before wiggling to be put down again.

Josh raised his eyebrows.

"It sounds like he thinks you're his mother. Doesn't that bother your aunt? I mean, considering what happened with her daughter."

Catherine shook her head.

"She prefers it. She wants to be his grandmother."

"That's good." He got to his feet and shoved both hands into his pockets.

An awkward silence settled between them broken only by the noise of the baby rummaging through his basket of toys. Catherine peered at Josh from beneath her lashes and saw how stiffly he held himself. He was a refugee from the past; their past. Teetering on the edge of uncertainty, she took a chance and guided by impulse, plunged ahead.

"Would you like to stay for dinner?" she asked softly.

His entire body visibly relaxed.

"Yeah. I'd like that very much. Thanks."

"I'll go tell my aunt to set another place. You're in luck; she's making her fantastic lasagna." She started to walk away, but stopped with a mischievous gleam in her eyes. "Have you ever changed a baby's diaper?"

He blinked in surprise before his mouth tilted in a slow grin.

"No, I can honestly say that's never been one of my adventures, but I'm willing to learn, especially if you're going to be my teacher."

She felt happiness spread slowly throughout her body until her skin glowed.

"That would be me. I'll be back in a minute to give you your first lesson."

Josh's grin widened, as little Tommy toddled over to him. "I look forward to it," he said and got down on his haunches to take the toy car the baby thrust at him.

>>>>*dreams*<<<<

Catherine had just finished her shift several days later and was getting ready to leave when Ryan came up behind her.

"Heading home?"

She felt herself stiffen, but turned to him with a smile. "Yes. How about you?"

"I still have a couple patients to see yet. I hoped I'd run into you. We seem to be working different shifts lately. Did your aunt tell you that I called?"

"Yes and I apologize for not getting back to you. I meant to, but I've just been so busy with work and the baby." She swallowed. "I also had to go out of town."

"I know. Your aunt told me. She said you were in Alaska."

Her cheeks flushed with embarrassment while her stomach twisted with guilt. She fiddled with her purse strap trying to give herself a few seconds to regain her composure.

"I went to Alaska to find Josh."

"I see. So that's where he's been living all these months?"

"Yes. I took your advice and went to see his family. His mother tried to keep me away, but his brother-in-law told me where he was." She inhaled a deep breath. "Josh followed me back at my invitation. I was going to tell you. I just haven't had the chance."

"I'm a friend, not your Father confessor, Catherine. I'm happy for you. It's what you needed to do. That's why I encouraged you to go. I hope things are going well."

"Not too bad. I guess you could say we're in a cautionary stage right now."

"That's probably a good place to be under the circumstances. It's been a difficult time for you both. I'm sure with enough patience everything will work out for the best."

"I . . ." She stopped, swallowed and began again. "That's very generous of you."

"Take care of yourself and remember if you need anything I'm here."

Tears of gratitude welled up and she had to blink several times to clear her vision.

"I don't deserve to have a friend as wonderful as you, Ryan, but I'm thankful that I do."

"You deserve a lot of things, not least of all to be happy."

She wanted to reach out to him, but there were too many prying eyes watching their exchange.

"Thank you for being so understanding and for . . . for everything."

"Seeing you content is thanks enough," he said and walked down the corridor.

She realized the door to intimacy they'd tried to open between them had closed for good, but she hoped the door to friendship would always remain ajar. She turned on her heel and hurried away, her mind quickly switching to thoughts of Josh. Tonight would be their first night alone since his return from Alaska. He was taking her out to dinner, but the glint of desire she'd seen in his eyes easily convinced her that food wasn't the only thing on his mind when he'd issued the invitation.

She hadn't exaggerated when she'd told Ryan things were in a cautionary stage. Josh hadn't touched her. There had been too many harsh words and bitter feelings to smooth over before they could make a fresh start. Butterflies fluttered inside her now at the thought of making love with Josh after so many months apart. Her body tingled with excited anticipation, as she drove out of the parking lot ready to accept her new destiny.

She took special care preparing for their date. She rubbed her body after her shower with the scented lotion he had always liked, applied her makeup with all the expertise of an artist at her canvas and left her hair loose to flow in long shimmering waves down her back the way she knew he preferred. Her body tingled with anticipation as she put on silky scraps of pale pink lingerie beneath her outer clothes. He arrived a few minutes early, but she was more than ready and answered the door herself. Seeing him standing there with a small bouquet of violets made her feel as though she might melt and end up in a puddle at his feet.

He handed her the flowers.

"I hope you still like violets."

"I do," she said, allowing a quick smile to touch her lips. "Thank you, Josh. They're lovely."

"Not as lovely as you." His eyes did a slow perusal of her body stunningly sheathed in indigo silk.

"You look beautiful. Make that seriously gorgeous."

Priscilla came into the room and offered to put the flowers in water. Catherine handed them over and let Josh lead her outside. She couldn't believe how tense she felt. It reminded her of her first date when she was a freshman in high school.

"This is going to sound silly, but I'm actually kind of nervous."

"That makes two of us. It's like prom night all over again." He opened the passenger door for her. "I didn't think about it until I was driving here tonight, but I guess a pickup truck isn't the most elegant vehicle for a guy to take his best girl out."

The fact that he'd admitted to being nervous helped her relax, knowing she wasn't the only jittery one.

"You could have brought a skateboard and I wouldn't care."

He treated her to a grin and helped her climb into the front seat. "Hmm, maybe we'll have to try that some time."

"Where are you taking me?" she asked once he started driving.

"It's a surprise."

Catherine could feel joy leaping inside her the minute he pulled up in front of the restaurant where they'd had their first dinner date. She was even more amazed when he ordered them the same two meals they'd eaten that night. She hadn't forgotten each detail, but to have Josh remember delighted her.

They finished their food and sat lingering over a bottle of champagne. He'd been staring at her so intently the last half hour that Catherine had to fight the urge not to squirm. He made her feel as though he wanted to lap her up like a bowl of cream. Her nervousness returned and was playing havoc with her senses.

"What are you thinking?"

"I'm thinking I'd like to get us out of our clothes and sheathe myself inside you." His voice was a low, intimate sound that sent tiny shivers zinging straight to her heart.

The raw desire in his voice made her gasp and glance quickly toward the table nearest to them.

"Not so loud. Those people might hear you and kick up a fuss."

"Something's up all right," he told her before glancing down at his lap. He laughed when her face turned bright red. "What are you blushing for?" he teased. "I'm the one that has to figure out how to walk out of here without embarrassing myself."

>>>>*dreams*<<<<

Later, in his apartment, Catherine felt the thunderous pounding of her heart at the sight of Josh's aroused body. The time for waiting was over. It was all about wanting and need. But when she saw the scars on his chest, the horror of what he must have had to suffer made her hesitate.

"Wait! I don't think I can do this right now. How did you . . .?"

"Yes you can," he cut through her protest. "Touch me, Catherine. I want your hands on me." He kissed her then and she forgot everything except the need to surrender.

Lost now in their mounting desire, they literally tore into each other stealing breath, savoring flesh, as their mouths and hands plundered with hungry urgency. Wild kisses that branded ownership and promised to fulfill every need had them both gasping, as the hot rush of emotion shot through them like acid etching into glass.

"I've needed you for so long. God, you're driving me insane." The words sounded like a ragged prayer. He ran his hands restlessly over her and groaned, before tearing impatiently at her dress sending the tiny pearl buttons scattering like snowflakes.

They clung to each other with a tenacity born of deprivation; a craving that throbbed deep within. Their bodies awakened anew to the insatiable hunger that had always existed between them, igniting in flames of passion that threatened to consume.

He lifted her hips toward him.

"Brace yourself,sweetheart. It's going to be one hell of a ride."

Every ounce of energy was absorbed while they poured themselves into each other, equally giving and taking; heart to heart, flesh to flesh. They continued to moan in unison rising again and again until they were ready to erupt in a frenzy of fiery passion.

Josh's head reared back.

"Mine!" he roared seconds before they erupted.

Moments later, fighting to breathe, Catherine shifted beneath his weight."

Josh?"

"Not yet," he panted. "Let me enjoy being a part of you a little while longer."

When he rolled away a few seconds later he kept one hand resting possessively across her stomach. They lay in the dark, their bodies slick with sweat, wrapped in the afterglow of their lovemaking, and the intense pleasure they'd given to each other.

He smiled and wound a hand through several strands of her hair before letting it flow away like threads of spun gold.

"It was always good between us, wasn't it?"

"Better than good," she agreed.

He cupped her face and brought their mouths together in another searing kiss, leaving her breathless and clinging to him. His eyes flamed with desire when he looked at her again. "I want you here beside me when I wake up. Stay with me tonight."

"I wish I could, but I have to work the early shift in the morning."

He groaned and pressed her against his rapidly hardening body.

"Call in sick," he demanded before rolling her onto her back and positioning himself between her thighs.

They took their time with their second joining, stretching out their lovemaking until it spilled out of them in a sweet symphony of movement and sound. They were together again, but there was still the blankness of all the lost months, and unlike the marks on Josh's chest, unseen blemishes that one felt, but could not see.

She pressed her lips to his scars, whispering words of empathy. The thought of the agony he must have suffered made her eyes fill with tears until they dripped onto his chest. She felt him stiffen and quickly wiped a hand over her cheeks.

He lifted her head and made her look at him.

"Why are you crying?"

"I'm thinking of your pain." She touched his scars. "How did you get these?"

A muscle danced in his cheek.

"You don't want to know."

It wasn't that she was morbidly curious, but she thought perhaps if she knew what had happened in the jungle it would make it easier for her to fill in some of the missing gaps.

"I thought it might help me to understand if I knew what happened."

"So you want the gory details, do you?" he said, his voice dangerously quiet. "If you had my memories you wouldn't want to be digging them up again, Catherine."

She heard the faint warning in his voice and the beginning of temper that she sensed he was fighting to control.

"I'm sorry, Josh. I didn't mean to upset you."

"I know you didn't; and while I realize you think you're doing the right thing in trying to get me to talk about it, I can't go over all that again. I've had enough trouble trying to forget the degradation of what I went through and move on as it is."

"That was very insensitive of me. You've been through enough. It wasn't my intention to make things worse. Just forget I ever mentioned anything," she babbled on until a catch in her voice made her stop. She tried to wipe away newly forming tears.

He blew out a noisy breath.

"Come here," he said and hauled her into his arms, pressing her to him. "Please don't cry, Catherine. It makes me feel like a damn heel."

"I shouldn't have brought it up. It's not a very good way to end our lovemaking."

"Who says we're finished?" He treated her to one of his devastating smiles before his lips began a slow trail along her neck to her shoulder and down to her breasts. She scraped her nails across his back and felt his mounting passion and recognized the desperate craving that would soon push him out of control.

His hands were everywhere, gliding over her, creating currents of pleasure that rushed through her body like a flashflood. He groaned out her name. Catherine bowed her body and offered him all she had to give wanting to blot out the bad memories for him in the only way he would allow.

"I love you," she said, but somehow knew the words weren't going to be enough.

A deep shudder tore through him. He pulled her to him and surged forth piercing the very core of her until their release came in a glorious shower of glittering sparks.

Chapter Seventeen

The weeks passed as they continued to slowly reconstruct their relationship. But because there was still so much unsaid between them, Catherine couldn't help feeling they were building on shaky ground. She could see that Josh had changed. Although on the surface he seemed to be trying to return to his old carefree self, she sensed an underlying edginess in him.

This was especially true at night when he'd awaken her with his body shaking and shouts of distress. She'd rouse him as gently as possible fighting to keep her voice calm in an effort to lead him out of his nightmares. No one knew better than she did about dreaded visions that invaded sleep and made you feel as though you were losing your sanity. It was like having a monster living inside you that took control of your brain.

The look in his eyes worried her, as she watched him struggle to fight his way out of the trauma and return to the present. She suspected he was suffering from posttraumatic stress disorder, but he refused to talk about his dreams. All she could do was give him what comfort he'd allow by holding him in her arms.

His old company hired him back and he confessed he was still bored with the job, but appeared to lack the ambition to try for anything else. He rejected old friendships and refused to cultivate any new ones. He spent as much time with her as possible and soon became so possessive there were days Catherine felt as though he was suffocating her. He questioned her every move when they weren't together, begrudged her time with her friends, and insisted on having her work schedule to keep track of her hospital hours.

He condoned his behavior by saying he was making up for their time apart. He talked of marriage, but she worried he was driven more by a nameless fear rather than confidence in forging any kind of permanent happiness. As much as she loved Josh, Catherine began to wonder if love would be enough to make their relationship work.

She angered him when she told him they needed more time to get used to each other again and she upset him further by turning down his suggestion that she move in with him, using the excuse she didn't want to leave the baby or take him from her aunt.

She was spending another night at his apartment and as usual most of the time had been spent in bed. It wasn't that she didn't enjoy their lovemaking, but it was beginning to trouble Catherine that it seemed to be their only form of communication. There were times Josh seemed almost desperate to have her be a part of him, and he'd make love with such intensity they were both left feeling totally exhausted, but strangely unfulfilled.

But tonight had been one of their gentler couplings, as Josh teased her body into sweet surrender with soft kisses and hands that moved slowly over quivering flesh. He stretched his length alongside her now and hooked a muscular leg over her calves. His expression, filled with lazy satisfaction reminded Catherine of a large contented feline.

His lips trailed up the side of her neck lingering in the small hollow beneath her ear causing her to shiver. He gave her neck one last nuzzle before propping himself up on an elbow.

"I checked your schedule and you don't have to work this weekend."

"That's right. Do I take that to mean you've made some kind of plans for us?"

"Yes and I hope you'll agree with them. I want you to come with me to my folks and bring Tommy. I'll make all the arrangements and promise we'll only stay one night."

He'd asked her to go with him before, and so far she'd been able to put him off.

"My aunt and I were planning on taking him shopping this weekend. He needs new shoes and a couple of outfits," she said, hoping to once again stall the inevitable.

"We both know you can do that any time. You must admit my family has been more than patient waiting to see him. We've circled around this before and to tell you the truth, I don't understand why you haven't suggested getting together with them yourself."

She didn't miss the slight censure in his tone and felt herself stiffen.

"I'm not exactly your family's favorite person," she said carefully, dreading the conversation.

"That's my fault after the way I carried on about you. Everything is fine now."

"I'm not so sure about that. They all knew Tom loved Nancy and that she was the baby's mother, but they still let you go on believing I was having an affair with him."

"How do you know they didn't try to tell me the truth? I was pretty out of it."

"There was time when you'd recovered. They think they're right about me."

"What makes you say that?"

"I was with Tom when he told them about you being kidnapped. They assumed I was his girlfriend until I told them about our relationship. But your mother still thought Tom and I would want to sleep together that night. After you told the family Tom and I were having an affair and I'd given birth to little Tommy, they were angry and felt that I had deceived them. Jerry was the only one who gave me the benefit of the doubt."

"Okay, maybe they did, but I'm telling you everything's been set to rights."

"Has it? I think they still need someone to blame for what happened to you."

"The hell with that. They can't go on making you the scapegoat for Pete's sake. If that's what's worrying you, I'll talk to them."

"I'd rather you didn't. Defending me might cause more repercussions and I don't want to add to the problems your family already has with me. They need time to come to grips with everything." She wanted to tell him it was his mother who had caused the riff and who continued to foster a grudge, but she was afraid he wouldn't believe her.

"They've had enough time already. You're an important part of my life and my future, Catherine. They'll have to learn to accept that. Come with me. Everything will be fine. You'll see. It'll be a good way to smooth out any grievances by having the baby there with us. Nobody's going to be able to stay angry with you once they see him."

Thinking of Ivy made her feel as though she was deliberately heading for the spider's web.

"I hope you're right. I don't have your confidence, but I'll go because I know Tom would have wanted them to see his son."

"He would. I've really become attached to the little guy." He leaned down and brushed her lips in a gentle kiss. "Maybe someday we can make him our son together?"

She realized it was another way to get her to marry him.

"We might some day if that's what you think you need," she said peering at him from beneath her lashes.

He moved on top of her and grazed his teeth along her jaw before moving down to the soft curves of her breasts. She rose up against him and caught her breath when a tingling sensation ran all the way down her arms to her fingertips while warmth coiled and unfurled in her belly.

"You are what I need, Catherine," he groaned and flipping over, pulled her on top of him. "That's all my family has to understand and they'll come around when they do."

She wanted to believe him, but Catherine knew Ivy wouldn't be anxious to accept her back into Josh's life, even if it was what he wanted. She couldn't stop that little nugget of doubt even as she responded to the pressure of his body's demands.

>>>>*dreams*<<<<

Anyone who knew Ivy understood that she liked being in control, especially when it came to her family. Josh gave her anxious moments with some of the work assignments he insisted on taking, but none were as terrifying as the one in the Amazon when he'd gone missing for all those months. She had grieved with a broken heart thinking he was dead.

Once she found out that he may have taken the job for extra money to marry Catherine, Ivy's anguish turned to hostility that quickly transferred to the young woman. She'd disliked Catherine at first sight. She was envious of her delicate beauty and intelligence, but most of all she was jealous that her son desired Catherine.

When she discovered Josh had gone to Catherine first, instead of coming home upon his return, Ivy had been consumed with resentment. By the time he finally did arrive on their doorstep, a shattered man consumed with fear that he'd lost Catherine to Tom, Ivy despised her with a fury that knew no bounds. Layers of anger continued to build until she'd encased herself in a shell of hatred too thick for empathy to break through.

Ivy set herself up as judge and jury and plotted revenge against Catherine as meticulously as a general going to war. She would have preferred that Josh stay close to home, but she'd consoled herself with the knowledge that taking the job in a remote area of Alaska had kept him away from Catherine, until Jerry had intervened.

Now despite all her careful planning, Josh had come here with all the appearance of settling back into a relationship with Catherine. Because he seemed blinded to the fact that she was wrong for him, Ivy knew it was up to her to rescue her son from his own confused emotions. She had no qualms about using any means at her disposal to accomplish her goal, including Josh's obvious attachment to Tom's child.

It hadn't surprised her that Tom had taken his own life. The man had always been weak and apparently he'd entangled himself with a woman as feeble in spirit as himself. Although she cared nothing for their baby, Ivy had seen that he would be a convenient tool in implementing her plan. Now all she needed to do was get Josh alone.

>>>>*dreams*<<<<

He wandered into the kitchen where Ivy was washing dishes. She dried her hands and smiled at him.

"Where's Catherine?" she asked, hiding her animosity.

"Upstairs putting the baby down for a nap."

"He's like a small replica of Tom, isn't he?"

"Yeah. Sometimes it almost hurts to look at him knowing Tom is gone."

"I know, but we have to be thankful that Tom left this wonderful little bit of himself behind." She pointed to a coffee pot. "Will you join me for a cup? It's fresh."

"Sure." He pulled out a chair and sat down.

"Where's Dad?"

She touched her cheek.

"At the dentist. A filling fell out last night." Ivy filled the mugs and brought them over to the table. "Would you like another piece of cake?"

Josh shook his head and patted his stomach.

"No thanks, I'm about to bust as it is from everything I shoveled in during lunch. The food was great as always, Mom."

She sat across from him. "It's so wonderful how you've gained back your weight. It was hard seeing how emaciated you were after your return from South America."

"I guess I did resemble someone out of a horror movie."

"I don't like to think about it." She touched a hand to her heart. "It hurts too much knowing that you suffered and I was helpless to do anything to stop it."

"I made you suffer, too and I'll always be sorry for that."

"Well, you're here now and that's the most important thing." She waited a heartbeat. "I'm glad we're having this opportunity to talk in private because I have some things I need to tell you. They're not pleasant, but they have to be said."

"What things?" he asked warily.

Despite his guarded look, she was determined to go on knowing she had enough salient facts to add credence to the story she'd concocted. "I'm talking about Catherine's behavior while you were away."

"I was afraid of that." He shoved himself to his feet. "I don't want to hear it. I'm trying to put negative stuff behind me. It'd make things a lot easier if you would, too."

She clutched his hand to keep him from walking away. "Darling, listen to me, please. You know how much I love you. The only thing that matters to me is for you to be happy. I would just as soon cut my tongue out than say anything that might hurt you, but there are things you don't know about Catherine. If you still want to be with her after I finish, then I can't stop you, but at least I'll know I did my best to try and save you."

"Save me? Don't you think that sounds a bit melodramatic?" He jerked his chair back and sat down again. "Tell me something; why do you dislike her so much?"

"Because she's a selfish, deceitful woman. She barely showed any concern that you'd been kidnapped. She only cared about her own self."

Ivy allowed the ice inside her to coat her words now.

"You have no idea what went on while you were gone. No matter what she's told you, she did have an affair with our poor hapless Tom. She led him on all the way, and he followed along like a puppy on a leash."

Chapter Eighteen

"You're wrong, Mother. They wouldn't do that to me," he insisted. "I don't know why you'd think they would. Anyway, you haven't any proof."

"Oh, but I do." He shot her a surprised look and Ivy began to relate her carefully constructed tale. "For one thing, she was at his apartment practically every time I called, and they slept together when they came here that night to tell us about your kidnapping."

"I don't believe you. Tom wouldn't have shared a bed here in your house."

"I went upstairs to see if they needed anything before I went to bed. I could hear Tom's voice in Catherine's room and believe me he was doing more than talking to her."

"Were you spying on them?" he demanded. "Jesus Mother, that's sick."

"Of course not. I told you, I merely wanted to see if they were settled in." She watched, as he shook his head obviously refusing to accept her explanation. "Josh, I changed the sheets. Tom's bed hadn't been slept in and Catherine bedding reeked of sex."

His chest heaved.

"Why are you doing this? Do you enjoy tearing me apart?"

"You know better than that. I have to tell you the truth. My conscience simply won't allow me to sit back and watch Catherine continue to hurt the innocent. I blame her for Tom's death. You know how sensitive he was. She led him on until he was hopelessly enthralled with her. Then she decided she wanted some widowed doctor at her hospital and went after him. Successfully, I might add, as their affair went on for quite a while."

His hands curled into tight fists.

"Who told you she was with another man?"

"Tom. He called me one day literally crying his heart out over her defection."

"Who is this doctor? Do you know his name?"

"I do. It's Ryan Wade. You can check with the hospital if you don't believe me. But right now you should be more concerned with what happened to poor Tom. He was beside himself and when he tried to continue on with Catherine, she manipulated him into a relationship with her cousin, so she could concentrate on her affair with the doctor. Tom ended up eloping with the girl to Las Vegas because she got herself pregnant."

"It wasn't exactly the Immaculate Conception, Mother. From what I understand Tom was very much in love with Nancy and he was devastated when she died. The family should have been there for him. I know I couldn't be, but what about the rest of you? Now that we're on the subject, why didn't any of you try to help Tom?"

She wasn't about to admit that she'd waited several days after Catherine's call before she told the family about Tom. Nor would she admit how, when John suggested contacting Catherine, she'd convinced him the girl didn't want to have anything to do with them. Hearing Josh's accusing tone made Ivy dig in her heels like a bull preparing to charge. "Because Catherine told us she and her aunt preferred to have us stay away."

"That doesn't make sense. She knew Tom was like family." He frowned. "Maybe he was so in love with Nancy that he felt he didn't need any of us as much as he used to."

"Perhaps. But how do you know he loved this Nancy? We only have Catherine's say so. Men get women pregnant every day without marrying them. I think Tom took her on because she was the cousin, so he'd have an excuse to stay close to Catherine. As for us not being with Tom, we didn't know about his wife's illness or death because Catherine couldn't be bothered to tell us until it was too late. How could you even think that we would have let him suffer alone? If only Tom would have contacted us himself we might have been able to save him."

"She said Tom didn't want to upset you because you had to deal with what happened to me, but she felt he needed us and when she did call, you hung up on her."

Ivy shook her head and clucked her tongue.

"Oh Josh, you know I would never have done such a thing to our Tom. She's lying like she's lied about everything else. Look how she's kept little Tommy from us and if that isn't bad enough, she's using the baby to lure you back into a relationship because the doctor dumped her."

"He dumped her?"

"He certainly did – and to save face, she told everybody she broke it off herself because you had returned and asked her to marry you. She even had the audacity to spread the rumor that you two were secretly engaged before you left."

"How could she tell everyone we were going to be married when she didn't even know I had returned from South America until I confronted her at her aunt's?"

"We did know, dear. I never told you, but Mr. Marsh called us. I telephoned Tom right away to let him know you were back and of course he told Catherine."

"She certainly didn't act like she knew, and I asked Marsh not to say anything."

"Catherine is quite an actress. But please don't be angry with Mr. Marsh. He thought it would be best to prepare us because he could see you were so ill. I didn't tell you before now because I gave him my word I wouldn't mention that he called."

"He shouldn't have said anything," he grumbled.

"I disagree. We had a right to know considering your health. As for Tom, he was upset because Catherine insisted there was no way that they'd ever be together again."

"He was upset because his wife died," Josh contradicted.

"That may have been a small part of it, but it was really Catherine he wanted. Despite having that adorable baby boy to live for, he didn't even try to bond with his son. I'm afraid dear, misguided Tom still had illusions of being with Catherine. He committed suicide when he finally realized there wasn't any chance that she would take him back."

"If you called Tom and told him I had returned, why didn't he try to contact me?"

"Oh darling, please don't ask me that. It's been hard enough for me as it is being the one to tell you all this." Ivy hung her head while she whipped up a few quick tears.

"Why stop now? You've told me everything else you may as well spill the rest."

"Well, if that's what you want." She let out a heavy sigh and dabbed at her tears with her apron. "He told me he was too ashamed to face you after he'd betrayed your trust by sleeping with Catherine. I'm sure all that guilt was another thing that contributed to him taking his own life. That's another reason I blame her for what happened."

"He could have kept the affair a secret. I need never have known."

"Too many people had seen them together. Someone was bound to slip up and tell you sooner or later. But even if no one did, Tom was so eaten up with shame he probably would have ended up confessing to you himself. How could things ever be the same between you once you learned how he'd carried on with Catherine? Tom was your best friend, but he violated that friendship and she encouraged him every step of the way."

He sucked air through his nostrils like a man fighting to breathe.

"I hate this."

"I know how difficult all this is for you." She sighed again. "Tom was such a pragmatic soul. He never saw the world exciting like you. Everything was drab to him."

"What did you expect from him considering the way he grew up?"

"He could have overcome it if he tried. Whatever joy he did have came from your relationship and look how he repaid you. But Tom always was weak, and I'm sure that's why Catherine was able to take advantage of him. I hold her responsible for his betrayal more than I blame him. His actions were clearly manipulated by her influence."

"Tom never was very good with women. Maybe if I had known any of this I could have talked him out of thinking things were so bad he had to kill himself."

"No, I say it's a good thing you didn't know what was going on. God knows what you might have done if you had heard about his involvement with Catherine."

His brows lifted.

"Do? What, to myself, or her?"

"Both. You don't belong with a woman like her. You could do so much better."

"Why is it so difficult for you to accept that I want Catherine?"

"Because I don't happen to think you know your own mind. I see what she did to Tom and how she's twisting you to her will. She only cares about herself. The woman is poison to every man she touches."

He got up and walked over to lean against a counter. "She told me she loved me."

Ivy waved her hand in the air, as though she might be flicking at an annoying insect.

"Until the next man comes along she decides she wants. She is incapable of fidelity. She has no heart. She's pure ice inside. Can't you see she's playing you false?"

"I don't want to believe these things, but I admit you've made me feel uneasy. If what you say is true and Catherine's pretending to need me to soothe her ego, then I have a right to know, but it makes me sick to think she might be responsible for Tom's death. I can't believe she's been deceiving me all this time. I wanted to make a home with her." He closed his eyes for a moment and when he opened them again his inner turmoil was reflected there. "I thought we'd cleared things up and put the lies behind us for good."

"That's what she wants you to think. Please don't let her hurt you again, son. God knows you deserve to be free from her treachery after all you've been through."

He sank back down on a chair. "If this is true, it looks like I've come full circle."

She reached over and laid a hand on his shoulder. "I'm so sorry I had to spoil what you think you have with Catherine, but I'd rather do it now than later before she ensnares you even more. I have little doubt that she'll deny everything I've said, so whatever you do is up to you. But I will ask you on behalf of Tom that you give your decision careful thought. You owe him that for the years of friendship you had before Catherine came along and ruined it all. She's the one responsible for destroying Tom."

"So you're saying me wanting Catherine makes a mockery of his death."

"Well, can't you see in a way it does, dear? But you can make it right. It's our responsibility to Tom to consider his little boy's future. We're fighting for him now."

"What do you mean? I told you Tom asked Catherine to take care of him."

Ivy delivered her final salvo.

"Again, we only have her say so. How do we know she didn't lie about that, too? Given her past history, I for one seriously doubt her claim. Surely you don't want such a lying woman to be that sweet baby's mother?" She reached over and gripped his hand. "We must not fail Tom in this."

"So what would you have me do to try and make things right?"

"Take the baby, and kick Catherine out of all our lives once and for all."

Chapter Nineteen

The throbbing headache that had plagued Catherine over the last few hours still held her hostage, as she sat next to Josh while driving to her aunt's place from the airport. Despite his earlier assurance that all of his family would be willing to give her a warm welcome, Catherine had sensed Ivy's silent malice as soon as she walked into the house.

To make matters worse, Ivy invited Robyn, a woman who'd gone to school with Josh and Tom, to join them. The invitation supposedly was issued to give Robyn a chance to see the baby, but it didn't take Catherine long to see she was more than just an old friend. The way she looked at Josh and touched him at every opportunity told its own story.

"He's adorable," Robyn cooed patting Tommy's plump cheek while fluttering her eyelashes at Josh, as he sat next to her holding the baby on his lap. "I'm so glad I'm finally getting the chance to meet him. We've all been wondering why it's taken you so long to bring him here," she said looking around the room to include his family.

Josh's eyes strayed to Catherine.

"Things have been kind of complicated."

Ivy stood.

"Well, the fact that you're here now is a step in the right direction. Of course we'll expect more frequent visits in the future, so that we can get to know the baby." She looked at Robyn and then Catherine. "I'd like you two to come help me with the coffee."

Shocked and somewhat suspicious to be involved in the invitation, Catherine reluctantly followed them to the kitchen where Ivy immediately excused herself and left.

"Ivy felt it would be best to give us a few moments alone," Robyn explained.

"I can't imagine why she would think that."

Her eyes that had glowed with warmth for Josh suddenly turned cold.

"I know you're sleeping with Josh, but he doesn't love you. He's only using you for sex. It's all about availability. You live near him while I have to stay here to take care of my parents. We've loved each other since we were in grade school, and he wants to marry me."

An idea nudged its way into Catherine's brain.

"You sent me that note warning me away from him." She knew by Robyn's expression she was right and actually felt pity for her. "Don't you think Josh would have married you by now if that's really what he was planning?"

"Everything would have been settled if you hadn't talked him into taking that terrible job in the Amazon. What he went through in that jungle and what you did to him when he got back messed with his head. It's your fault he's been so confused."

"You're giving me too much credit. I don't have that kind of influence over Josh."

"That's not what Ivy says – and she knows him better than anyone. She said I had to let him go to Alaska, so he could heal. I agreed because I knew it was best for him."

"If Josh didn't want us to have a relationship he wouldn't be with me."

Robyn pressed her lips together. "You don't have a relationship. You're just another one of his meaningless affairs. He always comes back to me. I'm the one constant woman in his life. He needs me and when he walks down the aisle I'm going to be on his arm."

"Are you sure about that?"

"Yes. Ivy said she'd see to everything, and she's very good at handling things."

By the time Robyn left, it didn't surprise Catherine when Ivy insisted Josh walk her out. He returned to the house several minutes later with a smudge of lipstick on his mouth. It didn't take much imagination to know they'd done more than shake hands.

But Josh's jovial mood had vanished by the time they'd sat down to dinner last night. It'd been a dismal affair. It was difficult enough having to tolerate his mother's iciness, but Catherine was more concerned with the alteration in Josh's behavior.

He'd barely spoken to her and Catherine hadn't missed his cold stares when their eyes did meet. The undercurrents had continued to swirl between them and it was a relief when she could use the excuse of putting Tommy to bed in order to escape upstairs. She had no idea where Josh slept and wondered if he'd been with Robyn. She tried to tell herself she didn't care, but knew deep down she wouldn't hurt so much if that were true.

She'd wanted to skip breakfast to avoid a repeat of the atmosphere at last night's meal, but she knew Tommy would have to eat. Luckily having the baby to care for gave her a good excuse not to focus her attention on Josh and Ivy. John, in his usual mild manner was the only one who made an effort to be pleasant to her.

But Catherine knew she couldn't avoid Josh on their way home. And, as she expected, the flight had been a nightmare in strained silence. She didn't know what had caused the abrupt change in him, but she was certain Ivy was behind the problem. The tension seemed to radiate from him making her feel the weight of it like a constant pressure.

Despite Josh's assurance to the contrary, it was obvious that his mother wasn't willing to forgive and forget the wrongs she felt had been committed. Catherine didn't need Robyn's presence to realize Ivy wasn't going to be happy until she forced her out of Josh's life and installed Robyn in her place. The hope that they'd be able to progress beyond what they shared in bed was once again slipping away with Josh's latest mood.

Priscilla came running out to meet them when they drove into the driveway. Catherine handed her the baby and let her take him inside. Josh leaned against the truck with his arms folded across his chest, staring at her. He reminded Catherine of a man ready to do battle.

"Something is obviously bothering you, Josh. Are you going to continue to give me the silent treatment, or tell me what's on your mind?"

He unfolded his arms and shoved his hands into his front pockets.

"I think it would be a good idea if the baby stayed with my parents for a while."

"What in the world are you talking about?"

"I know I was out of the loop for a long time, but some facts have recently come to my attention that we need to discuss. In the meantime, I'd like Tommy to go to my folks." He pulled his hands free. "You needn't worry. They'll take good care of him."

She paced back and forth for a few seconds struggling to keep her temper under control.

"Is this your idea or your mother's? I'll bet she's involved. I told you it was a mistake for me to go with you. I felt her spitefulness the minute I walked into the house."

"You're mistaken. My mother's just naturally reserved. Maybe the real reason you didn't want to go was because you were having an attack of guilty conscience?"

She stopped.

"No. Why should I? I don't have anything to feel guilty about."

"Are you sure about that? What about Dr. Wade?"

"You mean Ryan?"

"So you're on a first name basis I see. Then you admit you know him?"

"Of course I know him. He's on the staff at the hospital."

"How convenient. It must have helped to simplify matters for the two of you."

"What's that supposed to mean?"

"I'm sure you found his bedside manner particularly welcoming."

Shocked and insulted by his insinuation, she spoke very deliberately through clenched teeth.

"Go to hell."

He shoved away from the truck and grabbed her by the arms.

"I've already been there. Remember? Is he the reason you won't marry me?" He gave her a little shake. "You said you loved me and that makes you mine. I don't want Wade or any other man touching you."

She pushed him away, oblivious to the hint of desperation in his voice.

"You're acting like I'm some kind of possession. Is that what you think love is really all about?"

"You know I didn't mean it like that."

"Well, however you meant it I'm not yours to control and for your information Ryan is a good friend. He supported me through some very difficult times."

"I'll bet. Did he give you his home address for some private consultations, too?"

He had accused her of having an affair with Tom and now this. She could hardly believe it was happening again. It took every bit of her will power not to scream a denial.

"It's none of your business if I did or didn't go to Ryan's house and while we're at it, you don't see me bringing up Robyn and the way you two played kissy face."

Dusty red color spotted his cheeks.

"We grew up together for God's sake."

"How convenient," she mocked using his words. "She told me you two are getting married." She rushed on. "I'm sure I have your mother to thank for inviting her to the house along with convincing you that I slept with Ryan. She'll say anything to discredit me and you absorb her lies like a sponge. Did you know she told me you were getting married to keep me from going to you in Alaska? You certainly have a lot of would be brides lining up to get your ring on their finger."

"That's crazy talk. I think you're making this up to make Mom look bad."

"I'm not. You're mother's the one who's the mistress of deceit here, but you don't see it." She pressed fingers to her temple trying to ease the pounding pain. "Oh, what's the use? We've already been through all this. I told you how things were with Tom and now I'm telling you Ryan and I were never lovers. In fact, he was the one who encouraged me to try and get back with you. Everything I've said is the truth."

A quick flash of uncertainty flickered in his eyes before a shutter came down.

"Since I wasn't here when a lot of things happened, I have to choose who I trust. How do I know you're telling me the truth?"

"Because I have nothing to hide; I've never lied to you, Josh."

"So you keep saying. But, I happen to have a slightly different perspective on things; and I want what's best for little Tommy."

"And you think I don't? What about my aunt? Aren't you forgetting about her?

The baby is all she has left of Nancy. How could you be so cruel as to even suggest taking him away from her?"

He ran his hand around the back of his neck.

"I don't want to hurt her. She's not the one at fault here. I'll make sure my parents give her generous visitation rights with him."

"My God, what makes you think you have the right to make that decision?"

"You're forgetting that Tom was a part of my family long before your cousin entered the picture. She only had a few months with him, while he was ours for years."

"There you go again, acting like people are property. You talk like he was a piece of furniture instead of a human being. Tom loved Nancy and that love brought little Tommy into the world. He means everything to my aunt, and she doesn't deserve to be punished by you or your malicious mother."

"This is between us, Catherine. Stop trying to drag my mother into this."

"How can I not when I know in my heart she's the one who's twisted your mind against me? The pathetic thing is you don't recognize her treachery or seem to realize how she bends you to her will. Well, I'm sick to death of trying to explain myself to you and that manipulative woman. If two people are going to make it together there has to be trust. Go away Josh. And while you're at it, you might want to try learning how to be your own man."

"You don't have to tell me what I need to do. I know where my duty lies."

"I doubt it." She retaliated. "If you did, you wouldn't have left. It's getting so I don't know what to expect from you. You make me feel like someone pulling the petals off a daisy asking myself will you stay or will you go. Well I'm not the one who went away. I promised Tom to take care of his son and I intend to keep that vow."

He tugged her by the hand.

"We can't work this out if you walk away."

Provoked beyond her endurance, Catherine jerked free.

"Oh no, you're the only one who's allowed to walk out on people and slam doors in their face."

"I've already apologized for that. I can't change what's in the past. What more do you want from me? You're making me sound like some kind of monster when all I'm trying to do is rectify some of my mistakes. Let me take the baby and make up for . . . ."

She cut him off. "You're a little late. You could have been here when Tom needed you if you'd thought about someone besides yourself." They'd worked their way up to the front door now. "He always tried to support you, but when he asked you not to take the job in South America it didn't stop you from leaving him, did it?"

"I can only take desk work so long. Tom understood how things were with me."

"Yes he did, which is certainly more than you can say about him. I doubt if you ever considered his feelings. You'd take off knowing he'd be here waiting. Have you forgotten how much he admired you? The poor man was practically subservient to you."

"That's not true."

"No? If you don't know that, then you never really understood what your friendship meant to him. It wasn't about power or control for Tom. It was about doing whatever he could to please you. You were his idea of perfection. He wanted to be you."

"Now you're being ridiculous."

"Like I said, you obviously didn't understand him." She spun around and slipped inside, shutting the door in his face and flicking the lock before he had a chance to reply.

He huffed out a breath.

"Well, I sure as hell didn't win any points here today."

>>>>*dreams*<<<<

Heavy brooding and deep nagging uncertainty pushed Josh into a dreadful nightmare that night. Caught in the crossfire between the two most important women in his life, he felt anxiety and doubt whittling away at him as he struggled to deal with their conflicting stories. One of them was obviously lying, but which one was the guilty party?

The question pounded inside his head, as he continued to toss and turn ensnaring himself among the bedding. He labored to bring each breath to the surface, as images continued to torment him. Faces lurked among the shadows of his mind before bursting forth to confront him with guilt, accusations, and ultimatums that made him pull back as though he was stepping too close to the edge of a very dangerous precipice.

Tom, pale in death with long strands of seaweed trailing from his body stood before him, eyes filled with sadness. Ivy's face, distorted in fury appeared next, spewing her hatred of Catherine like spears that jabbed him in the heart until he cried out in pain. A solemn Catherine, stood bravely, with her chin held high, and shook her head at Ivy while she continued to clutch little Tommy to her breast.

Although his body was slick with sweat, his insides felt chilled to the bone by the time he managed to claw his way to wakefulness. Yanking the covers aside, he shot up in bed fighting to draw air into his tortured lungs. He reached a trembling hand over and snapped on the bedside lamp causing a modest pool of light to shine into the room.

His throat ached for water, but he didn't trust his legs to carry him. He swung them over the edge of the bed and pressed his feet to the floor needing to anchor himself to something solid. His fingers plowed through his hair. The nightmare had so unnerved him that he couldn't help feeling empathy for what Catherine must go through when her night terrors involved people she cared about.

He usually dreamed about his time in the jungle and being pursued by Orlando. He never shared those nightmares with anyone because they made him feel like a coward, which was bad enough, but tonight's episode filled him with a different kind of dread.

Despite what his mother said, he still clung to the hope of marrying Catherine. He knew she was having a problem with the idea, but he hoped she'd eventually accept his proposal. Now that goal seemed to be slipping away. Their relationship reminded him of an intricate mosaic pattern with its complicated blend of promises and love, misgivings and betrayals. Once again he was afraid he'd wasted too much time and energy longing for what he was never going to have.

His entire being rebelled at the thought of losing Catherine, but jealousy and insecurity was causing him to destroy their relationship. It seemed the more he wanted her, the more he drove her away. He couldn't seem to get things right between them and his mother wasn't helping matters any.

He'd been so sure their saga would finally have a happy ending when he'd followed Catherine home from Alaska, only to become embroiled in this latest dispute. The more he went over their most recent confrontation and the things his mother had told him, the more disillusioned he became. How could he ever hope to figure things out when he kept getting so many conflicting stories thrown at him?

Desperate to know the truth, he thought of swallowing his pride and calling Catherine, but knew she'd probably hang up given her present mood. The sound of her door closing had twisted his insides. There was something agonizingly final about the gesture and he knew there was no way he could leave things like this and keep his sanity.

If only he could talk to someone who knew the real story. It would certainly make things a lot easier if Tom was here to defend himself. He thought of Pricilla, but rejected the idea knowing she wouldn't say anything to hurt Catherine.

He needed to find a person who knew the true facts; someone unbiased enough to be fair to everyone involved. Josh feared it was the only chance he had to try and stop the erosion of his future happiness before it slid away from him for good. But who would be able to tell him what really had happened while he'd been gone? Could there possibly be anyone out there with the answers to his questions?

Chapter Twenty

To say Ryan was surprised that Josh would be calling him was an understatement. But hearing the obvious turmoil in Josh's voice made the physician in him feel compelled to offer whatever professional help he could. He knew enough from Catherine to guess that Josh had apparently experienced a difficult time during his stay in South America. Ryan also had to admit the personal side of him was curious to meet the man who had kept Catherine from accepting another man's love. He invited Josh to come to his office.

"Come in, Mr. Dallas." He held out his hand in greeting and Josh shook it after a split second of hesitation.

"I'm sure you're very busy. I appreciate you taking the time to see me."

He nodded and pointed to a chair.

"Have a seat."

Josh sat down while Ryan perched on one corner of his desk, as each man quickly measured the other.

"You said you wanted to talk to me about Catherine," Ryan prompted when Josh remained quiet.

"Yes. There are some things I . . ." He let out a long shuddering breath.

"Take your time."

"Have you ever dug yourself into a hole so deep you're not sure you'll get out?"

"A time or two. Burrowed pretty far down, are you?"

Josh grimaced.

"I'm damn near halfway to China."

"As bad as that? Not an enviable position."

"I realize we don't know each other, but I hope you'll be upfront with me." Josh inhaled. "I need to know what Catherine is to you. She says you're just friends."

Ryan crossed his arms over his chest.

"That's right, but I'd be lying if I said that's all I wanted from her. However, she never allowed what we had to go beyond friendship. So if you're worried whether or not we slept together, we didn't."

Josh closed his eyes for a moment and opened them again, his face still twisted in anguish.

"I appreciate your candor, but I still have another hurdle to get over." He raked a hand through his hair. "Did you ever meet my friend, Tom Wolden? His wife gave birth to a son in your hospital while I was away, but she was very ill and died soon after."

Ryan uncrossed his arms.

"Yes, I remember them quite well. Their situation was one of those tragedies we sometimes have to deal with in my profession, but their particular case touched all of us in the hospital very deeply. Your friend sat by his wife's bedside day after day refusing to leave her. It certainly took its toll on him. Catherine and her aunt suffered right along with him. You knew Mrs. Wolden was her cousin?"

"Yes." He cleared his throat. "I thought maybe Tom and Catherine might have been, you know, comforting each other while I was away," he mumbled and quickly looked down at his hands while deep color worked its way up his neck.

Ryan's voice lost some of the earlier friendliness when he spoke. "If you mean in an inappropriate manner, then you're doing them both a grave injustice."

"I must sound like a first class jerk to you."

"I don't know you well enough to make such a judgment call, but I'm afraid your imagination is more vivid than the reality of what actually happened. It was a case of two good people being thrown together in extremely tragic circumstances. They took solace in their friendship, but never abused it."

"You're right, you don't know me, and I'm beginning to think I don't know myself. I used to be so sure of everything – cocky enough to think I could have it all. My life started to change when I met Catherine. I'd begun to think about marriage, but I wasn't quite ready for the responsibility of a committed relationship, so I went away."

"Is that when you decided to take the job in South America?"

"Yeah. I wasn't sure if you knew about that. I thought I could take off and come back and pick up where I left off. But things haven't gone the way I thought they were going to, and I can't seem to get back on track."

"Maybe you need to try a different path?"

"I don't know what that would be. I keep wishing things could go back to the way they were before I left. My life was certainly a lot less complicated then."

"We should all probably be careful of what we wish for. Maybe you were forced to grow up while you were away," Ryan said with a bluntness only a stranger would dare.

Josh's eyes flashed in anger, and he rubbed a hand across his chest.

"It wasn't a very pleasant way to gain maturity, believe me."

"It wasn't my intention to play down what you must have gone through, but I'm sure you realize if you continue to dance through life you're eventually going to step on some toes and have others step on yours."

"You're right, my ego did need taming down, and Catherine made me take stock of where I was going with my life. I made all kinds of vows after I was rescued on how much I would appreciate her, but instead I've made a God awful mess of things."

"Perhaps because you lost Catherine once you're afraid of losing her again, so to protect yourself you continue to drive her away, even though you actually want her in your life. You might also consider the possibility that you feel guilty for leaving and that could make you think you don't deserve her."

He stared at Ryan with the look of someone who'd just been jolted into coming to his senses.

"I never thought of it like that. I love Catherine and I'm sick at the thought of losing her, but I've been acting like an idiot, hounding her with accusations and making outrageous demands. You'd think a thirty-four year old man would be able to do a better job of handling his personal life." He rubbed his forehead. "Everything's so tangled up inside me I don't have faith in my feelings enough to do the right thing to keep her."

"You can't have love without trust."

"You medicos are on the same page. That's what Catherine said. I really screwed up when I accused her and Tom of being lovers. He was like a brother to me and I know in my heart he would never have done such a thing, but I threw it in her face not once, but twice. What kind of a person does that make me?" he asked in self-disgust.

"I'd say a foolish one as well as a man who lacks confidence. You went to South America and returned a different person. You and that man have to learn to get to know each other. Catherine fell in love with you the way you were, and she needs time to adjust to the change. There's more to love than sex. The rest is different for each individual, but to have a truly meaningful relationship you have to want a person as much out of bed as you do when they're in it. My advice is not to allow anyone or anything to come between you until you get the correct balance. You'll know when you have everything right."

He thought of Ivy. "What if it's someone you've known and trusted all your life?"

"This is between you and Catherine. Love carries certain obligations and one of those responsibilities is that you have to believe in the other person as much as they believe in you. Love doesn't guarantee we'll always make the right decisions, but personally, I'd do whatever I had to do to keep a woman like Catherine in my life, even if it meant crawling on my hands and knees."

"I'm not sure if she'll be willing to give me another chance after the way I acted."

"You won't know until you try. We're all hanging by a fragile thread most of the time, but you'd be surprised at how much strength can come from our weaknesses. Your life changed because of a series of dramatic events. You can't alter the fact that they happened, but you can learn from them. It's your call to try and make the right choice."

"I'd say it's about damn time I do." He cleared his throat and shifted uneasily in the chair. "Um, I'd appreciate it if you'd let me tell Catherine about this visit."

"Understood. She's a good friend and I'd like her to be happy."

"So would I." Josh stood up and offered his hand with much more enthusiasm than he'd felt when he first arrived. "You've been a great help. Thank you, Dr. Wade."

"Make it Ryan. Helping people is what I do. Go put things right with Catherine for both your sakes. Life can get to be lonely when you lose someone special."

Remembering his mother saying that Ryan had been widowed, Josh felt compelled to say something.

"I know you lost your wife, Ryan. I'm very sorry. She was obviously a very lucky lady to have snared a guy like you."

"I was the lucky one, but my luck ran out. Don't let that happen to you, Josh."

Deep in thought, Josh left the office and headed for his car. If he'd been more willing to believe Catherine, things would be a lot easier between them now. He could forgive himself given his emotional and mental state the first time he'd rejected her words, but there was no excuse for his latest accusation.

For some inexplicable reason his mother had crossed an ethical line using lies while she hoarded the truth. He couldn't understand what had made her do such a thing, but her efforts to turn his mind against Catherine had nearly worked.

Josh felt revolted with himself remembering how he'd insulted Catherine using his mother's trumped up story. Now he must see her to apologize, although he knew simply saying he was sorry wasn't enough to make up for the way he'd treated her.

At least he hoped he'd have another opportunity to make things right and like Ryan, he didn't care if forgiveness came with groveling. He intended to confront his mother about her duplicity, but right now he needed to make another phone call.

He picked up his cell phone.

"Mr. Marsh, this is Josh Dallas."

"Josh! How are you, my boy?" he asked in a warm voice. "It's been a long time."

"Yes sir, it has. I'm well, thank you."

"I'm so glad. When I last talked to your mother she said you'd had a breakdown."

"I guess I did. Um, I was wondering if you've spoken to my mother since then."

"No I haven't. I did ask her to keep me informed, but she never called back. I thought of contacting her, but decided it was best not to intrude in the event there were complications with your recovery. Jenny will be so pleased when I tell her you're well."

Josh thought of the woman who looked so much like Marie that she'd jolted his brain into remembering everything he thought he'd lost.

"How is she?"

"A bit of a saint for putting up with me," he chuckled. "I got her to marry me."

"That's wonderful news. Congratulations to you both."

"Thank you. Now, how about you, did you ever marry your young lady?"

"No, but I still want to very much. Unfortunately we've had some setbacks."

"I'm sorry to hear that, but take my advice and don't waste time when you find that special someone or you might miss out."

"I'm trying, but I'm confused about a few things. Did you call my parents after we parted at the airport to let them know I was coming home?"

"Why no. I thought you said you wanted to surprise your family."

Josh barely managed to stop himself from blurting out a vicious string of cursing remembering how easily he'd been duped by his mother's skillful lying. He pushed back the throb of temper that wanted to beat against his temples.

"So you weren't in contact with my mother at that point?" he stressed, needing to be sure, but dreading the answer.

"Not then, no. But she did call me later wanting to know what had happened to you after the kidnapping. She said you were too distraught to communicate properly and thought if she knew the details she would have a better chance of helping you recover."

"Did she happen to mention Catherine at any time during the conversation?"

He hesitated.

"Yes, as a matter of fact she did."

"Do you mind if I ask what she said?" Several seconds of silence followed his request making his pulse hammer knowing the reply wouldn't bring comfort. "I'm kind of lost here and I need some direction. Any help would be appreciated." he prodded.

"I understand, but I don't want to be the cause of any problems between you and your mother. It might be best to leave that part of the conversation alone, Josh."

"It's important that I know what she told you and you don't need to gift wrap it."

"Well, if you're sure that's what you really want." But he still hesitated until once again Josh urged his cooperation.

"All right then," he let out a breath. "Your mother insisted Catherine was the real cause of your breakdown and that it was up to her as your parent to protect you from having to deal with her. I'm afraid my suggestion that she step back and allow you and Catherine to work things out on your own wasn't received very well."

"How do you know she felt that way?"

"Because she hung up on me after a few final blistering words to let me know what she thought of my advice."

Josh's fingers tightened on his phone recalling how his mother had looked at him with such pleading while she spun her tale of deceit like a spider creating its web. His gut burned with the disgust and anger churning inside him.

"I'm sorry she was so rude."

"I admit I was shocked by her reaction, but considering your condition, she had a right to be upset. It couldn't have been easy for her seeing you in such a state."

"I was pretty out of it," he agreed. "But she shouldn't have taken it out on you."

"Don't worry about it. I hope I've helped you. You're obviously experiencing some problems in communication and I certainly wouldn't want to make things worse."

"You haven't. You've told me what I needed to know. Thank you for being honest with me."

"Well, I certainly wish it could have been a happier conversation for you. I hope you can make things work out between you and your Catherine."

"So do I. She's means everything to me, but I have a feeling I'm going to be involved in quite a battle. I'll let you know what happens."

"I hope you will. And as to that battle, some things are worth fighting for."

"Yeah, especially when you know it's your one chance to win the war."

Chapter Twenty-one

Priscilla watched from the doorway, as Catherine deftly folded another set of clothes for Tommy and laid them in the small suitcase lying open on his changing table. She grabbed several disposable diapers and began stuffing them into a diaper bag.

Catherine looked up.

"Did you get everything set up with Meg to use her condo?"

"Yes." Priscilla came into the room. "Luckily she doesn't have it rented right now."

"How about the shop? Is she going to be able to work the extra hours?"

"It's all set. We had discussed when I hired her that she might be needed to take over from time to time since we have the baby. How long do you think I should stay away?"

Catherine closed the suitcase. "I'm not sure, but hopefully not too long. I'll update you as soon as I can. I'm sorry about this, Aunt Pris. I realize it's an inconvenience asking you to drop everything on such short notice and take off. I might be over reacting, but I can't take the chance that Josh will make good on this threat."

"I can't believe he would really come here and try to take the baby from us. What does he hope to gain? He has no legal rights where Tommy is concerned."

"He thinks his long relationship with Tom takes precedence over blood ties."

"Well, I wish he'd make up his mind instead of just threatening us. One minute he's saying he wants the two of you to help raise Tommy together, and the next thing I know you're saying he wants to take the baby out of our lives." She shook her head. "I still don't understand why he'd even suggest something so selfish."

"I don't think these legal threats and hostility are coming from Josh. I'm almost certain his mother has put the ideas in his head," she said, while gathering up a few more toys and other essentials for the bag.

"Considering the way she treated you when you tried to contact him earlier, and now all this turmoil makes me dislike her all the more. I can't understand why she insists on wanting to hurt us. We would have happily shared Tommy with her."

"Ivy Dallas doesn't believe in sharing." Catherine's voice cracked with anger as her hands tightened on a toy soldier.

>>>>*dreams*<<<<

Ivy was rolling out pie dough when Josh silently entered the kitchen. He cleared his throat to alert her to his presence. She looked over her shoulder and instantly smiled.

"Why Josh what a lovely surprise. Why didn't you tell us you were coming?"

"As you said, it's a surprise." He came further into the kitchen, and she lifted her cheek for a kiss. He gave her a quick peck before stepping back.

"Where's Dad?"

"Out fussing in his vegetable garden, Ivy said, wiping her hands on a towel. We can have a nice private visit. Would you like something to eat or drink?"

"No thanks. I'm not here for food or drink. Sit down, Mom. I need to talk to you."

Her eyebrows slowly drifted upward, taking in the full view of her son.

"Oh? What about? Nothing serious I hope."

"Please." He added, pointing to a chair.

She sat while he stood leaning back against the counter gripping the edge with both hands braced on either side of him. His body remained taut; his eyes watchful.

"You seem upset." she observed while staring at him. Her expression twisted into a hostile mask. "Don't tell me that troublemaker Catherine has been bothering you again."

"Why did you make up all those lies about her?" he asked, fighting to keep his voice level. Shocked at the hatred in her eyes, he wondered how he'd missed it before.

Bright color flushed Ivy's cheeks while her eyes raked over him with disapproval.

"Obviously something has happened to send you here questioning me as though I were on a witness stand," she said in a censorious tone. "Catherine did get to you, didn't she? I was afraid this might happen. She's like an addictive drug to you. I warned you she would deny everything I said. I didn't make it up. She's a lying whore just as I told you."

Josh felt as though something fetid had crawled inside him making his gut churn with nausea. Unable to contain his inner rage any longer, he surged forward and slapped the flat of his hand on the table with enough of a bang to make Ivy jerk back in her chair.

"Don't call her that! And stop your lying, damn it! Can't you see how this charade of yours demeans us both? Do you have any idea how difficult it is for me to stand here and tell myself that I still love you knowing how you tried to destroy my happiness?"

She shook her head in a quick denial. "I did not try to destroy it. I was trying to preserve your chance to be happy. I wanted to ensure myself that you'd have a decent future ahead of you. Catherine puts you in jeopardy, but you don't seem to realize that."

"Mother, all she's ever done is try to love me. You've got to stop blaming her for my mistakes. Catherine is not responsible for any of the things that happened to me."

Ivy stood up so quickly her chair rocked perilously back on two legs.

"Oh yes she is! You would never have taken that job if you hadn't wanted extra money to marry her."

"She didn't know about that until I got back and she did beg me not to go. I could have borrowed money if I really needed it, but I went because it was something new and I was feeling bored at work. I took the job because I was so egotistical I thought I could leave her dangling until I got back. As usual, I was only concerned with what I wanted."

"Why shouldn't you be? You have every right to do what you want without having to answer to her. She's obviously been chasing after you from the first moment you stepped into her hospital."

"I was the one doing the chasing. I chose her. I was lucky to get our first date."

"Bad luck, if you ask me. I don't care what you say, she doesn't deserve you."

"You have it all wrong. I'm the one who doesn't deserve Catherine."

Now it was Ivy's turn to smack her hand on the table.

"How can you say that when you almost died because of that woman?" she shouted displaying her own fury.

"You've got it all wrong. I stayed alive because of her. Even in my amnesia my subconscious mind knew she was one of the main reasons I wanted to live. If I'm fortunate she'll forgive me for doubting her and give us another chance to be together."

Ivy let out a derisive snort.

"Where was your precious Catherine when you were so ill?" she practically snarled. "I was the one who nursed you back to health, not her."

"Only because you wouldn't allow her to come here." He raked a hand through his hair. "Do you know how humiliating it was for me to have to go crawling like some beggar to strangers trying to glean information, so I could find out the truth? I'm not sure if I'll ever be able to forgive you for lying to me about Catherine's supposed affairs."

She started to speak, but he held up his hand to cut her off.

"I want no more of your lies. I don't know how you can live with yourself knowing you deliberately used Tom, especially knowing he was dead and unable to defend himself. It makes me sick to my stomach just thinking about it," he said not bothering to hide the revulsion he felt.

"You weren't here when they came to stay. I could see he was attracted to her. I'm still convinced they carried on with each other."

He blew out a hard breath fighting to keep his temper in check.

"You don't give up, do you? Now I see that you hated Tom, too. How it must have galled you all those years that I wanted him for my friend." Josh stared at her as if he was seeing a stranger. "I never realized what lengths you were willing to go to in order to have your own way."

She reached out to him, but dropped her hands when he stepped back out of reach.

"Please don't look at me like that, darling. It's never been about what I wanted. You're my son. I needed to protect you like any mother would that loves her child."

"I know you thought you should shield me like you've always tried to do, but it has to stop. Your interference has put my future in jeopardy. I'm giving you fair warning, I don't ever want to hear you say another disparaging word about Catherine again. If you do, I really will be dead to you."

Genuine tears began to run down Ivy's cheeks and dripped off her chin. She used the hem of her apron to wipe them away.

"You wouldn't be saying these cruel things to me if you knew the agony I suffered thinking you had died in that horrible jungle."

"I'm sorry for the pain I caused you, but you have to move beyond that now."

"You know what you mean to me, Josh. I only have your best interests at heart."

"I wonder." His eyes probed deep. "Or maybe it's more what's best for you."

"How can you even think such a thing?" she whined, her hands clenching her apron and tears continuing to fill her eyes.

"What would you expect the way you've been carrying on with your trumped up stories? I'm not a little boy. I'm a grown man. I need to fight my own battles. You can't keep me tied to you forever," he said forcing himself to use a more gentle tone.

"I wasn't trying to do anything of the kind and in time you'll see I'm right about Catherine. I chose Robyn for you because she's the perfect girl for you and she deserves your allegiance considering all the years she's waited for you to marry her."

"You chose her? Do you have any idea how ridiculously archaic that sounds? I've never wanted to marry Robyn and you were wrong to make her think otherwise."

She reached for him and this time he allowed her to clutch his arm.

"But . . ."

A tall figure stood in the doorway partially hidden in shadow.

"Let him go, Ivy."

She snatched her hand away and spun around at the sound of her husband's quiet voice.

"What are you doing sneaking in here? I don't appreciate being startled, John."

"I am not sneaking, Ivy. I do believe I still live here."

Her eyes snapped with impatience.

"Josh and I are trying to have a conversation. A private conversation I might add. I would have let you know if you were needed here."

"I've heard enough to know what's going on. You didn't want me because you knew I wouldn't approve." He then looked at Josh. "You go to Catherine with our blessings."

Ivy shrieked her displeasure.

"No! I'll never give my approval to that woman." She pulled on the front of Josh's shirt. "Don't listen to him. Your father has no right to try and shove Catherine down my throat. I will not tolerate being anywhere near her."

"I said let him go, Ivy." There was steel behind his voice now.

She pulled her hands away from Josh and turned at John's unaccustomed commanding tone. She stared at him with astonishment clearly showing on her face.

"What on earth has come over you? You've never spoken to me like that before and I don't have time right now to deal with whatever you think you're doing. Now go back to your squash and tomatoes and let me work out this little misunderstanding with Josh."

He came fully into the room and stood gripping the back of a chair until the tan skin covering his knuckles turned white.

"I'll thank you not to dismiss me in my own house as though I were some pesky child."

"Oh for heaven's sake," she ground out with irritation. "You don't understand what's going on as usual. There's a history here you know nothing about."

"Because I haven't said anything before doesn't mean I don't know what you've been doing. I understand more than you realize and I won't stand by while you distort things to suit your own needs. Josh has a right to live his life without your interference."

"I know what's best for my son and I don't like you butting in," she admonished.

"He happens to also be my son too, and at this point I don't care what you think."

"How dare you talk to me like that!"

Josh looked from one to the other and frowned.

"I had to come here and try to clear some things up, but I didn't mean to cause trouble between you two."

"You needn't concern yourself about us. You have more important matters to take care of. You go find your Catherine and make things right with her. She's a good woman and I'd like to see you have her in your future."

"I'll not have you speak for me. I forbid you to go to that woman, Josh," Ivy said.

"You forbid me?" His expression mirrored his frustration. "What part of me telling you I'm a grown man didn't you understand? I do happen to have a mind of my own, and it's about damn time I start making my own decisions without you butting in. You've got to resign yourself to the fact that I love Catherine and I want to be with her. Now let's leave it at that before we both end up saying something even more regrettable."

She snorted out a harsh laugh while pointing an accusing finger at both men.

"What's regrettable is how gullible you both are. If you had listened to me you wouldn't have allowed yourselves to be duped by that lying bi . . ."

"That's enough!" Fury racing through his blood, eyes black with rage, Josh thrust himself toward Ivy making her stumble back. "I told you not to talk about

Catherine like that. You're slandering the woman I love. It's like plunging a knife into my heart when you insult her, and if you really do love me as much as you claim, you wouldn't say such awful things."

John stepped between them and touched Josh on the arm before Ivy could say anything else.

"I think it's time for you to leave now." He looked over his shoulder and gave Ivy a warning glare when she started to speak.

Josh felt his insides clench. If he hadn't been a part of it he wouldn't believe he'd actually had this shouting match with his mother.

"I'm sorry for the way things have gotten so out of hand. That wasn't my intention when I came here."

"I'd say you've shown remarkable restraint considering the damage that's been done. I hope Catherine will understand." He squeezed Josh's shoulder. "Good luck, son."

"Thanks, Dad. I have a feeling I'm going to need it. I'll be in touch."

He stared at Ivy for a few seconds. She reached out her hands to him, but he shook his head and walked away without allowing her to make contact. As soon as the door closed, she whirled around to lash out at John with the wrath that boiled inside her.

"Well, I hope you're satisfied now that you've turned Josh against me."

"That was not my doing."

"You think not? I didn't notice you doing anything to help defend my position. That's what a good husband would have done for his wife. I've only been trying to protect Josh. Am I to be condemned for wanting what is best for him?" she demanded.

"You need to give that question some serious thought. Josh knows what he wants and it's about time you realized it. Instead of casting blame on others, you should try examining your own motives. If you don't want to kill whatever love Josh still has left for you I suggest you don't abuse that love because he wants to share it with others."

"I don't care if he shares it with others; just not Catherine."

"Because she represents competition for you? That's pretty pathetic, Ivy. Did you really believe you were going to be able to keep Josh as your own exclusive pet forever?"

Her cheeks brightened with a surge of color. "That's a disgusting thing to say."

"Call it what you will, but you had better get used to the idea that you either learn to share Josh, or not have him at all. In the meantime, you owe Catherine an apology."

"I don't owe her anything. She deserves to be punished for causing all this."

"You're never satisfied until you've squeeze out every last drop of pain, are you? You thrive on making people your victims. How sad that you'd do it to your own son. Well know now that I'll not support you in continuing to drive Catherine out of his life."

She watched him go and shoved his words aside. She neither needed nor wanted his help. Her anger was coupled with frustration at Josh's rebellion. Despite his threat, Ivy was confident he would never push her out of his life, but Catherine was definitely swaying his judgment on where his priorities should be, and that she could not allow. No one had ever bested her and no one would; certainly not a little nobody like Catherine.

The annoying girl was like an unwanted weed in a garden. Some were more stubborn than others, but Ivy had always prided herself on knowing how to get rid of weeds. She went back to her pie dough, her brain a whirlwind of activity, and by the time she'd slid the pastry into the oven the expression on her face was positively evil.

Chapter Twenty-two

Catherine roamed restlessly around the empty house. She felt unsettled, but she reminded herself it had been her idea to have her aunt take the baby away for a few days. Although, like Priscilla, she doubted if Josh could legally take little Tommy, she didn't want to risk him coming here and upsetting her aunt.

She hadn't realized how much she'd taken for granted her aunt's friendly chatter and the baby's presence. Now, the quiet was beginning to close in around her. Feeling the need for some fresh air, she wandered outside to the patio. A light breeze ruffled her hair while the mélange of scents tickled her nose. Her aunt loved gardening and had planted a profusion of flowers in the yard and around the patio in various pots and tubs.

This had always been a special place for her; and now with Josh's latest cold attitude toward her, Catherine needed the warmth of happy memories. Her father had helped her uncle pour the cement here. She'd only been five years old at the time, but Catherine could remember how the two men had insisted on having her and Nancy's small handprints pressed into their handiwork before the concrete dried.

She couldn't help smiling as she recalled how their mothers fussed over them afterward making sure all the thick grainy mixture had been thoroughly washed off. Special attention had also been added to be sure their tiny fingernails were spotlessly clean again. The fathers had allowed each girl to print her name next to her own handprint. Catherine recalled complaining that it had taken her longer than Nancy because of the extra letters in her name.

She stretched and inhaled deeply. The morning sun was a bright yellow ball in the sky and felt good on her skin. She turned her face upward to catch the warm rays and closed her eyes. Her aunt's gardening had produced a cornucopia of color and fragrances. Catherine opened her eyes when she heard the sound of bees busily humming nearby, as they flitted among the flowers.

She gradually grew tired of her own company and went inside again. Wondering what she could do to fill in the time, she decided it was a perfect opportunity to shop for her aunt's birthday gift. She enjoyed the annual ritual, and the thought of getting out around people was suddenly very appealing, especially when visions of Josh kept intruding in her thoughts. Reenergized, she retrieved her purse from the bedroom, approving the sexy image peering back at her from the full-length mirror on the closet-door, and headed for her car.

Although there were several malls to choose from, she drove to the one closest to their house. She knew from past experience there were some shops there her aunt favored. As soon as she entered the shopping center she filled herself with the sights and sounds so unique to such a busy place.

She wove her way around people with pleasant memories guiding her steps directly to Pricilla's favorite shopping area and the first store of choice. Although it carried some other types of merchandise, it specialized in music boxes. If there was anything her aunt enjoyed as much as flowers, it was her collection of music boxes; the more whimsical the better.

Catherine took her time strolling around the shop and doing her best to ignore the hovering saleswoman while she made her selection. It wasn't easy. There were dozens to choose from, each one quite distinctive. She finally chose one she hoped would please.

Its dusty rose exterior was decorated with dozens of miniature flowers in various colors and topped with a smiling fairy. Catherine touched a fingertip to the delicate coil of blonde curls and the wispy looking wings. But it was the tiny creature's mischievous smile that caught her attention.

The artist had painted the little mouth in such a way that the fairy seemed to be conveying the idea that whoever looked at her was in for a special treat. When she lifted the lid and heard the first notes of, "You Light Up My Life", she knew this was the right one.

As soon as the box had been gift wrapped, she headed for a bath shop where she purchased a trio of lotion, bath spray, and soap in the raspberry scent her aunt preferred. From there she made her way to a candy store and added a brightly wrapped box of chocolates to her medley of gifts.

Catherine strolled back to her car feeling happy with her success. She toyed with the idea of having lunch at a little bistro near the mall, but decided instead to wait for another day when her aunt could join her. By the time she arrived home and carried the bags inside, she was in a better mood knowing her shopping trip had been a success.

She stashed the gifts in her bedroom closet and changed clothes before padding barefoot into the kitchen for something to eat. She'd just opened the refrigerator and was looking over her choices when she heard footsteps. She immediately let go of the door and felt her pulse leap when she saw Josh standing there watching her.

"Don't you ever knock?" Her happy mood vanished in a flash.

"I did, but I guess you didn't hear me. I hope you don't mind that I let myself in."

"As a matter of fact I do. You are no longer welcome to come and go here as you please; and if you came for the baby you're too late." She braced her body in a gesture of defiance. "I made my aunt take him away for a few days."

"You didn't have to do that. I'm not here for him and it was wrong of me to suggest such a thing. I'm sorry you felt they needed to leave. I didn't come to cause trouble."

"Unfortunately trouble seems to follow you around."

She folded her arms over her chest.

"Just why are you here, Josh?"

He stepped forward, reached into his pocket, and set a small frog made from thick green glass on the counter next to her. She looked at it and let her arms fall to her sides.

"What in the world is that for?"

"I read somewhere that the Japanese believe the frog is a symbol of good luck for things like keeping travelers safe on their journeys."

Instinctive compassion softened her expression for a moment. "It's too bad you didn't have it with you in South America."

"Maybe I would have if I had known about it then, but now I'm about to embark on another, more important journey and I need all the help I can get."

Disbelief turned her heart to stone.

"Some things never seem to change. You still think running away is the answer. So where are you off to this time?" she asked, not bothering to hide the bitterness she felt. "Outer space?"

He shoved his hands in his pockets.

"Not quite, although I'm sure that's where you'd like to send me. I'm taking the uncertain road to my future, but there could be problems along the way because I've thrown up some formidable roadblocks."

"Yes, as I said, you do seem to excel at that kind of thing."

"I know. That's why I need your help. I want to get it right this time."

"What is it you want me to do, take you by the hand and lead you? You'd be better off getting yourself a good compass." The sarcasm in her tone had deepened.

"I was hoping you'd walk beside me," he said watching her with a steady gaze.

"I'm not in the guide business. You'd be better off recruiting Robyn."

"I don't want Robyn; I've never wanted her. There are all these empty spaces inside me that only you can fill. I want us to be together again, Catherine."

"Seems to me I've heard that before. There was an imbalance in our relationship from the very beginning, but I thought we could eventually work things out. I was wrong. We obviously have different needs and too much has happened for things to ever be right between us now. You must know we can't go back to where we began."

"I told you before I'm not interested in the past." He pulled his hands out of his pockets and let them hang loosely at his sides. "I want to go forward with you – only you."

"That's what you say now, but experience has told me it would only last until the next time your mother comes up with another one of her fabricated stories and brainwashes you. No thanks, I'm not interested in running her gauntlet again."

"There won't be any more of that kind of thing."

She rolled her eyes toward the ceiling.

"No? You believed all the lies she told about me before. How do I know you won't be swayed once more?" She held up her hand before he could answer. "You don't seem to be able to see her for what she is or the vicious tales she spins. I refuse to subject myself to her mendacity ever again."

"You won't have to. I've stepped outside the realm of her influence for good." He paced a few steps back and forth before facing her again. "Please try to understand how it's been for me. I had to accept that someone I loved and trusted all my life was deliberately lying to me. I realize it doesn't change what she did or justify her motives, but my mother really believed she was doing what was best for me."

"Anything to keep her baby boy close to her," Catherine scoffed.

"It was wrong of her and it makes me sick to know what she's done to us." He dragged long fingers through his hair. "If only I could make you understand what I've been going through. You told me to go away and grow up. That's what I'm trying to do."

"I believe I said learn to be your own man."

"Seems like the same thing to me. Ryan Wade told me I'd probably changed in South America and both you and I need to learn to get to know the person I've become."

Her brows instantly snapped up in surprise.

"You talked to Ryan?" She shook her head. "You couldn't have, you don't even know him."

"I introduced myself. I've been so mixed up about everything I needed to talk to someone who might be able to set me straight. He seemed to think given time you'd be able to accept me again. I know I treated you badly, but I've hurt myself, too. I can't erase any of the foolish things I said or did, but I'm willing to do anything to have you forgive me. Can't you see the power you're capable of wielding over me?"

"If that were true I would have been able to make you stay. You've hurt me too deeply and too often. I've been punished by your leaving and then coming back only to reject me. I prayed for your safe return, but in the end nothing ended up being right."

"That's because I've acted so stupidly, but I'm here to change all that. Give me the opportunity to make it up to you. I know I can do better this time."

She shook her head.

"You're too late, I no longer want you."

His entire body seemed to clench at her words.

"You can't mean that."

"Haven't you listened to anything I've said? You think I haven't suffered? I had nightmares; terrible visions of you in torment. Do you have any idea what it was like knowing you were in pain and not being able to do anything to help you?"

"But can't you see that proves we share a special link?"

"That's not the way I see it. I'm the one who felt the link, but it was one-sided. You've made it impossible for me to get you out of my heart and let anyone else in."

"I don't want another man having you because I can't make myself want anyone else, either. That's why I was so possessive of you. I didn't doubt you. I was mistrusting myself. I know it was wrong to treat you that way, but I was afraid of losing you. If you need more time, I'll give it to you, but please don't send me away for good."

"I have to for both our sakes because I don't believe you can really change. We'll end up driving each other insane the way your feelings vacillate. Whatever honest love I thought I received from you I felt like I had to steal. God, I sound as pathetic as Robyn."

"Something that's freely given isn't stealing."

"That's the big problem. You want my body, but you don't give your love freely."

"I am now. I want all of you and I want to give all of myself to you in return."

"If you really meant that you wouldn't be so easily influenced by your mother – and we wouldn't be having this conversation."

"I told you I've changed. Give me the opportunity to prove it to you. You loved me once. I'm asking you to give that love another chance."

"I can't," she whispered heartbroken, knowing she was letting him slip away.

The muscles in his throat contracted as he swallowed.

"Can't, or won't?"

"What difference does it make? If something gets broken often enough you eventually end up with too many pieces to be able to have anything worth keeping. Past events should convince you of the impossibility to mend our relationship."

"Then we'll forget about reviving old hurts and start building new, happier memories. I tried living without you before and it wasn't living. I don't think I can go through that again. One more chance; that's all I'm asking of you, Catherine."

She'd spent her career administering to the needs of others, but now she longed to be comforted herself.

"We had our time together, but now it's over."

"Please don't say that."

"I can't help it. I don't have the emotional strength for this anymore, Josh."

"What more can I say to make you change your mind?"

"I don't want you to say anything. I just want you to leave. I'm tired of playing this same scene between us. Maybe you enjoy being a masochist, but I don't."

He stayed very still for several seconds looking at her, as though he might be imprinting her image on his brain.

"I'll go, but I wonder if you're ever going to be able to forgive me for ignoring your warning not to go to the Amazon."

"Can you forgive yourself?" she countered.

He flinched. "Touché. If you change your mind I'll be at the motel where I stayed when I came back from Alaska. My landlord's having my apartment painted."

She nodded toward the little figurine. "Don't forget to take that."

"Let it stay and allow me the small pleasure knowing that it's here with you."

She watched him leave. She'd made him beg and she hated herself for it. The man had bared his soul to her and she'd been cruel. Not for revenge or to punish, but to protect them both, she reassured herself. She picked up his little frog.

"If I kiss you, will you turn into my real prince?" she murmured past the emotion that clogged her throat.

Chapter Twenty-three

Josh knew this had been his last chance to win Catherine back and he'd failed, but there was still a part of him that couldn't help but cling to hope. As slender as that hope might be it was all he had left. God knows not every path was smooth enough to lead a way free of uncertainties. The hardships he'd endured in the jungle and now this new trouble made him more aware than ever that life was not a journey without peril.

He thought of the little frog he'd left with Catherine. It took more than manmade symbols of good luck to protect against pitfalls, but each individual chooses their own way and certainly some more wisely than he had. Hadn't he wasted enough time wandering around taking too many wrong turns like a blind man bumping into walls?

Catherine was the most important person in his life and yet he had allowed his mother's poisonous lies and his own jealousy to undermine their relationship until he'd destroyed her love for him. Her dismissal had hurt even more than he'd imagined it would. The pain chipped away at him, sharp edged and unrelenting. He knew he was strong enough now not to go to pieces as he'd done before, but he still felt mired in misery at her rejection.

When she hadn't contacted him by the end of the third day, Josh was so distraught it felt as though the walls were closing in on him. Not knowing where to go or what to do, he drove around until he found himself at the ocean. He parked and walked down to the sand. A brisk wind blew off the water bringing with it the salty scent of the sea. It ruffled his hair and made his clothes flap against him while biting into his thin jacket.

He let himself slip back in time to recall a day he'd spent here with Catherine.

They'd played in the gentle waves splashing like children before chasing each other out of the water where they laid on a blanket and basked in the sun. But there was no sun now and the clouds had begun to chase across the sky with an approaching storm.

The first rumble of thunder and ensuing flash of lightening startled him out of his reverie. Josh knew he should seek shelter before the rain came, but he couldn't summon up the energy to move. He was tired. Tired of always running, trying to find his niche in life. Now that he finally knew where he wanted to be, it was too late. What he needed only Catherine could give, but she no longer wanted what he had to offer.

Filled with the utter fruitlessness of his attempt to win her over, Josh stood there with his feet anchored to the sand. He stared with impassive eyes, as angry gray waves rushed in to assault the shore. He couldn't make out where the sky ended and the sea began. Lights blinking from a ship in the far distance reminded him of how Tom used to joke and say if he had the guts he would get on a freighter and sail around the world.

Thoughts of him filled Josh with fresh guilt. No one could have asked for a truer friend, but he had taken Tom's faithfulness for granted. The thought of his own selfish behavior disgusted him. As his feelings of misery increased, he sank down until his knees pressed into the sand. Josh was never more acutely aware that he carried the burden of needing his friend's forgiveness than at this very moment.

"I'm sorry for being such a lousy friend, Tom," he whispered in a strangled voice.

He knelt there with his head bowed low while his fingers gripped handfuls of sand. Everything he'd hoped for and everything he had been through meant nothing now. He felt so utterly alone it was as though the entire world had shut him out leaving him in total isolation.

He looked up as the sliver of moon suddenly broke free from the dense cloud cover. The light reflected on the water like a shimmering path that seemed to suddenly be beckoning to him. Josh struggled to his feet reeling from the raw force of his emotions and the wind that buffeted against him. He moved toward the water's edge feeling immune to the rain that had begun to fall in large drops striking his body, soaking him.

Waves rose and fell in their ancient rhythm with long foamy fingers that gripped the beach and rolled back only to claw their way forward again. They seemed to be reaching out, luring him ever closer toward the mysteriousness of their domain.

Maybe Tom had the right idea. When you realized you can't have the one person in the world you want to share the rest of your life with what was the point of going on without them? He pictured his future stretching out before him solitary and bleak. He'd had enough experience living a half-life to know it wasn't something to look forward to.

Mesmerized by the hypnotic surf, Josh began to move closer to the water and stopped at the edge where the sea licked at his feet. He kicked off his shoes and twisted out of his jacket. He vaguely realized he couldn't distinguish the difference between the roaring of the sea and the pounding inside his head, as he stepped into the water.

>>>>dreams<<<<

Jenny watched Douglas from beneath her lashes. He'd been pacing around the apartment like a caged animal for most of the morning and she'd grown tired of waiting for him to tell her what had him so stirred up.

"Okay, enough already. What's wrong?"

He jolted to a stop and blinked at her.

"What do you mean?"

"When you pace like you've been doing I know something is bothering you. Either tell me what it is and stop wearing a hole in the floor, or please go outside."

He gave her a sheepish smile.

"You're too perceptive for my own good."

"I don't know about that, but I do know something is worrying you, as I said and I'd like to help you if I can."

"It's Josh," he said with a heavy sigh.

"What about him? Have you heard something I don't know? Is he all right?"

"That's just it; I don't know. I expected to hear from him by now. I told you he'd called me. I asked him to keep me informed how things went after he met with his lady friend Catherine, but it's been too long now. I'm beginning to think his silence is a bad omen. I can't shake the feeling that something's wrong."

"They're probably so wrapped up in each other he just forgot. I think you're fretting over nothing." She patted the sofa. "Come sit down now," she urged.

"I'm too worked up to sit. I can't stop thinking about how he questioned me concerning his mother's interference. It sounded like she's caused a great deal of trouble between him and Catherine. Apparently he had a lot of ugly accusations to answer for, and I'm worried he wasn't able to repair the damage enough to get her to marry him."

"Oh dear, that would be a shame. I remember that's all he could talk about on the plane coming back from South America."

"I know. That's what keeps cropping up in my mind. He's in love with that girl and despite what Mrs. Dallas said to me, I'd like to believe the feeling is mutual. I've never been one to interfere when I'm not wanted, but I don't like to ignore my gut feelings, either."

"That makes me think of a line from Shakespeare's King Lear."

He cocked a brow.

"Which one?"

"*Speak what we feel, not what we ought to say*," she recited and handed him their personal telephone book. "If you believe he's in trouble and you think you can help, then do what you can to make things right. Those two people deserve to be together."

>>>>*dreams*<<<<

Catherine left work and stared up at the leaden sky that matched her mood. Rain had threatened all day and as she hurried to her car the first drops began to fall. A few escaped inside her coat collar and sent cold chills down her back. She slid inside her car just as the sky opened up and seconds later began to rapidly pour forth a torrent of water.

Her mind had been in turmoil ever since Josh's visit, wondering if she'd done the right thing in sending him away. To make matters worse, she'd started having bad dreams about him again; visions of him kneeling and in emotional pain. What was it about the man that affected her like this? It was like a strange kind of psychic connection.

She still wasn't convinced that he was ready to make their relationship the priority it deserved. But she was afraid she'd continue to have these dreams about him if they remained apart. If only Ivy would leave them alone. It was obvious she'd try to keep Josh bound to her forever. He'd insisted he was his own man, but Catherine had her doubts.

The rain was coming down in heavy sheets hammering against the roof of her car like the beat of a hundred drums. Catherine hated driving in wet weather, especially at night. She reached over to start the car when her cell phone rang. It was her aunt.

"I wanted to let you know you're going to be getting a call in a few minutes from a man who was most insistent that he speak to you. It sounds important, so I gave him your number."

Catherine frowned.

"Who is he and what does he want with me?"

"I'll let him tell you and please hear him out, dear. Believe me, it's imperative that you speak with him."

"At least give me an idea what this is all about."

"It'll be better if he explains. I don't want to tie up the line. Drive carefully."

"But Aunt Pris . . ." Catherine stared at the silent phone in exasperation.

Who on earth was the mysterious caller and what was so urgent that it couldn't wait until she got home? She couldn't help feeling irritated with her aunt for putting her in such a position. She was willing to humor her to a point, but Catherine decided if the man didn't call within the next five minutes he'd have to catch her at home. She refused to drive in this weather while talking on her phone.

It rang a minute later.

"Ms. Ashley?" a gravelly male voice asked.

"Yes, this is she. Are you the person who just spoke with my aunt?"

"That's right. My name is Douglas Marsh and I'm calling you from Hawaii."

The name sounded vaguely familiar, but she felt too impatient to think it through, and she didn't know anyone in Hawaii.

"What can I do for you, Mr. Marsh?"

"I'd like to talk to you about Josh."

"Josh? Why would you want . . ." His name clicked inside her head. "I remember now. You're the CEO of the company that hired him to go to the Amazon, aren't you?"

"I was, but I'm retired from that position now."

"I see. Well, I can't think why you'd be calling me."

He cleared his throat.

"There's no delicate way to tiptoe around this, so I'm just going to come right out and ask: Are you and Josh together?"

She was so taken aback by his query she thought she must have misunderstood him.

"I beg your pardon, sir; But, what did you just ask me?"

"I know you two were estranged, and I was wondering if you had managed to work things out and are back together again."

She pressed her mouth into a stern line, wondering if Josh had gone to this man with his concerns as he'd done with Ryan. The thought filled her with embarrassment. The way he was going, the next thing she knew he'd be taking out an ad in the newspapers or make an announcement on the radio and TV about their private lives.

"We're no longer friends! And I must tell you that I don't appreciate these tactics, especially if Josh put you up to this." She made no attempt to disguise her resentment at such a possibility. "Now if you don't mind, Mr. Marsh, I just got off work and I'd like to get home before the rain here gets any worse."

"Wait. Don't hang up! This is strictly my own decision and the last thing I want to do is further complicate things, but I feel compelled to speak on his behalf. Please Ms. Ashley, let me explain the reason I've involved myself; that's all I'm asking."

Irritation cut right through her. It seemed she was destined to be burdened by begging males. She wasn't happy with this man's pleading anymore than she'd been with Josh's appeals, but decided she'd better listen to him rather than be plagued by possible doubts later. She looked at her watch.

"All right, you have two minutes."

"Thank you. I'm going to plunge right in here. Josh strikes me as a man with impulses that sometimes cause him to make bad decisions. But he's a good man at heart and is willing to rectify his mistakes, especially where you're concerned. Are you going to give him another chance to do right by you, or will you continue to make him suffer?"

Chapter Twenty-four

"You're being too personal considering I don't even know you," she snapped.

"I realize that, but there's too much at stake here for the proper etiquette. I know his mother is largely responsible for what's caused the split between you and Josh."

That surprised Catherine.

"You know his mother?"

"Only via telephone, but we had what you might call a difference of opinion because I disagreed with the way she was handling things between you and Josh when he was so ill. I personally think she's a wretched interloper. She had no business getting involved. She acted as though she was speaking for a child," he snorted in disgust.

Knowing that he felt the same way she did about Ivy made Catherine's temper soften, but not enough to sway her opinion.

"I agree, but it was Josh's choice to take her side. He's an adult, but he allows her to make too many of his decisions. I'll admit he did try to apologize to me, but I've had quite enough of all this love/hate business."

"Your attitude sounds rather cynical if I may say so."

"After what I've gone through with Josh, I prefer to think of it as being realistic. I'm simply not open to any reconciliation, Mr. Marsh – if that's what this call is about,"

"Perhaps it would help to understand his motives if you take into consideration he felt a certain allegiance to his mother. Obviously she was very convincing."

"What about his loyalty to me? Every time he goes, he robs a little piece of me."

"I don't imagine he found it easy being forced to choose between his mother and the woman he wants to marry. Whatever she said to him obviously wasn't anything good, but if Josh apologized I'd say you're the one he believes now."

"For how long? He's so wishy-washy I don't think he knows what he wants. He doesn't understand what the concept of ever after between a man and a woman means."

"He's frightened, Ms. Ashley. Here's a man who thought he had control over his world only to have everything taken away from him. Sometimes things happen in a person's life that changes who they are. Unless Josh is willing to share his innermost feelings, none of us will ever know the exact nature of what he went through. But I had the opportunity to talk with the missionaries who found him in South America. I know you've probably seen the scars on his chest, but they said his body showed evidence of brutal beatings besides. They felt that he was more dead than alive when he came to them."

She couldn't prevent the sharp gasp and felt her anger begin to slide away.

"Add that to the fact he was forced to watch helplessly while his colleague suffered . . ." his voice cracked with emotion, as he struggled to regain his composure. He cleared his throat and continued, ". . . while she suffered her own physical abuse at the hands of their despicable captors. Then he had to watch her die because he couldn't get her the help she needed. Small wonder Josh is 'wishy-washy' as you put it."

Catherine's stomach lurched as she listened to his harsh description.

"I'm sorry. I didn't mean to sound so callous." An image of Josh the day he'd returned flickered inside her head. "I knew he must have suffered, but I had no idea how much. I hadn't heard about the missionaries. The last I knew he'd disappeared with a native woman."

"I thought Josh would have told you the details about his stay with them."

"He didn't. I've seen the scars on his chest and can only imagine the pain he must have endured, but when I asked him to tell me what happened, he refused to talk about it. He obviously had a very difficult recovery to stay with those people as long as he did."

"I don't think any of us can have the remotest idea of what it must have been like for him being so weak and not knowing who he was, or where he came from."

"What do you mean he didn't know who he was? I'm sorry, but I don't understand what you're talking about."

"Why, his amnesia of course."

Catherine's heart leaped like a bird beating its wings against a cage.

"Amnesia?"

"Do you mean to tell me you didn't know the reason Josh was gone all that time was because he didn't know his name or why he was in South America?"

"I had no idea about any of that. I did try calling his parents, but his mother was almost maniacal on the phone ranting that everything was my fault. Then he disappeared again and it was months before I knew he'd gone to Alaska."

"Alaska? That's news to me. But you got back together for a while, right?"

"Yes we did, but his mother made up disgusting lies about me having affairs with his best friend and a doctor I work with. I tried to tell Josh the truth, but he wouldn't listen and by the time he finally did decide his mother had lied, I'd had enough."

He swore under his breath, but loud enough for Catherine to hear.

"I apologize for my language, but Mrs. Dallas does seem to bring out the temper in me."

"I know the feeling. The woman obviously doesn't have a conscience."

"Not much of one, anyway. Please don't allow that woman to get away with her vile schemes to keep you and Josh apart. You were all he could talk about when we were bringing him back. Despite what you think to the contrary, he does love and need you."

"Then why didn't he say so in the beginning? He could have told me everything that happened to him. He must have known I'd be sympathetic."

"He wants your love, not your pity. Let the man have his pride. He's suffered physical pain, but the pain in one's heart is often much worse. I know what it's like to love someone, to say the wrong things and never have the opportunity to make it right."

It might have been the words or perhaps the quiet earnestness in his tone, but Catherine couldn't ignore the underlying plea. If Josh had confessed his feelings for her to this man to move him so, then perhaps she'd been too hasty in sending him away.

"You've told me things I didn't know; important things that have made me look at the situation in a different light. I only had a sketchy outline of what happened before, but now you've filled in the details to give me a more complete picture."

"Then you will call Josh?"

She heard the anxiousness in his voice.

"I'll do better than that; I'll go see him."

"Good girl! I hope you'll forgive an old man's meddling in the affairs of the heart. It's not something I'm accustomed to doing, but I felt strongly enough about this to butt my big nose in."

She smiled into the phone.

"Josh is lucky to have a friend like you, Mr. Marsh."

"I felt he needed someone in his corner. Thanks for taking the time to listen."

"I'm the one who should be thanking you, and for the record I think you make a very good matchmaker."

He chuckled. "Well, it's not a job I'm used to, but I'm grateful you've been willing to hear my bumbling attempts."

"Not so bumbling since you got me to go to Josh. I hope he still wants me."

"I bet he'll welcome you with open arms, but I'm crossing my fingers, too."

>>>>*dreams*<<<<

As soon as they hung up she made a quick call to her aunt before heading to Josh's motel, praying he would still be there. She realized she was driving much too fast for the weather conditions when she went through a large puddle spraying muddy water onto the hood. She gripped the steering wheel and eased her foot up on the accelerator.

Her mind was a jumble of chaotic thoughts and her nerves felt as taut as piano wires. Catherine realized now that Douglas's phone call had been the catalyst she needed to do what she'd probably subconsciously wanted to do all along. Everything between her and Josh had come down to this moment. What could she say to undo her rejection?

She pulled into a parking place in front of the office. The motel was small and there were few cars, but she didn't see Josh's truck. She grabbed her purse, scrambled out of the car, and rushed through the rain to duck inside the building. The woman clerk wouldn't give his room number, but shared the news that Josh hadn't checked out.

Catherine went outside and stood beneath the slender overhang, wondering if she should call his cell phone when she saw Josh drive in. She watched him pull into a space and waited. It seemed to be taking him an awfully long time to get out of his truck. When he finally emerged she was surprised to see that his clothes were drenched. Wherever he'd been he must have gotten caught in the rain.

Catherine felt as though her heart was in her throat, as she walked through the rain toward him. She couldn't seem to make her legs go any faster even though she wanted to run. The rain was coming down harder now pelting her with heavy splashes of water.

Her lips moved silently, forming his name, as he stood struggling to unlock the door. She frowned when she saw how much his hands were shaking. Catherine realized he was obviously cold and considering their last conversation, probably upset as well. She had to close her eyes for a moment fighting against the guilt knowing that part of the reason she'd sent him away was to make him suffer for the times he's doubted her fidelity.

The rain darkened his hair plastering the strands against his head like a skullcap. Drops streamed in rivulets lining his face. He looked gray with fatigue and the shadows beneath his eyes told their own story. He was suffering. She had done this to him. The realization filled her with shame. He really did need her. She felt her insides crumble in a way they did only for him.

She finally managed to say his name, but he didn't react and she realized the water gushing through the roof's drain near their heads was drowning out all other sound. He'd just shoved open the door when Catherine stepped closer and repeated his name, louder this time. He whirled around. She heard his quick catch of breath before he rubbed his wet fingers over his eyes, as though he might be looking at a mirage.

"Catherine?" It sounded almost reverent. "Please tell me this isn't a dream."

He smelled of rain, and if she wasn't mistaken, seawater.

"Not this time."

"I'd given up. I thought you weren't coming. Oh God, Catherine, come here. Let me hold you." A hoarse moan escaped him and he reached out to snatch her to him.

She thought he sounded like a wounded animal suddenly being relieved of some terrible torment. Love for him moved in and crowded out every other emotion. It simply imploded inside of her until the breath was literally sucked right out her.

They stumbled into the room locked together in each other's arms. She pressed against him. He immediately captured her mouth in a hard kiss and they fed on each other's lips like manna from heaven. They clung together frantically gripping each other, as they poured out turbulent emotions until his shivering made her lift her head.

"How is it that you're sopping wet? Where have you been?"

"To the end of the road," he mumbled after a few seconds hesitation.

Catherine wasn't sure she understood what he meant by his cryptic remark, but she could feel the tension that emanated from him. His teeth chattered making her frown.

"You have to get out of your wet things and into a hot shower."

It amazed her that she could think coherently, let alone talk with the emotions she felt tearing through her. He took her by the hand and led her to the bathroom.

"Looks like you got wet yourself. You can shower first," he offered and reached in to turn on the taps.

"How about we shower together? I'm not ready to let go of you yet."

His eyes still blazed with heat, despite the shivers of his chilled body.

"I was hoping you'd say that."

They watched each other hungrily, as they peeled the sodden clothes from their bodies. When they stepped into the stall together the hot steamy water cascaded over them warming their icy flesh. Josh brushed his knuckles down the side of her face and then his lips followed, moving across her shoulders and down to her breasts.

"Do you have any idea what you do to me?" Her eyes traveled the length of his rapidly hardening body and felt her own muscles tighten. His mouth continued to move over her, torturing, pleasuring. "I want you so much it's like having a volcano ready to erupt inside of me."

She framed his face between her hands.

"Then it's time we explode together."

Chapter Twenty-five

He took her hands and draped them over his shoulders. She felt herself shiver when he licked drops of water that had settled in the tiny hollow at the base of her throat while his hands traced her shape and molded themselves to her curves. He backed her against the wall and pressed her there with muscles straining, his body hard and aroused.

"I love your taste and the feel of your skin," he said, his voice thickening.

His mouth descended, taking her breath away. By the time he reached behind and turned the water off, Catherine understood the feeling that she would explode any minute. He took her by the hand and led her away from the stall, grabbing a couple of towels as they went. They dried off in haste before Josh pulled her against him again. His tongue caressed her lips with soft swirling strokes before diving inside her moist sweetness for a more thorough taste. She moaned into his mouth inviting him to deepen the kiss.

Long minutes passed bringing precious moments to savor while tender flesh ached to be possessed. The outside world had disappeared. They were alone in their own universe. Intoxicated by a beautiful world they had created for themselves, they began to turn the dingy little motel room into their own special Eden. Driven by pure sensation and hunger, they were ready to soar into the upper peaks of passion.

They fell onto the bed with arms and legs entwined. Her skin gleamed alabaster white against the dark quilt. He pulled the spread aside until they lay on the sheets.

"Our hair. We need to dry our hair, Josh."

"I haven't got time for that now," he groaned and lowered his pulsating body to Catherine's waiting arms while he shivered and let himself sink into her scented flesh. Filled with a powerful sexual force neither could stop, they began to shudder out of control. Each demanded more than they had ever sought before. Raw, naked yearning drove them on until their emotions crested and burst forth in a series of blinding flashes of light leaving them spinning out into another dimension. They rode the luminosity in concert, basking in its glow until they gradually floated back down to earth as one.

Completely drained, yet strangely invigorated, they lay in each other's arms. Somewhere between the sound of the rain and her long drawn out sighs, Josh's voice penetrated Catherine's brain.

"This is going to sound kind of corny, but I feel like I've just been reborn," he said and burrowed his face against the side of her neck. "I'm tired of running, Catherine. I meant it when I said I'm not going anywhere ever again unless you're with me. I'm yours to do with what you want now."

She lifted his head and reached up to touch loving fingers to his face. He had given himself to her at last to mold to her will. His humbly spoken surrender brought a vulnerability she hadn't expected from him. Emotion filled her throat and tears slowly began to seep from beneath her lashes. She wept for the time lost, the challenges they'd never confronted, and the mistakes that had been made by themselves and others.

He rolled them onto their sides and held her in a tight embrace.

"I thought you'd be happy. This isn't exactly the reaction I expected from you," he said and stroked her hair. "I certainly never wanted to make you cry. Don't tell me I've messed up again?"

She buried her face against his chest.

"I'm crying because I am happy. To be here with you and knowing that we're going to be together at last is like a dream come true."

He kissed the top of her head.

"For me, too. It's good to know that our dreams sometimes turn out the way we hope they will."

"I had begun to think I was a jinx because so many people I cared about, my parents, Nancy, Tom, all left me. Even you went away."

"I understand that kind of pain now that Tom is gone and how I almost lost you, too. I'm sorry that I failed you in so many ways, but I vow that I'll never leave you again. My world is wherever you are. I don't need to look any further ever again."

She sniffed and wiped away tears.

"No more traipsing off on another jaunt?"

"Like I said, not unless you're with me, but I have a feeling life with you is going to be all the adventure I'll ever want."

"I'll try to make it worth your while."

He laughed and kissed a few stray tears away. "I have little doubt of that."

"What will you do if your mother still refuses to accept me?"

"She knows she has to, or she loses me." His mouth tightened. "Right now I'm having a difficult time forgiving her for interfering in my personal life. She lied thinking she was protecting me, but in doing so she very nearly caused me to lose you."

"She did. If it hadn't been for a phone call from Mr. Marsh revealing so many things about what had happened to you, my stupid pride might have kept us apart even longer."

He stared at her with surprise clearly showing in his eyes.

"When was this?"

"Tonight. He caught me as I was leaving work. He convinced me to give you another chance." She felt him go rigid and saw the tension in his expression. "You aren't angry with him are you? He's very fond of you, Josh. He did the right thing, you know."

"Maybe. Maybe not. Did you come here only because of his phone call?"

"Of course not. I'm here because this is where I'm supposed to be. I knew that all along. I just needed someone like Mr. Marsh to give me a push in the right direction."

"I owe him big time, then. He's a good man. You'll like his wife, too."

"I'd like to meet them some day to thank him in person." She snuggled against him and kissed his chest. "Now I think we both could use some shuteye. Nurse's orders."

He stroked her lips with the tip of his finger.

"I'd much rather make love again."

"We will, and it'll be even better once we've rested. I have a feeling you haven't been sleeping very well lately. I know I've certainly done my share of tossing and turning."

His mouth replaced his fingers in a quick kiss. "Okay, you're the boss.

>>>>*dreams*<<<<

But later, after he heard her breathing deeply in sleep, Josh still hadn't closed his eyes. There were too many emotions chasing around inside his head. He thought about how he'd almost ended it all like Tom had. He very well might have if he hadn't caught his toe on a child's plastic pail half buried in the sand at the water's edge. It made him think of little Tommy and how he suddenly realized he wanted to be his father. He'd decided even if Catherine didn't want him, he owed it to Tom's son to stick around.

He'd done a lot of thinking and soul searching about his life on the drive back. He recognized he'd wasted too much time on what wasn't important and cared too little for the things that should have mattered. It hadn't been easy admitting that he'd been way too arrogant and full of himself chasing after empty pursuits. While there was no way he could erase the mistakes he'd made, he could at least try to be better in the future.

This was especially important when it came to how he'd handled his relationship with Catherine. He couldn't blame all the mistakes that had been made on his mother's interference. He'd hurt Catherine deeply by his own selfishness and mistrust. It terrified him to know what a near thing it was that he would never have her in his life again.

How many chances did a person have to clear away the blunders they'd caused in their life? His actions had put him on a risky seesaw ride long enough. He barely held back a shudder knowing if fate hadn't finally worked in their favor, he wouldn't be here with Catherine lying in his arms.

>>>>*dreams*<<<<

The next time Catherine opened her eyes Josh was propped on an elbow smiling at her.

"Good morning. How did you sleep?"

She gave him a sleepy smile in return.

"Great." She decided she'd tell him later about the dream she'd just had of them exchanging wedding bands. "How about you?"

"Changed my mind about sleeping. I'd much rather watch you."

"You'd better get used to it because I plan on hanging around for a long time."

"I think I can handle it." He leaned down, nipped her chin with his teeth, grazed her jaw, and tugged on her bottom lip making her moan.

"I do believe this nurse ordered you to get some sleep."

"Sleep is over rated. I've more important things to do right now."

His voice sounded ragged before his mouth covered hers in a kiss so hot it was a wonder it didn't singe her lips. Long clever fingers, bold and daring, stroked her body, touching her quivering flesh in all her secret places making her whimper with such intense pleasure it came close to becoming pain.

"Josh, please . . ." she gasped, as his fingers danced over her breasts seconds before his mouth followed the same path. She rose toward him, offering, begging.

He stared into her eyes seemingly captivated by their seductive depths.

"Do you want me, Catherine? Tell me! I need you to say it," he insisted in a voice gruff with lust.

"I want you, Josh. You know I do," she barely managed to moan before he dove forward and sheathed himself within her honeyed sweetness.

His weight pressed her down into the mattress while his mouth devoured. His body gave her everything he had to offer and demanded as much from her in return until their world rocked off its axis. Blinded by need, lost in a sated haze of passion, they collapsed together and lay limp and weightless, fighting to breathe.

Catherine's hands slid off Josh's slick shoulders. She felt her heartbeats slowing and waited until they'd settled back into a normal rhythm. But she still hesitated, wondering if what she was about to say was the right choice. Fate may have brought them together, but it hadn't always treated them with a kind hand. Perhaps she was being unfair to catch him at a weak moment like this, but she was counting on the power of love to help her cause.

Catherine could only hope Josh would be more receptive now that he was so relaxed after their lovemaking. She was either going to destroy their relationship, or set them free. She prayed it would be the latter.

"Josh?"

He nuzzled his face between her breasts.

"Hmm?

"You shared a lot of important information last night and I want you to know how much I appreciate that, but there are still some things you didn't talk about."

He lifted his head.

"Which means they're probably best left unsaid."

"I don't think so."

He heaved a heavy sigh and rolled off her.

"All right then, what things?"

"I think you already know the answer to that." She touched his face before letting her fingers trail down to the bumpy ridges on his chest. "These. I need to know what happened to you when you were in South America. All of it, especially your feelings."

He pulled her hand away, pushing them down between their bodies and clasping their fingers tightly together.

"I thought you said Douglas told you."

"He could only tell me what he knows. You need to talk about your nightmares."

"Why is it that women always want to know so much?"

"Because the more we get; the more we can give in return. It's important that you tell me the rest until there's nothing left. We skipped that in our last reconciliation. I can't help but think that's part of what went wrong."

He let go of her hand and turned his back to her. "I told you before I'm trying to forget about all that. I thought you understood."

"I do understand, but you said Ryan told you I needed to get to know you again. I can't do that if you only give me snippets. I don't want to cause you more suffering, but you know as well as I do that emotional pain can leave scars, too."

"Then why bring it all up again? Why dig up the past?"

Going with what she hoped was the correct instinct honed by her love, she continued.

"Because the more you try to shut some things away, the more they try to get out. Remember those roadblocks you talked about before? Let's knock all of them down for good. Then I give you my word we'll never speak of this again. Please Josh, do this for me – and of more importance, for yourself."

"Death came looking for me Catherine and that's one door I'm not going to regret slamming shut. Add that to the fact I tortured myself thinking I'd lost you. Those are only some of the memories I'm trying to hold back. If you were in my place would you want to put out a welcome mat?"

A bone-chilling cold settled inside her at the icy sound of his voice, but she forced herself not to back down.

"I would if it meant I'd never have to worry what would happen if I did open those doors again."

Seconds became long agonizing minutes. Josh shifted his body restlessly and rolled onto his back, but remained silent. She leaned over and looked at him trying to read his expression, but it was as closed as the tight set of his mouth.

She gnawed her lip and felt her heart sink. She was beginning to wish she had waited before bringing up such painful thoughts. Had she made a mistake to ask this of him now? Perhaps their newly formed bond was still too fragile for him to confide in her.

Afraid that her carelessness had ruined their reunion while it was still in its infancy, she waited while her unanswered questions pulsed inside her head like a hammer pounding out a persistent beat. Had her probing made him barricade the door for good?

Josh's continued silence lingered while other less important sounds filled the room. A car alarm went off somewhere in the distance, someone coughed in the next room, and the dripping showerhead suddenly seemed terribly loud.

She knew if he couldn't bring himself to tell her what had happened, she'd have to accept that. She was about to tell him when he began to speak and the first words out of his mouth made her heart ache for what this sharing was obviously going to cost him.

Chapter Twenty-six

"I can't seem to get the stench of my own fear out of my mind. Or forget how it felt holding Marie's dead body in my arms. Orlando, the leader of the men who took us, haunts my dreams. It's like having the devil himself coming after me again and again. I swear to God fire shoots out of his eyes every time I see him and the pain starts all over."

She heard the torment in his voice and reached for his hand offering him comfort. He laced their fingers together, squeezing tightly as though he needed that lifeline.

"I can see you're still emotionally attached to those horrors even though you don't want to be. That's probably why you have the nightmares. They won't go away until you either let go of those negative emotions or better yet, exchange those feelings for a list of more positive options. I'd like to hope our building a future together would be at the top of that list. But if this is too much for you to talk about right now, we can wait for another time as long as you'll promise me there will be another time."

"No, let's get the mess over with. You're right, the sooner I get everything out and start working on replacing the bad images with healthier choices the better off I'll be." He rested their joined hand on his scarred chest.

"This might take me a while."

"Take all the time you need."

He sucked in a deep breath, filling his lungs before letting the air slowly escape.

Once he began to talk, it was as if flood waters were flowing over a dam.

"The natives gave us the only relief from the horrible circumstances, but they were limited in what they could do. In many ways they were innocent as children. Their eyes held ancient knowledge, but they existed out of time. I don't think they understood the barbarism of the modern world."

"Are you referring to the kidnappers as being the barbarians?"

"Yes. They were the real savages. Poor Marie. Her motivation in going to the Amazon was to search out undiscovered plant life for medicines, so she could help people. But her dedication was rewarded by appalling cruelty. Orlando slapped her around, and every time I tried to stop him he'd have me beaten. I began to hate him in a way I never thought I was capable of."

"I'd say that was understandable considering the way he was mistreating you. But I don't see why he abused you with so much money at stake. Surely he had to know he must keep you both in good health to collect the ransom."

"I thought that at first, but he had a vile temper and he liked to see people suffer."

"He must have been a brute, but also a coward for wanting to hurt innocent people. I feel so sad for Marie when I think she only wanted to do good things."

"Yeah. I cried when she died; broke down like a baby. That doesn't exactly make me sound like the big brave explorer does it?"

"Crying has nothing to do with being brave. In my profession I've seen plenty of strong men cry. It takes courage for a man to let his guard down and expose his emotions like that. You were mourning the loss of a friend; one who had suffered unfairly. You had every right to be upset." She squeezed his hand. "I know how hard this has been for you."

"There's more," he said in a grim tone. "I went berserk the last time Orlando was getting ready to go after Marie, and he set his thugs on me. They tied me to a tree and beat me with their fists. Then they gave me these souvenirs," he touched his scars.

"I can't begin to fathom the pain you must have suffered."

"Imagine the sensation of being repeatedly sliced with a razorblade or having several giant paper cuts magnified a thousand times tearing into your flesh. It got even worse when my sweat added salt to the wounds and then the insects started in on me. I was still tied to the tree, and Orlando wouldn't let the natives help me at that point. As I said, he enjoyed seeing people suffer and watching me gave him a real charge."

Catherine couldn't choke back the sob that escaped her.

"Oh my God, Josh."

"You said you wanted all the gory details," he reminded her. "The pain was so excruciating I prayed to die. I probably would have if it hadn't been for Sad Eyes."

"Sad Eyes?"

"She was the native woman who took me to the missionaries. It was just a name I made up. I never knew her real name. Orlando and his men had left the encampment for a few days. I assume to go back to where they'd nabbed us to see if anyone had turned up with the ransom money."

"Was Marie ill with fever then?"

"Yes, but I don't think Orlando knew how bad she was. I certainly didn't. She died not long after he left, and I had to bury her right away because of the climate. Sad Eyes immediately insisted I leave the camp. I almost stayed in the hope that a rescue team would come, but then I thought about Orlando's reaction when he found out Marie had died. I knew he'd be furious and given his temper God only knows what he would have done to me in retaliation. I wasn't in any shape to go through whatever punishment he'd end up inflicting, so I went with Sad Eyes even though I had no idea where she was taking me."

"I'm surprised she thought you could travel if you were so sick."

"My illness didn't really hit me until after we left. That's when the fever kicked in and made me pretty delirious for a good part of the journey. I remember all that green closing in on me as we made our way through the jungle labyrinth. It was like being trapped in a pot of pea soup."

"It must have been unnerving."

"More like a weird hallucination, actually. I collapsed as soon as I arrived at the Daniels' house and when I finally came to I couldn't remember anything. I lost months floundering around in a fog." He looked at her. "My last rational thought before I went under was how it looked as though your dream had come true."

"Thank goodness Sad Eyes was able to get you away from that horrible Orlando."

"I take it you don't know about my second encounter with him, then."

She shot into a sitting position and stared at him in disbelief.

"Second encounter? You mean to say Orlando came after you when you were with the missionaries?"

He drew her back into his arms.

"No. It was later when Marie's mother, Jenny, asked me to take them to the spot where our team had camped. They unknowingly hired Orlando as one of the security guards for the trip. He tried to abduct Jenny and when he couldn't get her, he took another crack at me."

"I don't believe this! It must have been like a never ending nightmare."

"You got that right. He would have succeeded if one of our other men hadn't shot him. I watched while Orlando's blood seeped out of him. The more he bled, the better I felt. My only regret is that he didn't suffer more. I actually wanted to kill him with my bare hands. As gruesome as that sounds, I'm not going to pretend otherwise."

"Why should you? No one could blame you for feeling that way."

He drew in a deep breath, like a man would that had just completed a long, difficult journey.

"That's everything, Catherine."

She pressed her lips to his mouth, lingering in the kiss.

"I can't erase what you went through, but I'll do everything I can to help you put it behind you."

"It still might take me a while to get rid of these nightmares," he warned.

"I know. I understand about bad dreams, but I'm going to fill you up with so much good stuff you won't have room for anything else. We've got plenty of time because I plan on us being together until our teeth fall out and oatmeal dribbles down our bibs."

His mouth twitched in a smile.

"Sounds wonderful." He pulled her on top of him. "I'd say there's no time like the present to start filling me up with the good stuff. Or better yet, how about I fill you?"

"I didn't know the clock had started."

"It has now," he growled.

She loved that he was letting her be in control. She sucked on his bottom lip, nibbled at his neck, and tormented his male nipples with her teeth until he groaned. He let her push his hands over his head and hold them there while she assaulted his lips in a breath robbing kiss. She took the kiss deep, and then deeper using her tongue to explore the inside of his mouth.

She slowly scraped her nails down the length of his arms and continued along his ribcage making his muscles twitch with need. She trailed her lips wherever she could reach, arousing him to fever pitch before straddling him. When he finally couldn't take any more of her sweet torture, he thrust his hips upward and she was there to receive him.

They rode together in a heart pumping, muscle straining ride that had sensations tearing through them. Their rhythm increased bringing them both ever closer to the peak of ultimate pleasure. Bodies strained and giving one last mighty effort, burst together in a deep, shuddering climax. Catherine fell forward onto Josh's chest and lay there limp and sated while listening to his heart beating a mad cadence.

Ignoring the sweat that slicked their bodies, they cuddled and enjoyed the afterglow of their lovemaking. They talked of the future and made plans; plans that were all the more cherished because they both knew they might never have been.

Josh frowned when Catherine finally eased herself out of his arms and scooted off the bed.

"Where are you going?" he asked raising himself up on one elbow.

She gave him a quick kiss on the mouth.

"To the shower. I have to go to work."

"Can't you call in sick?"

"I would, but two nurses are out on maternity leave. I'm sorry, but duty calls. You know I'd much rather stay here with you."

"No, you're right. I've got an obligation to take care of myself."

She quirked an inquiring brow at him.

"What obligation?"

"I've been asked to go back to Alaska and tie up some loose ends."

"But you've already been gone for so long."

"I know, but they still want me."

He tossed the covers aside and stood up making her stomach quiver at the sight of his naked body.

"I just got the call yesterday. They've asked me to finish up the job I was working on and I kind of hate to turn them down since I left in such a hurry."

"No, that wouldn't be very professional. How long will you be gone?"

"Depends on the weather, but hopefully no more than a week."

"A week! It's going to seem like forever."

He groaned.

"Tell me about it."

"Well, it can't be helped. Why don't you bring your things and come home with me now? My aunt is still gone." She looked around the shabby room and made a face. "It'll get you out of here."

"I happen to have grown very fond of this place in the last few hours. I'm thinking of asking the management if I can put a plaque outside declaring this as the spot where Josh Dallas stepped out of the mists and into the light."

"How sweet. Let me know if you succeed. I'd like to be here for the unveiling."

He gathered her in his arms and rubbed his mouth along the sensitive cord at the side of her neck.

"What time do you have to be at work?"

"In a couple of hours and I need that shower first." He surprised her by lifting her into his arms and carrying her back to the bed.

"What are you doing?"

"What do you think? We've still got two hours and I'm not about to waste them."

"What about my shower?"

"We can shower together later and as a special treat I'll let you wash my back."

"Oh you will, will you? And what reward will I get for such services?"

He gave her a wicked grin and proceeded to show her in a very satisfying way.

Chapter Twenty-seven

Catherine managed a quick break later that afternoon and called Josh before he left for the airport.

"Be sure and call me as soon as you arrive," she reminded him.

"You got it. God, I miss you already."

"I miss you, too." She looked at her watch. "I've got to go."

"I love you."

She closed her eyes for a moment, savoring the words.

"I love you, too. Come back to me, Josh, as soon as you can." Her voice wasn't quite steady.

"Damn it, this is killing me. Do you want me to stay? Just say the word and I won't go. I'll tell them I broke my leg or something."

Just hearing him say that he wouldn't go made her heart swell with love recalling how there had been a time he wouldn't have given her a choice.

"No. That wouldn't be fair to the people who are counting on you, but it means a great deal to me that you're offering. We made it being apart for a year; we should be able to do a few days."

"I guess so, but this damn coming and going is a hell of a way to carry on a courtship. When I finish this job in Alaska I'm going to stay put if I have to encase my feet in cement."

"Don't think I won't help you if those feet of yours get the urge to take off again."

He chuckled.

"I think you would, too!"

"Go now and please be safe, my love."

"Yeah, and right back at you. Don't forget to save my place in your bed."

"The reserve sign goes up tonight."

"I'd better hang up before I change my mind and end up back on your doorstep."

>>>>*dreams*<<<<

Catherine left work the next night in a drizzling rain. It had been an unseasonably wet winter and she was tired of all the rain, especially driving in it. She was more than anxious to get home tonight. Her aunt was due back in the morning, and she wanted to pick up a few groceries and do some light housekeeping.

She was going over a grocery list in her mind when her cell phone rang. She snatched it up while being careful to keep her eyes focused on her driving.

"Hello?"

"Is this Catherine Ashley? I need to talk to her right away. It's rather urgent."

The connection was poor and she didn't recognize the muffled voice. She couldn't tell if it was a man or a woman speaking.

"Yes, this is Catherine. Who is this?"

"You wouldn't know me even if I gave you my name and that's not important right now. I'm calling about a Priscilla Mills. I found your name and number in her purse. I called what I assumed was your house first, but got your answering machine."

A flicker of fear made the hair on the back of Catherine's neck stand up.

"Priscilla Mills is my aunt. Is anything the matter? Is she all right?"

"She's here in my house, but I'm afraid she's not able to come to the phone."

Fear spread making her heart pound. She had to force herself to focus, as a chill rode slowly across her shoulders.

"What do you mean? Has something happened to her?"

"To tell you the truth, I'm not sure what the problem is except that she's been crying hysterically ever since I found her wandering in front of my house. She keeps going on and on about losing a baby. She doesn't appear to have any physical wounds, so I thought you'd rather come for her than have me call the police or an ambulance."

"Oh dear God! Something must have happened to Tommy."

"Who's Tommy?" the woman asked.

"Her grandson. Doesn't she have a little boy with her?"

"No, she's alone. Oh my, you mean there actually is a child involved?"

"Yes. I'll come right away. Where is your house located?"

"It's a bit difficult to find. I live way up in the hills, you see."

Catherine listened carefully to the directions.

"I'll be there as soon as I can, and perhaps if you tell my aunt I'm on my way it might help to calm her down."

"I doubt it since she's pretty far gone, but I'll do the best I can."

"I appreciate that, and thank you so much for calling me."

"Oh, you needn't thank me. I'm only doing what should be done."

Catherine frowned when she hung up. There had been something almost familiar about the tone of that voice just then. But she shook the thought away and gave all her attention to following the directions she'd been given. She was heading into an area she'd never been before and with the bad weather, she knew she needed to concentrate.

Once she left the lights of the city behind and began the long slow climb into the hills, the night seemed to close in on her. The higher she went the more she tried not to think about the way the embankment dropped off into utter darkness. The only illumination came from her headlights casting eerie patterns over the narrow ribbon of road and the sparse vegetation lining either side.

The rain was falling heavier here making the windshield wipers barely able to clear the water away. Her hands gripped the wheel, as she leaned forward straining to see the winding route, while she cautiously negotiated each hairpin curve.

Driving so slowly had her nerves edging up to panic. The need to get to her aunt and find out about Tommy was making her nearly hyperventilate, and she had to keep reminding herself to take in slow, even breaths in an effort to keep calm. If her aunt was as hysterical as the woman said, Catherine knew it wouldn't help if she fell apart, too.

So far there hadn't been another car or any sign of lights to show that there were any houses up here. Could she have misunderstood the directions? She prayed not.

Looking around, she couldn't imagine why anyone would want to live in such isolation.

Now that she had the time to think about it, Catherine couldn't imagine what in the world her aunt would be doing up here. The only thing that came to mind was that she must have somehow gotten lost. Worrying what could have happened to the baby and what state of mind her aunt must be in filled Catherine with renewed dread.

She peered through the windshield wishing she'd thought to get the person's telephone number. Then again, she doubted if she'd be able to get a signal on her cell phone up here. If only she'd known the drive was going to be so treacherous she would have asked the person to call an ambulance and meet her aunt at the hospital.

She'd about given up the hope of finding anything when she finally spotted lights up ahead. A sigh of relief shuddered through her and she dared to accelerate a bit more in her anxiousness to reach her destination. Catherine realized she must have finally made it to the top of the mountain when she saw that the road appeared to have come to an end.

But she felt immediate disappointment when she saw what appeared to be the headlights of a car rather than lights coming from a house, as she had expected. She'd obviously made a mistake and drove all this way for nothing. But Catherine began to worry that her aunt might be in the car. She had to be sure.

She pulled up alongside the vehicle and waited for someone to acknowledge her. But when no one appeared after several seconds, she pulled up the hood of her coat to cover her head, opened her own door, and stepped out into the pouring rain.

It was too dark to see inside the car. She tapped on the window expecting it to be rolled down, but it remained tightly closed. Something was very wrong here. For all she knew this might be some nut who had gotten hold of her aunt's purse. What if it was a man who had lured her here intent on doing her harm? Her heart skipped a couple of beats, but Catherine knew she couldn't walk away if her aunt really was in trouble.

"This is Catherine Ashley. Are you the person who called me about my aunt?"

She tapped on the window again.

"Hello? Is anyone in there?"

No answer.

The night was silent except for the rain and the sound of a nocturnal animal rustling through a nearby bush. The notion that it wasn't the only thing that might be out hunting made her wonder if she'd been lured into a trap. A sudden image of Robyn warning her away from Josh popped inside her head followed quickly by Ivy's spiteful words. Would either of them go to such elaborate lengths to scare her off? Surely not.

But that didn't mean she was going to hang around to find out the identity of the person inside the car. Whoever they were obviously had a sick mind scaring her half to death about her aunt being in danger. If only she'd thought to double check and call her aunt before she'd started the crazy drive up here. She was hurrying back to her car when she heard the other car's engine start up. Catherine spun around and saw with horror that the vehicle was coming straight at her.

As unbelievable as it seemed, she realized that whoever was driving intended to run her down. For one split second she froze like a deer caught in the headlights before her survival instincts kicked in and she ran around to the other side of her car. She cowered there shaking, barely able to believe this was happening. A scream rose in her throat, but refused to budge. But it didn't matter, since there was no one to hear her except the monster inside the car.

The other vehicle began to creep like a giant insect turning to follow her. Looking down at herself, Catherine realized her face and white pants were reflected in the car's lights making her an easy target. Keeping her light hair hid in her hood, she dropped to the ground and rolled in the mud while scooping up a handful to smear over her face.

For one hysterical moment she was reminded of how some women used mud packs as a beauty aid. She pressed close against her car and drew herself into a tight knot hoping to blend in with the ground. But the menacing headlights were seeking her out again. The vehicles were so close she heard metal scraping against metal. The blood was pounding in her ears making her feel as though her head would explode any minute.

She knew she couldn't protect herself by staying put. She'd have to get away from the car. Every nerve in her body wanted her to run, but fear rendered her helpless for the next few seconds until she heard a maniacal laugh that sent chills down her spine.

Despite her body shaking in violent shudders, she gathered her courage, pulled herself to her feet, and took off running, slipping and sliding trying to gain traction in the mud, as she scurried away. But surrounded by so much darkness, she knew she had to be careful that she didn't plummet off the edge of the cliff.

Her one thought was to get away from the fiend so intent on running her down. If she could ease herself over the rim and find some bush or tree roots to cling to, she might be able to conceal herself enough to make the maniac think she had fallen. The very idea of how close she was to plunging to her death made the breath stop in her throat, but she had no other choice. If she tried to dash out in the open, the car would run her down.

Catherine saw with fresh terror that her nemesis was driving straight for her again. She dropped to her stomach and crawled over the rocky edge cruelly scraping her body through the thin material of her clothes, as she groped in the darkness for handholds. She feared she hadn't gotten out of reach when the car kept coming at her.

Her hands continued to dig into the rocky soil until she became aware that the driver had obviously realized too late he'd misjudged how close he was to the edge. Terrified, Catherine pulled herself away from the car's path, as the front wheels dipped over the rim and hung there teetering like a clumsy beast on a seesaw.

She watched with a mixture of relief and horror, as the vehicle rocked for several seconds before it was carried forward by its weight. She heard a woman's high pitched scream, as the car tumbled down into the darkness of the labyrinth below.

Catherine closed her eyes. This had to be a nightmare and she'd wake up any minute. But her eyes snapped open when she felt herself slipping. She clawed at the ground in a frantic attempt to stop her own downward momentum. Her body twisted while her mind fought through a haze of panic struggling to save herself, as she began to slide downward. Her mouth opened and she released her own scream of terror.

Chapter Twenty-eight

Priscilla pulled into her driveway and frowned when she saw the house was dark. When she'd talked to Catherine earlier her plan was to come home in the morning, but she'd had a sudden change of heart and decided to arrive tonight. She had to admit it was disappointing that she was apparently coming home to an empty house.

She expected Catherine to be home and anticipated surprising her niece – especially when Catherine mentioned how much she missed them. She sincerely hoped the poor girl hadn't ended up having to work another late shift. It seemed to be happening quite a bit lately.

Priscilla knew she couldn't be out with Josh because he was in Alaska. She smiled recalling how happy Catherine had sounded on the phone telling her about their reconciliation. Knowing how much she had suffered over the man, it was a relief to realize they had finally been able to put their differences behind them. As far as she was concerned they'd more than earned the right to be together after going through their long, painful saga of separation.

She parked the car, lifted the sleeping child out of his car seat, and hurried through the rain to the house where she took him directly to his crib. Priscilla was glad she'd had the foresight to put on his pajamas before she started the drive home. She covered him with a blanket, flicked on a nightlight, and tiptoed from the room.

Considering the weather, she decided to wait until morning to unload their things from the car. Right now she was longing for a cup of coffee and a nice hot shower. She checked the phone to see if there were any messages and not seeing a flashing light, headed for her bedroom, unbuttoning her jacket as she went.

Twenty minutes later, after slipping into her nightgown and robe, she checked on Tommy to assure herself that he was still sound asleep. She made her coffee and a slice of toast then carried them into the living room and turned on the television to wait for Catherine.

Priscilla didn't realize she had fallen asleep until the baby's crying made her jerk upright in her chair. She rubbed a hand over her eyes and pushed herself to her feet, calling out reassuring words as she hurried to his bedroom.

"Grandma's coming, love."

Once she had changed his diaper and rocked him back to sleep, Priscilla was surprised to see how late it was, or early, depending on one's point of view. She glanced into Catherine's room noting the bed had not been slept in. Her car was not outside either. She looked at the clock again and frowned. Catherine had obviously not been home.

She could be out with friends and spent the night. Priscilla knew it was a definite possibility given the fact that Catherine wasn't expecting her home yet. She walked to the front living room window and stood looking out. The amount of rain they'd had this season had broken all records making her weary of the seemingly endless wet weather.

The rain came down in long silvery streams splashing against the windows in watery disarray. If

Catherine worked another shift, Priscilla disliked the thought of her driving in this latest storm. Visibility would be poor and streets flooded forcing detours.

She hated it when negative thoughts popped into her head, but it was impossible not to think Catherine could have had car trouble or, God forbid, been in an accident. Nerves danced up and down her spine sending tiny tremors to other parts of her body.

The concerned woman turned from the window and began to pace the room. Twisting the bathrobe's tie around her fingers she tried to wish away the all too familiar sense of panic beginning to creep in. It was something she'd never quite been able to get over because of the terrible accident that had taken her husband and Catherine's parents.

She continued to pace until pain in her fingers made her look down. They had turned blue from the way she'd wrapped the bathrobe tie around them. She pulled her hand free and flexed her swollen hand. Looking at the clock again, she gave up trying to convince herself to get through this worry on her own. She simply had to make some telephone calls before allowing another moment to pass.

Forty-five minutes later Priscilla sat at the kitchen table forcing herself to take deep breaths in an effort to calm her rapidly beating heart. A quick phone call to Catherine's hospital had confirmed that she'd left work hours ago. She tried friends her niece was known to sometimes spend time with, but despite their own anxiety, no one had a clue to her whereabouts. Other calls to area medical facilities and the police had not turned up any information.

She'd just gotten off the phone with Josh. Not meaning to upset him, she'd called in the hope that he might have heard from Catherine. Priscilla felt terrible now, realizing how frantic he'd been. She knew he felt utterly helpless being so far away. He begged her to get in touch with Ryan when she told him she didn't know who else to turn to. Frantic, she attempted to look up Ryan's number in their personal directory, but her hands were shaking so badly she couldn't seem to make her fingers work properly.

>>>>*dreams*<<<<

Josh shoved both hands through his hair and paced the room. There had been no mistaking Priscilla's concern and try as he might he couldn't stop his own worried thoughts. Where on earth could Catherine be? It wasn't like her to disappear without telling anyone where she was going. She was too responsible to be so careless.

There had to be a good reason for her to go missing for so many hours, but for the life of him he couldn't come up with any. Fear that something dreadful might have happened to her made his insides clench into tight knots.

Why was this happening? What kind of God would bring them together only to keep tearing them apart again? Hadn't they both suffered enough? What more must they give of themselves for the price of loving each other? He grabbed his phone and called the airport to check on flights. He needed to get home. He had to find Catherine.

>>>>*dreams*<<<<

The rain finally stopped shortly before dawn. A pale looking sun struggled to break through the thinning clouds when Jack Meredith's 1982 Chevy pickup wheezed around the last curve in the road. He was always grateful when the old truck was able to make another successful trip to the top of what he liked to think of as his private mountain. But he wasn't happy to see that he wasn't alone as he'd expected to be. He pulled to a stop and frowned at the lone car parked there.

He'd come back here to continue with the landscape he'd been working on that the rain had interrupted. The delay put him in a grumpy mood and having to share his precious solitude with someone didn't do much to improve his frame of mind. He didn't want strangers looking over his shoulder asking pesky questions.

He climbed out of his truck's cab and stood staring at the offending interloper. No other person was in sight. The thought of interrupting a couple of lovers crossed his mind but the idea didn't sit well. He didn't relish the idea of coming face to face with a couple of bodies locked in a passionate clench. He never could understand why some people thought it was romantic to have their rendezvous in a car.

Shoving his hands in the front pockets of his paint stained Levi's, he walked toward the car, but it didn't take long to see that no one was inside. He looked around. The person may have had car trouble and someone had come to pick them up, leaving the stalled vehicle behind. Shrugging, he started back to his truck to get his easel out when he happened to look down at the ground. He stopped abruptly when he saw deep tire tracks rutted in the mud.

He studied them for a few moments following the path of one set that veered off from the rest. When he realized what he was seeing his heart did a quick somersault inside his chest, as he ran over to the edge of the clearing where the tire tracks disappeared. He almost hated to look; afraid of what he might see.

His breath stopped in his throat when he saw a car resting upside down at the foot of the mountain. He quickly dug in his pocket for his cell phone while he scanned the area, and almost dropped it when he spotted a woman wrapped around a bush.

"Jesus God Almighty," he hissed through his teeth and immediately punched in 911. As soon as he reported the details he began to ease his way over the side.

>>>>*dreams*<<<<

Ryan stepped out of Catherine's hospital room and motioned to a hovering Priscilla.

"You can go in now, but try not to tire her out. She needs to rest. I've given her a light sedative, so don't be alarmed if she drifts off on you."

"Thank you, Ryan," she said choking back a sob.

He squeezed her shoulder.

"She's going to be fine, Priscilla."

"I was so scared when I couldn't find her."

"We all were."

"Oh dear, I forgot to call Josh. He'll be half out of his mind by now."

"I'll take care of it. You go to Catherine."

She nodded and hurried away. He waited until she'd disappeared into the room before turning to walk swiftly down the hall and out an exit that led to an adjacent building where he kept his office. He went in through the backdoor, picked up the phone on his desk, and punched in Josh's cell phone number.

"Josh? It's Ryan. Are you someplace you can talk in private?"

"Yes, but I was just about to head out the door for the airport. Do you have any news on Catherine?" he asked, his voice strained with anxiety.

"She was found this morning. She's going to be all right," Ryan hurried to clarify. "In fact, she's in remarkably good condition considering she spent the night outside clinging to a bush on the side of a mountain in a pouring rain."

"What! Are you kidding me?"

"I'm afraid not."

"What the hell was she doing outside in weather like that?"

Ryan pinched the bridge of his nose between his thumb and forefinger.

"I hope you're sitting down because if you're not you might want to be."

Josh sank onto a nearby chair.

"Okay, I'm sitting. What's going on, Ryan?"

"Someone called Catherine on her cell phone when she left work yesterday and told her Priscilla was at their house carrying on hysterically about losing a baby. Of course Catherine immediately thought something had happened to her nephew. The person claimed to have found her number in Priscilla's purse and gave Catherine directions to their supposedly house."

"What do you mean, 'supposedly'?"

"They had her drive into the hills where it's totally uninhabited. She'd never been there and didn't know this.

Once she arrived, they tried to run over her with their car."

Josh shot out of his chair.

"Why in God's name would anyone want to do such a thing? Did they catch whoever was responsible?"

"You could say that. Apparently they miscalculated the distance to the edge and ended up going over the rim themselves. Catherine, seeing the car coming at her was forced to climb over the side. Thankfully she was able to get out of the way and hold onto a bush when the car went literally flying by her, but then she couldn't climb back up."

"Jesus! Someone tried to kill her? Do you know who the maniac is?"

"Yes. Listen, this is going to be very difficult."

"It's obvious there's something you don't want to tell me? You weren't lying about Catherine being all right, were you?" he asked uneasily.

"She's suffering from hypothermia and shock as you might imagine, but she'll recover. She's here in the hospital resting right now."

"What, then? Come on Ryan, you're starting to spook me here, man."

"Josh, the person who tried to run Catherine down was your mother."

Chapter Twenty-nine

The sound of Josh sucking in his breath came clearly through the phone.

"What! No!" he cried out in horror. "There has to be some mistake. I know she didn't care for Catherine, but my God, my mother wouldn't have done something so terrible."

"There's no mistake. Her purse with a photo ID was in the car with her."

Josh sat back down.

"She's dead, isn't she?" he asked after a moment's hesitation.

"Yes. I'm sorry, Josh."

"Does my dad know?"

"No. I asked the police to wait until I called you. I thought it would help if you could make arrangements to have some family there when they contact him." He gave Josh a name and telephone number to call.

"My poor dad. He thinks she went down south to attend another one of those flower shows she likes."

He paused.

"He knew Mom had a problem when it came to accepting Catherine, but like me, I know he'd never think she would have gone this far."

"It's difficult to admit someone you love is flawed. He may have hoped she would change if he gave her enough time. Something or someone may have set her off."

"Set her off? Oh Jesus. I did. This is all my fault. I shouldn't have upset her with my ultimatum about kicking her out of my life completely if she didn't start being nicer to Catherine."

"You can't blame yourself for this. You're not solely responsible for your mother's actions. Anyone who would allow their hatred of another person to cause them to go to such extremes obviously was suffering from a deep rooted problem and needed counseling."

"So you're saying my mother was a nutcase?"

"Well, that's not exactly the medical term I'd use," he said trying to ease into his explanation. "I'd never met your mother, but I know from the things Catherine said she loved you very much to the point of being overly possessive. Sometimes when that happens people feel threatened by having to share that love."

"When you put it like that it does make her sound sick in the head."

"In her own way she was," he said gently. "Try not to hate her too much. She obviously believed it was in your best interests to have you break it off with Catherine."

"She told me as much, and that's when I tried to set her straight. You know my-way-or-the-highway kind of thing. I never thought she would crack up like this, but now that I remember how she looked when she talked about Catherine, I should have realized something was very wrong. My mother used her love as a shield to protect me and at the same time as a weapon to destroy Catherine." He exhaled a noisy breath. "It must have been like walking through a minefield for Catherine trying to deal with my mother. She'd have been a lot better off falling in love with you."

"I was never in the driver's seat on that. Is there anything I can do for you?"

"Take care of Catherine for me until I can get to her, will you? That is if she still wants to be with me after what my mother tried to do. After all, how many times can a person be expected to let bygones be bygones?"

"When you love someone? As many times as it takes, I would think."

"I may have used up my quota. Thanks for taking the time to call me personally."

"I just want to say one more thing before I hang up, Josh. Don't underestimate Catherine's capacity to forgive."

"I'll try not to, but if I was in her shoes and after all the things she's gone through with the Dallas family, I'd personally be inclined to say good riddance to the lot of us."

>>>>dreams<<<<

Catherine's eyes fluttered open. She swallowed, inhaled a shallow breath, and caught familiar odors that drifted around the room – hospital smells. Either she was hallucinating or she was finally out of the rain that had been her constant companion for hours. She closed her eyes for a moment and opened them again, half expecting to be back on the side of the mountain wrapped around the sturdy bush that had saved her life.

She moved her hands and almost whimpered in relief when she felt the firmness of a mattress beneath her fingers and the pillow underneath her head. Although a blanket covered her, she still felt cold with a chilling iciness that had settled deep into her bones. She remembered how numb her body felt and how she'd fought to keep her mind clear. But by the time the man had found her she'd been so exhausted she could barely form a coherent sentence.

Shock. There had been remnants of it despite her efforts to fight that, too. She couldn't stop thinking about how she'd scrambled over the edge of the mountain seconds before the car had followed her. She'd heard screaming – a terrifying sound that even now shuddered through her head. The horrible noise of scraping metal and human pain had echoed until she wanted to put her hands over her ears and block it out.

Filled with dread, her own sobs had burst from her throat when she realized she might very well join her tormentor if she continued to keep slipping. Then she'd crashed into the bush that became her salvation. She'd clung to the prickly branches and remained anchored there at the mercy of her own fear and the all enveloping darkness. By the time dawn's first light touched the mountainside, she'd been too numb to move.

She shifted slightly now, only to regret the movement when her aching muscles protested. Whatever she'd been given for pain had obviously worn off. Not wanting to subject herself to more drugs, she gritted her teeth against the discomfort.

A nurse came in seconds later. Catherine recognized her and tried to smile. It came out more like a grimace.

"Hello Susan."

"Hello yourself; and by the look of you, you need something a little stronger to help with the pain."

Catherine started to shake her head, but stopped herself fearing the discomfort it would probably cause.

"No, I'd rather not. I don't take well to drugs."

But Susan was already adding a drug into the IV hanging by the bed. She patted Catherine's hand and smiled.

"Stop trying to live up to the rumors that medical people make the worst patients and take your medicine like a good girl."

Catherine watched her leave and within seconds the drug had already begun to make her drowsy. Giving into the inevitable, she closed her eyes. The nightmare began almost immediately. She instinctively tried to fight her way out of it, but the drug was too powerful and kept her locked helplessly in its grip, trapping her in the unwanted dream.

Ivy stood there by the bed looking down at her. Catherine barely recognized the broken and bruised body, smeared with blood and grime, but the evil smile was all too familiar.

"I almost had you, you know." The voice came out as a blast of icy air.

Catherine pulled the sheet up in feeble attempt to shield herself.

"But you didn't."

The apparition raised bony shoulders in a shrug.

"This time."

"There isn't going to be another time. You're dead. You can't hurt me anymore."

"Don't be too sure. You're here in the hospital, aren't you?"

"It's only temporary. I'll be going home soon."

"It doesn't matter where you are because I live inside your head now."

"No you can't. I won't let you." Sweat popped out dotting her brow and glossing a thin coat over the rest of her body. *"Go away; just go away and leave me alone."*

"Never. You're mine," Ivy said, and filled the room with her deadly laughter.

Catherine's head tossed back and forth on the pillow. The sensation that cold fingers were closing around her throat made her gasp and claw at her neck. She continued to fight for breath until her screams brought Susan running back into the room.

>>>>*dreams*<<<<

The next time she awoke, Ryan was standing by her bed looking at her with a frown marring his smooth features.

"Catherine? Come now," he said in a gentle voice. "What's all this screaming about?"

She gulped back a sob and made a grab for his hand, needing to feel a warm flesh and blood human being.

"She was here. She came back. Don't let her get me!"

His frown deepened.

"Who was here?"

"Ivy. She . . . I couldn't breathe. Oh God, Ryan, she was choking me."

He squeezed her hand.

"You just had a bad dream. You're safe now."

Tears streamed down her pale cheeks.

"You don't understand; she's in here," she whimpered and pointed to her head.

"Ivy can't stay inside your head unless you allow it. She's dead."

"I don't think I can stop her. I didn't want her here, but she came anyway."

"That's because your defenses are down right now. Think about what you've been through in the last several hours. You're bound to be vulnerable. The sedative coupled with your exhaustion kept you under long enough for you to get tangled up in a dream."

"But why Ivy? I can't stand the woman."

"You know why. She was the last person you saw before you went over that cliff, and she was the one who drove you there. Give yourself time, but if thoughts of her continue to bother you I suggest you get some counseling. There's no need to suffer senselessly."

She thought of how she'd insisted Josh talk about his nightmares.

"You're right."

"Good girl. Your aunt is outside. She came earlier, but you were sleeping. Are you feeling up to seeing her now? I think it would help you both."

She wiped a few lingering tears from her cheeks.

"Yes, all right."

As soon as he left the room Priscilla came rushing in and hurried over to the bed.

"Thank goodness you're awake." She pressed a kiss to Catherine's forehead. "Oh, look at you, you're so pale, honey. I can't wait to get you home and start taking care of you."

"I'm all right. I don't expect you to stop working and become my nursemaid."

"Shush now. It's time someone looked after you for a change."

"Who's with Tommy?" she asked, steering the conversation away from herself.

"Meg has him." She fussed with the bedding. "Josh is out in the waiting room."

"He came back from Alaska? Does he know about my . . . accident?"

"Yes. I called him when I didn't know where you were. I wouldn't have bothered him, but I was frantic. I believe Ryan spoke to him afterwards. Do you want to see him?"

"Of course I do, Aunt Pris. Why would you think otherwise?"

"Well, we weren't sure after . . ." She stopped and shook her head. "Never mind. I'll go tell him before he wears a hole in the floor pacing."

Catherine watched her leave and immediately began to worry what she would say to Josh. After all, his mother was dead because of her. She thought of his father. She liked John very much and worried how he was taking the loss of his wife. Catherine wondered how she would ever be able to adequately apologize to him when Josh stepped quietly into the room.

There were new lines carved into his face she would have sworn hadn't been there when he left for Alaska. She commented on the dark circles under his eyes.

"Speaking of dark circles, you've a couple of smudges of your own."

"I'm just a little tired. I'm fine, really," she said hoping to alleviate his concern.

He lifted a brow.

"Are you? From what I'm told, you had a pretty rough night."

She heard the fury, barely veiled in his voice.

"It wasn't pleasant, but it could have been worse. Aunt Pris acted like I might not want to see you. Why would she think that?" He shoved his hands into his pockets, but not before she saw them clench into fists.

"How can you ask me that after all that's happened to you?"

Her heart ached at the hint of unsuppressed anguish escaping through his voice.

"Josh, please don't . . ."

"You told me before you thought it was better that we part ways. I've decided you're right. I hung around here to make sure you're going to be all right and to tell you goodbye. I'm leaving and this time I intend to stay away for good." He continued despite her gasp. "I don't deserve you; I've never deserved you. I'm setting you free at last."

Chapter Thirty

She had to fight not to give in to the black haze that suddenly swam before her eyes. This couldn't be happening again, but the way her insides felt as though they were splintering apart told her otherwise.

"Don't say such things. I'm sure you figured out after our night in your motel room that my sending you away had just been my pride talking."

"It's a wonder you had any pride left the way I'd trampled all over you. I should have left you alone a long time ago. It would have saved you a lot of heartache. You're in that hospital bed now because of your connection to me. But I'm going to rectify that. "

"Do you love me, Josh?"

"You know I do. Nothing can stop that. Not even my stupidity. You're my heart."

"Then why are you leaving?"

A spasm of pain streaked across his lean facial features.

"I have to."

"You love me, but you can't stay with me. Now there's an interesting bit of logic," she said in a lighter tone trying to diffuse his glum mood. "Where will you go?"

"I don't know; anywhere but where you are," he continued in a tortured tone.

"Why? You promised you'd never leave again. Have I done something wrong?"

"You? God, no. It's never been you. I'm just trying to make things easier." His jaw tightened. "You know who was in the car that tried to run you down, don't you?"

"The police told me. I'm sorry, Josh."

"You're sorry? For what? Jesus! I'm the one who should be apologizing to you."

"What happened wasn't your fault. I still want us to be together."

"How? You can't seriously want a man whose mother tried to kill you."

She reached out to him, but Josh shook his head and pulling his hands from his pockets held them toward her palms out, as though he were warning her away. His tension circled the room like a predator threatening to devour them both.

"What your mother did has nothing to do with who you are," she insisted.

"Now you sound like Ryan. I appreciate you trying to protect my image, such as it is, but there is such a thing as genetics. You know the old saying about how the apple doesn't fall far from the tree. My mother was twisted, Catherine. I realize that now. You'd be better off not forgetting that. I know I certainly won't be able to."

"So what are you trying to tell me? You think you might be tempted to murder me in my bed some night?" She let out an unladylike snort. "Come on, Josh."

"No, but I've been cruel enough to you in my own way to recognize I've obviously inherited some of my mother's less admirable traits."

"None of us are perfect, but we can try to control the part of ourselves we don't like. Remember, you told me you had stepped out of the realm of your mother's influence."

"I suppose I did say something like that, and at the time I really thought I was finally man enough to make a life with you without anymore mess ups."

"You did say it. And what's more, you thoroughly believed it."

"I'm afraid it was just a wishful dream that isn't going to come true."

"Don't speak to me of dreams. This is reality, Josh." Her nightmare speared its way into her head, but she willed it away knowing Josh surely would leave if she mentioned it.

"You're still letting your mother interfere with your decisions."

"I know it seems that way to you, but this decision is mine alone."

"Then why are you allowing her to destroy what we're trying to build together?"

"I'm not. You've given me so much more than I deserve, but between my mother's lunacy and my bungling our relationship, you've had the courtship from hell. I'm no good for you. It's time I end this and put us both out of our misery."

"Don't you think it's time we stop running and face our problems?"

"That's just it. We've been running. And now I'm going to stop all this drama once and for all. Life with me has been like being on a teeter-totter – up and down. Who'd want to continue living like that?"

"I would. I told you that life with you is like riding a roller coaster. I didn't think I wanted all the uncertainties, but you know how thrilling they can be.

Don't forget you asked me to walk the path with you into the future. I'm more than willing to do that now, Josh."

A nerve jerked in his cheek, as a look of hope flickered in his eyes.

"Are you sure that's what you want?" He held up his hand before she could answer him. "If I don't walk out of here right now you're going to be stuck with me forever."

"Is that a promise?" Her smile raised the corners of her mouth. "Of course I want you. Isn't that what I've been saying? Now will you please stop acting so noble and come over here and kiss me, or do I have to get out of this bed and attack you myself?"

"There are still going to be some shadows between us," he reminded her.

"We'll deal with them. I know in my heart we're destined to be together, Josh."

"So it would seem." He stepped forward to gather her in his arms letting his body relax against her in one long, fluid release.

She couldn't hold back a slight gasp as her sore muscles protested.

He quickly eased himself away.

"I'm hurting you."

"You'll hurt me a lot more if you don't hold me."

He leaned in again and held her gently against him, seeking and giving comfort.

"I would have died inside without you. I'd have let everything shut down and crawl into a dark pit," his voice sounded thick with emotion, as he buried his face against her neck.

"But you would have gone away," she reminded him, stroking his hair.

His lips brushed her mouth.

"I'd do anything possible to protect you, even from myself."

"I'm not as fragile as I look, Josh. You should know that about me by now."

"Whoever said women are the weaker sex was lying through their teeth."

He sought her mouth again.

There was more energy in this kiss, a greedy need that made her pulse begin to race. But when she looked at his face his expression still showed signs of too much stress. She decided to try using humor to hopefully make him forget what had brought her here.

"Does this mean you'll marry me? You should know I had a dream that you did."

His eyes opened very wide.

"Really? When?"

"The night at the motel. Are you going to ignore my dream this time?" she teased.

"Oh, hell no." He gave a mock shudder. "I don't dare."

"It wasn't exactly how I'd pictured it, but do I take it that's a proposal, then?"

He framed her face with his big hands.

"It is, albeit a very clumsy one. But know that you have my love and you'll have my ring as soon as I can get you out of here."

His words swirled around her heart like warm sunlight. She touched his face and felt the quick beat of love dance in her blood when he covered her mouth in a sweet kiss.

Chapter Thirty-one

Fresh from her shower, Catherine sat at her dressing table with its neat arrangement of perfume bottles, assorted boxes of hairclips, and hairbrush lined up along its smooth surface. She put her comb down and dug in her makeup kit, setting out the items she'd need. A silver frame with a picture of her and Josh on their wedding day sat on one corner with his little glass frog nearby. A larger double frame with pictures of Tom and Nancy in one and Tommy on the other stood next to it.

She liked being surrounded by family photos. There were others scattered throughout the house; pictures of her parents, her aunt and uncle, herself as a child standing with Nancy, and several of little Tommy in various stages of babyhood.

She applied the light touch of makeup she preferred and slipping out of her robe, went to the closet for her work clothes. As soon as she finished dressing she carried her empty teacup to the kitchen and put it into the dishwasher. She took a quick peek in the refrigerator and nodded to herself. Satisfied that everything was in order, she went back through the house and out the back door.

When she and Josh had mentioned to her aunt they were planning on buying a house she had offered hers for a modest price insisting she wanted a smaller place while still keeping the house in the family. Catherine was grateful for the suggestion. The wonderful old place always represented stability in her life when she needed it the most.

She stepped outside. The warm afternoon sun bathed everything in its golden glow bringing details into sharp focus. She put a hand up to shield her eyes from the brightness as she sought the shade of a large magnolia tree.

Her eyes stopped at the sight of Josh wrestling with Tommy on the lawn. The child's squeals of laughter echoed around the yard joined by Josh's deeper rumbles of amusement. Catherine watched as he maneuvered his big man's body around the little boy being careful not to crush his smaller frame.

Watching them so obviously enjoying each other made her own happiness sing through her blood like a bubbling brook. She had longed for carefree moments like this in all the dark days of Josh's absence, and even now it was sometimes hard to believe they were living out their dream of being together. Tears of gratitude gathered in her eyes.

"More, Daddy," the child demanded.

"That's enough for now, buddy. Let's put you on the swings for a while."

Josh scooped the little boy up and set him into a child swing, snapping a safety belt around his tiny waist. He looked up and saw Catherine standing under the tree. She was surrounded by pools of light where the sun had penetrated its way through the large leaves and around the huge cream colored flowers.

He gave the swing a push and jogged over to her in a loping gait.

"What's the matter?" He brushed a tear off her cheek with his thumb.

"Are you okay? The baby?"

She heard the concern in his voice and touched her protruding abdomen.

"We're fine. The sun's a little bright for my eyes," she told him and was rewarded by his instant look of relief. "It looked like you two boys were having a good time playing."

"Hey, we guys have to do our thing and for your information it's called male bonding, not playing." He snorted. "Playing is for sissies."

"Oh, is that so?" She laughed and brushed back a heavy wave of hair that had fallen across his forehead. "You're such a goofball."

"That's why you love me."

"Well, it's one of the reasons, anyway. I'll be leaving in a few minutes."

"I know, but I wish you didn't insist on working. I don't like the idea of you being on your feet so much. You know my new job pays enough for you to stay home."

She looked down at her protruding belly, as the child within her stirred. "Don't worry you're going to have me around plenty when my maternity leave starts. You're probably going to end up getting sick of me when I hound you to pick up your dirty clothes and put the toilet seat down."

"You do that already and I haven't complained." She raised a brow and he gave a sheepish grin. "Okay, maybe I whine a little, but you have to admit I'm getting better."

"At what? Controlling the whining or doing your little chores?"

He cocked his head to one side.

"Is that a trick question?"

Her mouth twitched in amusement. She loved that he'd gotten back his silly sense of humor. She'd never forgotten that it was one of the first things that had attracted her.

"Daddy! Daddy! Daddy!" Tommy chanted, interrupting their conversation.

"I'll be there in a minute, son. Demanding little beast isn't he?"

"That's why they call it the terrible twos. I also came to remind you about Ryan, Samantha, and Kiren coming for our barbecue tomorrow. Oh, and don't forget my aunt's going to bring her assistant Meg from the shop."

"I got it covered. Do you think Ryan will pop the big question to Sam?"

"I don't know, but I have a feeling it'll be any day now the way things are going."

"I hope so. She's a real keeper."

"Do I detect a bit of envy there?" She teased giving his shoulder a playful slap.

Josh grinned.

"Well, yeah, as much as any normal red-blooded male."

Samantha Farris was beautiful, friendly, and intelligent. She was also crazy about Ryan and his daughter. Fortunately, Kiren was as eager for her father to marry her as everyone else seemed to be. Catherine hoped Ryan might propose at their dinner tomorrow. Their friendship was special enough that she wanted to be in on the happy announcement if possible.

She also felt an unusually strong link to Samantha. The deep seated bond surprised her. Nothing like it had ever happened to Catherine before. She couldn't explain the feeling, so she simply accepted it. But curiosity did make her hope the strange connection would be explained some day.

"I suggest you rein in that testosterone before it gets you into trouble."

He smiled and laid a hand against her belly.

"Don't I know it?" The child chose that moment to kick.

"Whoa! That was a hard one. He's very strong."

"Yes he is and once more, he's getting restless to greet the world."

"Does it hurt when he moves around so much?"

"No, and I'd be worried if he didn't."

"I've been thinking about that list of names for the baby you gave to me."

"I certainly hope so, because time is getting short. Did you find any you liked?"

"I was wondering; did you put your father's name on the list?"

"No."

"Why not?"

She shrugged.

"I wasn't sure how you'd feel about it. His name was Michael."

"I think it would be nice to name the baby after him."

"You do?" She smiled, grateful for her husband's thoughtfulness. "That would mean a lot to me, but I don't want you to feel obligated. What about your dad? He's a good man, too."

"That can be his middle name. What do you think of the name 'John'?"

"Michael John – two strong masculine names. I like the sound of them together."

"Good. So do I. Michael John it is, then."

"Daddy, me swing!" Tommy called again with more insistence this time.

Catherine looked over at the swing set.

"He's getting impatient." She looked at her watch. "I'll go say my goodbyes and then I really have to get going."

Josh took her hand and laced their fingers together as they walked to the swing together. She looked at the child's face and saw Tom's warm brown eyes and Nancy's soft smiling mouth. She marveled at the wonderful little miracle they'd created together. She hoped they somehow knew that their love had endured, living on through their son.

Catherine pressed her lips to the satin smooth cheek and felt her own love swell inside when he reached up to wrap his tiny arms around her neck.

"Mommy go work?"

"Yes sweetie, Mommy's going to work. You be a good boy for Daddy now." She kissed him again and stepped back slowly, mindful of her ungainly balance.

"Hang on, son." Josh gave the swing another hefty push and was rewarded for his efforts when the little boy's gleeful laughter rang out.

Catherine smiled and waved her goodbye. "He's always such a sweet, happy child. I feel so privileged to have him to love."

"Yeah, I know what you mean. He has a way of wrapping around your heart."

"Sometimes I dream that Tom and Nancy are here watching him; watching us."

"I'm sure they are. Thank God not all dreams are bad. Sometimes they show us good stuff. It's like having windows inside our heads letting us see things that we might otherwise miss."

"What a lovely thing to say. I didn't realize you were so poetic."

"Is that what you call it?" He raised her wrist to his mouth and pressed his lips to the network of tiny blue veins there as though he was holding a fragile flower.

"I used to dream about you when I was in the Amazon."

His comment surprised her, as he rarely talked about his time there.

"I hope they somehow helped."

"They did." He squeezed her hand as though he understood what she'd been thinking. "Dreaming about you was my way to escape from the harsh reality at the time. That's what kept me going. In dreams we were always together. It was my mind's way of creating perfection in an imperfect world."

She thought about the disturbing dreams she'd had while he'd been in South America and her terrifying visions where Ivy intruded into her sleep.

"I'm glad."

He bent his head toward her mouth ready to kiss her when he was interrupted by Tommy's childish high-pitched voice.

"More swing, Daddy."

"The kid's got lousy timing. I'm going to have to teach him to pump himself," he said, but amusement shined in his eyes and the deep affection was there in his voice.

"Better get used to it. It won't be long and we're going to have two of them vying for our time. I checked the fridge. There's leftover spaghetti for dinner. Give Tommy frozen peas for his veggie and you can cut up an apple for dessert."

He made a face.

"Peas? Fruit? I was thinking more along the lines of beer nuts and beef jerky. If I'm going to do the male bonding thing with Tommy, I need to give him some real man food. They must fit somewhere in one of the basic food groups."

"You'd better be kidding about that, mister."

He gave a shout of laughter.

"Had you going there for a minute, didn't I?"

"Beast." She smiled before brushing his mouth in a quick kiss. "I've got to run."

"Whoa, I think we can do better than that, don't you?" he teased, before putting his hands on her shoulders and crushing her mouth in a kiss that left her breathless.

She leaned against him feeling lightheaded. He always had that affect on her making her wonder if she would ever get over the rush of excitement. Somehow she didn't think she would.

"You certainly know how to give a girl a first-class send off."

"All part of my strategy to keep in your good graces. How am I doing so far?"

"Not bad, but it's always a wise idea to keep practicing. Flowers are good and oh, don't forget to throw in a little chocolate now and then," she said enjoying their game.

"Guess I missed the memo on that one. Thanks for the tips."

He started to kiss her again only to have Tommy yell.

"Me want Daddy!"

Catherine laughed. "Your male bonding seems to be working quite well. You better go to him before he tries to climb out of the swing. I'll see you when I get home."

"I'll be here," he said, as he did every time she went somewhere without him.

She understood that it was necessary for him to say the words for both their sakes.

"I know you will."

Books Also Written by Olivia Claire High

An Angel Among Us (Nonfiction)

The Crystal Angel (Romantic Suspense)

Rose Cottage (Supernatural Romantic Suspense)